Francis Owen was born i… leaving secondary school st… evening newspaper.

Over the years he has w… regional and national newspapers, in the UK, Japan and Hong Kong, as well as for the BBC and the Reuters international news agency. *Heaven's Assassin* is his first published novel. Francis has been shortlisted in the annual awards organised by the UK Crime Writers' Association.

He is married and has two young children. He lives and works in north London.

A *PETER CHAN* crime novel

HEAVEN'S ASSASSIN

Francis Owen

Published in 2009 by New Generation Publishing.

First Edition

Published by New Generation Publishing

For Iris

HEAVEN'S ASSASSIN

1

TYPHOON WEATHER.

Rain spewed from an ash-coloured sky and scudded across the street. Inspector Peter Chan paid the cab driver then grabbed his umbrella from the back seat, silently congratulating himself that he had shown the foresight to bring it, only to discover on closer examination that his foresight had not extended to ensuring the umbrella worked. Three metal spokes were broken — before going ten metres he was drenched.

Head down, shoulders swaying like those of a middleweight boxer, Chan splashed across Johnstone Road. Typical, he thought, swerving to avoid a truck full of squealing pigs bound for the slaughter-house. I take two days leave for the first time in eight months and Hong Kong gets thumped by the worst typhoon to wander this way for fifty years. You should change your name, Peter. Why not call yourself Lucky? I bet no man alive encounters more good fortune. He had planned to go fishing. A friend had told him about the perfect place off Sai Kung, where the sea heaved with garoupa and yellow tail. Even Chan could catch something. Fishing was out of the question now. Only people with a death wish put to sea during typhoons.

He turned into the indoor market, which had become crowded with people stocking up — shops would close when weathermen signalled the official start of the typhoon. The market stank of raw meat, a smell that reminded him of dead bodies. He tried to think of other things. It was hard, though, when butchers carved up pigs barely two metres away from your face then tossed the entrails into baskets that oozed blood. He walked over to a stall which sold seafood. A pug-faced woman stood guard behind the counter, scraping the scales off fish with a cleaver. She rested the cleaver on a wooden chopping block and grinned.

"*Aheya!* You're getting as fat as me!"

"You say the nicest things, Ah Jun. Got any lobsters?"

"And your face! It looks like a bruised mango!"

"I think you're beautiful too. Have you any lobsters, or not?"

She gestured to the tank beside her. "What do you think are in here — silk pyjamas?" She thrust a mottled arm into the tank, fished out a grey-brown lobster and bound its claws with twine. She paused before handing it over. "Know how to cook it?" She stood back and eyed him slyly.

"Was Mao a communist? Of course I know."

She gave a raspy chuckle. "Make sure you have the number of Queen Elizabeth Hospital handy when you eat dinner tonight. If you're as good a chef as you are a liar, you're set for food poisoning."

"Not before you cut yourself with that tongue."

Outside the market, people crowded on buses and trams and piled into the MTR station, eager to get home before underground train services were cancelled. Workers hauled netting over restaurant windows. Police officers in dark green storm capes turned rubbish bins on their sides to stop them blowing away.

Typhoon weather.

Chan's daughter had been born on such a day eighteen years ago. He had spent what seemed like hours charging around rain-lashed streets like a lunatic, trying to summon a taxi, before calming down and using his police radio to call a squad car. Even then he had feared disaster — every time branches or rubbish had hurtled towards the car he'd felt sure they would crash. But they had reached Baptist Hospital safely, where Ah Fah had weighed in at a hefty eight pounds twelve ounces. Would she be safe during this latest storm? Should he call her university to make sure? No, he must stop clucking around like a mother hen. She was an adult now.

The harbour drifted into view. A ferry struggled through the grey-black swell as it headed for its base in Tuen Mun. The few junks and sampans that bobbed about like oversized champagne corks made for the safety of typhoon shelters at Causeway Bay and Yau Ma Tei.

Chan bought a copy of *Ming Pao* from the kiosk by his home then squished into his apartment block. He took the lift to his fourteenth-floor flat, changed out of his wet clothes, and then sat on the unmade bed and read the newspaper. Its main story was the typhoon and the damage it was likely to cause. He was drawn to an article at the bottom of the page about a Chinese army general's disappearance.

The general had been due to attend a meeting of Party chiefs two weeks ago, but had failed to turn up and had not been seen since. The writer of the article speculated that the general may have fled to Taiwan with military secrets. The general had been born in a Yellow River village near where Chan himself had grown up. Had they met in China? Chan stared at the picture accompanying the article. No. This man was a stranger.

The phone rang.

"Boss! Boss! ... That you?" said an excited-sounding voice.

"Of course it's me. What is it, Ah Wong?"

"Something wrong with your mobile? ... Been trying to reach you for ages … Because—"

"I switched it off," Chan said. "Like I always do when I want to avoid being hassled by sergeants called Wong on my day off."

"Patrol boys have found a body, boss. They—"

"I'm on leave, Ah Wong."

"Not any more you aren't."

"Says who?"

"Lam wants you over here in Mongkok — wants it quick, too. This one's big, see. It's … Boss! Boss! Can you hear me?"

"The whole block can. Why does Lam need me so badly?"

"Reckons you're the only one can do it, see ... Only one with the necessary experience ... Experience to handle something as big as this, if you get what I mean."

"I'll stand more chance of getting what you mean when you stop talking in riddles; something as big as what?"

"Adult male," Wong said. "Shot in the head ... Then stashed in the boot of a car."

"So why me?"

"Lam asked specially for you."

"A dozen other inspectors can investigate a straightforward shooting like that. And none of them are on leave either."

"It's *not* straightforward. There's the uniform, see, and—"

"Uniform?"

"Our dead man is a Chinese general."

2

THE BODY LAY in the car's boot.

Chan tried not to take many deep breaths: as well as a sickly-sweet stench from the corpse, the street reeked of blocked drains and rotting vegetables. Too late, he realised that he should have followed his usual practice; he should have shoved bits of carbolic soap up his nostrils to reduce the smell of death. The street was about two metres wide and ran gun-barrel straight for forty metres, enclosed by a low wall at one end, while yellow crime tape stretched across its open part. Despite the rain, journalists and curiosity-seekers crowded behind the tape.

Some of the reporters shouted questions at Chan. He ignored them. He walked over to where his police surgeon friend Eddie Gallacher knelt over the body, examining the gunshot wound in the victim's head. Chan leaned over and tapped the balding police surgeon on the shoulder.

"I need a closer look, Eddie."

Gallacher stood up and shuffled to one side. A sixty-year-old from Glasgow, a hangover from the British colonial days which had ended more than a decade ago, he was barrel-like fat. The effort of hauling himself to his feet made him wheeze like a man about to suffer a heart attack.

"Point-blank, Eddie?"

"Not exactly, old lad, but near enough," Gallacher grunted as he struggled to get his breath back. "Look close and you'll see powder traces embedded in the skin. To tattoo the skin with powder burns like that our killer stood no more than two feet away — the bullet entered the front of his head and came out at the back."

Chan knelt for a closer look. At the front of the skull, above the right eye socket, was a neat hole the diameter of a ten cent coin, barely large enough to probe with his little finger. At the back, where the bullet had exited, lay a crater big enough for his fist. Eddie had got it right: close range, but not point-blank. If the barrel had touched the head then gasses would have shot under the skin, expanded the skin and ripped it apart: point-blank hits always left ragged, star-shaped wounds.

"How long has he been dead?"

"Judging from the colour of the body, how it's swollen up and those skin blisters, at least four days." Gallacher pulled a pack of cigarettes from his pocket. "For a more exact time frame, you'll have to wait till we haul him over to the morgue." He grinned, revealing uneven teeth that had become stained black from his addiction to cheap mainland tobacco. "I take it you *will* be at the post-mortem, our Peter? Sitting in your usual front-row seat?"

It was an old joke. Gallacher knew about his friend's aversion to post-mortems. Ever since that first one in Shanghai twenty-five years ago, when he had been with China's Public Security Bureau, Chan had hated entering autopsy rooms. It wasn't the sight of the bloated blue-grey corpse hauled out of the Huangpu River that had so unnerved him but the smell; stale raw flesh, stale blood, stale piss — stale everything. The odour of four-month-old death had invaded his hair, saturated all his skin pores, penetrated his sinuses — taken a whole month of hot showers and scrubbing himself with carbolic soap to escape it. The corpse had been so decomposed that the Public Security Bureau's surgeon had worn a gas mask. No spare mask had been available. So Chan had sat on the floor, afraid that if he attempted to stand up he would fall over.

"I wouldn't miss one of your post-mortems for the world."

"In that case, I'll delay proceedings till you're sitting nice and comfy." Gallacher tried to light a cigarette. The rain and wind made it impossible. "That way you won't miss a single thing. You'll …"

He pointed down the alley at where Chan's partner, Sergeant Wong, had begun jumping up and down and waving like a man possessed. "I think our friend Doctor Watson wants a quiet word."

Chan set off towards Wong.

The sergeant signalled for him to hurry, but Chan maintained a steady pace. Experience told him Wong's news would not be as earth-shattering as the frantic waving suggested it would be. To call Wong excitable did him an injustice: he could announce that tomorrow would be another sunny day and make it sound like World War Three had broken out.

The rain grew heavier, the wind stronger. Despite this, the crowd behind the yellow crime tape had swelled: newspaper and TV reporters hurled questions that Chan ignored. Beyond the ranks of journalists, sex hotels jostled for space with bars, restaurants and karaoke joints. Illuminated purple and yellow signs dangled above the sex hotels. Beneath the signs remote-controlled cameras zoomed in on the street — staff watching TV monitors in the hotels would know that the police were about and would warn customers. A tall, long-legged hooker in tight leather pants glanced enticingly at Chan. Then, realising who he was, she glanced away.

Mongkok's vice business was in good shape, Chan reflected. Good enough for pimps to swan around in trendy Armani fashions. They toted portable phones and golf umbrellas and lounged next to sleek Mercedes automobiles. A teenage gang lolled beside the pimps, regarding them with the bug-eyed admiration that was usually reserved for pop stars. None of the gang looked older than thirteen. But judging from the colourful tattoos that decorated their biceps, they already saw themselves as 14K Triad members.

"So what do you think, boss?" Wong asked in the husky voice that always made him sound as though he had a cold.

"I think police sergeants should check their facts before they decide to wreck people's days off," Chan said accusingly. "You told me he was a general."

Wong held up flabby hands in a gesture of apology.

"I know, I know."

"No way is he a day over thirty," Chan said. When did China start appointing thirty-year-old generals?"

Wong tried to explain. "When I rang I hadn't seen him ... Only spoke to the officer who found him ... Inexperienced, see … Only on the force a month ... When he saw the uniform … Jumped to wrong conclusions … Tried to warn you, boss ... After I saw the body and realised I'd screwed up, I mean ... Rang your home to tell you ... Already on your way, though ... So—"

"Apology accepted," Chan cut in: fail to halt Wong when he was in full flow like this and he would babble on until doomsday. Chan brushed rain from his eyes. "I couldn't have gone fishing in this weather. And even if a typhoon hadn't been blowing, the odds would have been against me catching anything." He ducked his head to avoid pieces of cardboard blasted into the air by a strong gust of wind. "The way my luck's running right now, I'd probably have fallen overboard."

"So what do you think?"

"About what?"

"Heading for a fancy dress party, huh? That's why he's wearing that uniform, I mean."

"We found nothing to identify him?"

Wong shook his head.

"No wallet or credit cards? Passport, ID card?"

"Nothing."

"He wasn't a nobody, though," Chan mused. "That's a genuine diamond ring on his finger."

"He's wearing a Cartier watch too," Wong pointed out.

Chan nodded: "A watch that cost at least forty thousand dollars."

"Rules out robbery as a motive then, huh?"

"Have we checked the car registration on the computer?"

"Owned by a hire firm in Mid-Levels," Wong said.

"Who did they hire it out to?"

"Couldn't reach anyone to check with; staff at the hire firm went home early on account of the typhoon."

"Then we need to wait," Chan said, "until we check his prints with those on the ID card records." He brushed more rain from his face. "And we won't do that getting soaked."

"We go indoors?" Wong suggested enthusiastically. "Check the hooker bars and see if anyone knows, or saw anything, huh?"

"Be my guest," Chan said. "But don't get your hopes up. You've got more chance of winning the Mark Six lottery than you have of getting pimps around here to help."

"You're not staying?"

Chan shook his head. "Lam will spit fire if there's no report on his desk when he gets in tomorrow."

"Best go home and write it up then. I'll hang around a bit longer — maybe find us a friendly hooker or pimp."

"IT'S A DISASTER!" the man in Hong Kong wailed into the phone. Everything has gone wrong."

"Hush!" ordered the man in Beijing.

"But — but our target ... He's alive!"

"Calm yourself, Brother Li!"

"Our plan has failed!"

"Your plan, Brother Li, your plan has failed."

"The *wrong* man is dead!"

"Because of your foolishness."

"But — but he insisted. Yes, he insisted I give him the mission."

"You should have refused."

"And he had special talents! He could get close to our target ... Without suspicion ... So—"

"Using an amateur was bound to doom the mission to failure."

"I acted only for the best. I—"

"But our next attempt will *not* fail," said the man in Beijing. "I have recruited a professional and he never fails. Rest assured, Brother Li, we shall still have justice. This man will make sure Alan Yip pays for his betrayal."

3

OLD YUEN, THE caretaker-security guard at Chan's apartment block, sat at his desk in the lobby, fast asleep as usual. Just as well, Chan thought, considering that the old boy was pushing seventy-five. The firm which managed Chan's block liked to hire pensioners because the pensioners were prepared to work for near-starvation wages. It didn't seem to matter that they were also the world's worst security guards. If Old Yuen woke up he might have to confront an intruder. No way would he win that contest. He would only hurt himself, perhaps seriously. Better that he caught up on his beauty sleep — Chan closed the door gently.

However, the sound of the lift coming down woke the pensioner.

"Hey! What ... Oh, it's only you, chief ... You're soaked!"

"In case you forgot, a typhoon's blowing. Go back to sleep."

Old Yuen rubbed bloodshot eyes. "Hard sleeping in this sweat hole," he grumbled. "The management bastards turn off the air-con at night — then there's the lousy mosquitoes. I got no coils to burn to keep the mosquitoes away. The minute I shut my eyes they're all buzzing my head, biting my face and neck — last night one cheeky little bastard even flew up my trousers and bit my balls!"

"I've got some spare mosquito coils in my office," Chan said. "I'll bring them back for you tomorrow."

With a loud hiss, the lift doors opened. Chan said goodnight to Old Yuen and jabbed the button for the fourteenth floor.

"Hey! I nearly forgot," the caretaker shouted as the lift doors were closing.

Chan opened the doors. "Forgot what?"

"Your daughter came in an hour ago."

"Ah Fah's upstairs?"

"Unless she grew wings and flew out the window."

"Don't joke," Chan said. "With her you can never be sure."

"IS THAT YOU, dad?" Ah Fah called out. "I'm brewing some coffee. Want one?"

"If it's not the rocket fuel you usually make."

He went to the bedroom and changed out of his wet clothes. Then he moved into the living room where a tall, spiky-haired Ah Fah lounged on the sofa. She wore college rebel's uniform of Bruce Lee tee-shirt, camouflaged army cargo pants and cherry-red Doc Martens, but the hair was what really grabbed his attention.

Was this latest look completely new — it was hard to keep track with someone who changed their hairstyle almost every other week — or one of her old styles brought back to life? Most teenage Hong Kong girls wore their hair long and conservatively straight. Ah Fah had had her hair cropped short, then covered it with about half a tonne of industrial-strength hair jell and combed it to spike upwards, the spikes so sharp that you could have pierced apples on them.

"Here you go."

She leaned over and handed him his coffee so clumsily that she slopped half of it over his outstretched fingers. He danced around cursing and spilled most of what remained in his cup on the floor. Oblivious to his suffering, Ah Fah calmly explained why she had called round: "Missed the last train on account of this typhoon. So I … Oh stop prancing around like a ballet dancer! You're making me go all dizzy!"

He had trouble hearing her: she had tuned the TV to *Justice Pao*, a soap opera about a kindly and learned judge who tours ancient China punishing evil landlords. As usual, she had the volume loud enough to awaken the dead. He sat on the armchair opposite her and sipped the remains of his coffee. He winced. It tasted like treacle.

"You used too much powder again."

"Oh, stop complaining! It's not that strong."

"It's strong enough to send me three times around the moon!" He shoved the cup to one side. "And turn that TV down — it's giving me a headache!"

Grudgingly, she pressed a switch on the remote control and reduced the volume, from a level that would arouse the dead to one which merely destroyed brain cells of those living. She sat up straight, shook her head pityingly. "What happened, dad?"

"To what?"

"To the dashing inspector who my friends used to think was such a cool dude — when did he become the most miserable sod in Hong Kong?"

She dragged cigarettes and matches from her pocket.

He frowned. "I thought you were giving up."

She waved him away. "Oh shut up!"

"You could get cancer," he said. "It's medically—"

She interrupted.

"Shut up! You're becoming as big a chauvinist as that old wife-beater, Confucius — you'll ask me to bind my feet next! This is the *twenty-first* century, not the sixteenth."

"It's medically proven," he said. "People who smoke risk—"

"Okay, okay, you win." She replaced the cigarettes in her pocket. "Satisfied? I only wish Queenie could see you now, though, and see the tyrant you've become — I bet she wouldn't love you any more."

"Queenie?"

"Her real name's Po Tse, goalkeeper on our school team."

"The little fat girl with pigtails?"

"You remember?"

Of course he did: the world's worst goalkeeper, but one who had played with endearing passion. Yet so timid off the pitch that she'd blushed whenever he'd spoken to her. Thoughtful too; one season she had presented him with a home-made trophy for being the team's best supporter.

"Had a crush on you," Ah Fah explained. "Because you were the only parent dumb enough to watch every single game we played. She reckoned that there was something really noble about a guy prepared to torture himself week in week out like that."

"It wasn't torture," he said. "I've always liked watching a good game of football."

"Bullshit!"

"I beg your pardon!"

"Watching us was as thrilling as watching paint dry!" She levered herself from the sofa. "Tonight's *Justice Pao* is complete crap too. I'm going for a shower. The TV's yours."

She moved to the bedroom, walking in the confident bouncy way she always did, head bobbing from side to side. She toe-punted the door open then back-heeled it shut. Cupboard doors banged open and closed; she never did anything quietly. He heard her whistling and singing; she sang badly, couldn't reach high notes. On television, wise old Judge Pao told an evil landlord who had ravished a peasant's daughter that he would suffer the death of a thousand cuts, and what remained of his body would be fed to the fishes. The kindly and learned judge said he was sorry for the landlord, but ... well, rules were rules.

Chan reached for the remote. But true to form, Ah Fah had absent-mindedly taken it to the bedroom. He walked over and switched off the TV at the mains. A picture rested on top of the television: him clutching newly-born Ah Fah. Wrapped in a towel, yellow from jaundice, she stared up wide-eyed at an even wider-eyed father, who seemed scared that he might drop her. It triggered memories of her birth: three-thirty on a typhoon afternoon, sky the colour of cigarette ash, rain lashing leaden streets.•

She re-emerged from the bedroom. A pink towel was in her hands and running shorts had replaced combat pants. She gave the sort of yell *kung fu* film stars give when they chop enemies, kicked the bathroom door so hard she almost snapped the hinges, and lurched inside. He heard the sounds of running water and cursing — her blaming him because the water was too hot.

He glanced at another photograph.

A group shot of Ah Fah with school-friends he had hung this on the wall. Stood in the middle of the back row, she towered above the rest, and had she possessed the poise to go with her height it could have been different: she might have avoided those taunts. She had been ungainly, so kids had picked on her. It seemed only yesterday when she had fled home weeping after classmates called her the Ugly White Giant, and said she wasn't a proper Chinese but a half-caste. He had dried her eyes and told her not to get upset.

"They called me half-caste too. It's only a name."

In hindsight, the taunts had helped Ah Fah. They had made her resilient, encouraged her to develop a sharp tongue with which she could savage her tormentors — though perhaps it had become *too* sharp. Unless you knew her well, it was hard to realise these days when she was joking and when she was being deliberately rude.

The bathroom door burst open and she re-emerged. She had failed to dry herself properly and trailed footprints on the wooden floor.

"Going to listen to some music," she announced, kicking the bedroom door open.

"Well please keep the volume low."

"Don't I always?"

"Apart from last month, you mean?"

"Last month?"

"The people down the corridor say that you deafened them."

"Relax. I'll be as quiet as a mouse."

She slammed the bedroom door so loud that the walls shook.

4

CHAN POURED HIMSELF a glass of red wine; hopefully it would help him to sleep and chase away the nightmare about Liu Yan. It was strange how she had haunted his dreams for the past two weeks: normally the nightmare only troubled him when he investigated the murder of a teenage girl. His last such case had ended eleven months ago. Why then, a fortnight ago, had he begun dreaming about Liu Yan?

The approach of the anniversary, of course, the anniversary of that freezing January day twenty-five years ago; a day when stupidity, arrogance and … Screw it! Why should he feel guilty? He had done everything he could to prevent it. No one could have done more.

So why did he feel guilty?

He gulped wine. In the distance, thunder rumbled like cannon fire. Rain strafed the living room window. Another mouthful of red wine, then another: it was potent stuff; he sank further back into the sofa, felt himself starting to drift; felt his eyelids growing heavy; felt his grip on the wine bottle easing — *Aheya!* he was so tired. The rattling against the window eased, then stopped, and the rain changed to snowflakes. Fat snowflakes, like broken-off pieces of the steamed sugar bread he had loved to eat in China as a boy. He shivered as the room grew colder and darker and changed shape.

SNOWFLAKES FLOATED OVER the windscreen of his Lada automobile. The heater was broken and cold clawed his bones like a tiger. *Where were they?* He checked his watch: five-fifteen. The kidnapper was thirty minutes overdue. *Half an hour!* Would he ever turn up? Then Chan saw him; a hazy figure forty metres away who floated in the bronze glow of the Lada's headlamps. Chan shoved the door open and stumbled on to the icy road. The kidnapper got within twenty metres and then stopped, a slim silhouette cut from grey tissue paper. Chan stood transfixed as the kidnapper's breath turned to vapour in the freezing early-morning air.

"Got the money, *ah shuk*?"

It was the traditional Hakka greeting for a friend, but not the normal rasping voice of one of China's boat people. This was the velvet-like voice which had toyed with Chan over the phone and held him spellbound in the three weeks since the abduction of the Party official's daughter. The voice of a man not from these parts: perhaps from Guangzhou in southern China, maybe even from across the border in Hong Kong: the voice of a man in control.

"In the case" — Chan hoped the speed of his reply masked the tremor in his voice. "Front seat ... Where's Liu Yan?"

The kidnapper's body suddenly shimmied in the glow of the headlamps. Chan heard a click and his arm half-moved to the snub-nosed Makarov in his shoulder holster, before he realised that the kidnapper had only lit a cigarette.

"Wonderful *ah shuk!* I can see Buddha's fated us to stay friends."

"Where's the girl?"

"In my car — half a mile down the road. Don't worry, she's fine and she'll stay fine too. Providing you and your Security Bureau pals keep being nice. Tell me you'll stay nice, *ah shuk*."

Chan croaked a reply through lips that felt as dry as sandpaper. He had not intended it this way. He had meant to be cool and in control.

"Everything will be how you want it."

"Step away from the car." The voice had lost all its playfulness, now it cut through the freezing air with the sharpness of a scalpel. "And look ahead — if you want to see her alive. Wait five minutes after I drive off. Then, and only then, you get her. Understood?"

The kidnapper stepped out of the light and walked around Chan to the Lada, boots crunching snow. Chan waited, not daring to move, in case he provided an excuse to harm the girl. The car door opened and closed. The Lada's engine spluttered. Wheels churned against slush. The kidnapper drove past him. The Lada's taillights grew smaller and dimmer.

Five minutes passed.

He took a torch from his pocket and headed down the road. Wind sliced across the fields like a razor, but he didn't feel it as he strained to glimpse the kidnapper's car. After two minutes he had seen nothing; after five minutes, nothing.

He lied! There's no car, no girl!

Then he saw it. A dark-red lifeboat buffeted by a grey-white sea of snow and ice. The car was where the kidnapper had promised it would be. Everything would be all right.

He was twenty metres away when the car exploded.

Frozen ground rose up to club him in the face; he smelled burning gasoline, scorched rubber, the singed hair of his nostrils; tasted glass fragments. When he tried to get up, his body felt as though it belonged to someone without legs. Flames shot into the sky, illuminating the fields for miles.

Above the roar of flames, a girl screamed.

CHAN AWOKE BATHED in sweat. Twenty-five years on! In another twenty-five would Liu Yan still haunt him? As he swallowed clammy air, the phone continued to ring. He pulled it from the cradle.

"Boss! Boss! You awake?"

Chan fought to return to reality. "Yes, I … What's happening?"

"Won't like it … Better that our corpse had been a general … This one … It'll make waves, boss … I mean *big* waves!"

"Stop talking in riddles, Ah Wong, and calm down. Tell me slowly — what's happened?"

"It was when we lifted our corpse from that car," Wong said. "That's when we saw them ... Saw the pile of leaflets, I mean … Been lying on top of all these leaflets, see."

"Leaflets?"

"The garbage those Heavenly Ghosts screwballs hand out in the street," Wong said. "Crazy cult stuff … How joining them will save the world … Save it from all sorts of disaster, I mean … We found a wallet under the body too … And the ID card inside … Belongs to Alan Yip's son, Szeto … So now we—"

"*The* Alan Yip?"

"Our dead man is his youngest son, boss. Going to make some big waves, huh?"

Film producer Alan Yip was among the most powerful figures in Hong Kong. His influence extended far beyond the movie world. He was a friend of China's leaders. Wong was right about those big waves. If someone had murdered the son of such a powerful figure as Alan Yip, a storm would soon be raging.

"What now, boss? We contact Alan Yip, huh?"

"First we make sure it really is his son."

"The wallet proves it."

"Like that army uniform proved he was a general, I suppose. Our victim might have stolen Szeto's wallet. Get prints from the corpse, and then check them with ID records for Yip's son."

"Being done as we speak," Wong said. "Supposing the prints prove it's him?"

"Let's hope they don't."

5

DESPITE THE COLD breeze from the air-conditioner, Fai sweated. The sweat oiled his armpits, trickled down his neck and over his shoulder blades. Too late, he realised that he should have kept silent — he should never have spoken to his brother Szeto.

If he had stayed quiet he would not be constantly looking over his shoulder like this, wondering when the blow would fall, because sooner or later it *would* fall. A severe blow, too. In fact, when his secret leaked out the blow would not only be severe, but fatal.

He was at home on the Peak, the hillside enclave where Hong Kong's rich and famous live because it is less crowded and less humid than other parts of the island. Or rather he wasn't at home, he was at the luxury flat of his father — the bastard never let him forget that he owned this place, like he owned almost everything else in Hong Kong.

Fai had worked for his father, film producer Alan Yip, for ten years. He had worked hard, too: those movies would never have become so popular without his efforts to publicise them. The old man would never admit it, of course. He would have his nails torn out before giving anyone even a single ounce of credit. He would always claim it was him alone who had made the company, and who owned the company and everything in it. He's wrong, though, Fai thought. He doesn't own me. Never has. Never will. Others might fear him, but …

What was that?

Someone was moving around. In the bedroom by the door: the bedroom used by their Filipina maid, Angelita. Who had made that noise? He strained his ears for other sounds — then cursed his stupidity. Get a grip, he told himself. Of course someone's moving around — a typhoon is blowing the balls off Hong Kong! Sexy little Angelita has had to keep her cute little butt at home on her day off.

He moved to the window and stared out. The sky had turned crow black. Lights flickered jewel-like in waterfront skyscrapers. Victoria Harbour itself resembled a cauldron of swirling tar, broken only by splashes of grey as breakers reared up from the depths. Normally ships and boats of all shapes and sizes would be bobbing around in the harbour: fishing junks, sampans, ferries; container ships waiting to offload cargo into Kwai Chung's port.

Tonight, apart from a few container ships at anchor, patiently awaiting the storm's end, the black sea lay empty: the outlying island and Star Ferry services had all been cancelled; smaller boats had sought refuge in the typhoon shelters of Yau Ma Tei and Aberdeen.

Fai turned away from the window. Normally the majestic view from here helped to relax him. Not tonight, though, because tonight was not normal.

A photograph on the wall attracted his gaze: a large framed shot of himself and his younger brother, Szeto. The picture showed Fai at his best: flashing the film-star teeth he had always been proud of, smiling in the relaxed, self-confident way, that until recently he had often smiled. Just under six foot tall — five inches above average for a Cantonese man — with wide-set raven-coloured eyes, a tanned face that was still handsome despite the broken nose, and the broad-shouldered muscular build of a top college athlete, he had his right arm draped paternally around the shoulders of the much smaller and lighter Szeto, who squinted warily through steel-rimmed spectacles.

The photograph of the two brothers had been taken in much happier days, before the mad incident concerning the Chinese army general when … Fai shuddered at the memory; then cursed himself again. There was no reason to act scared like this. He had covered his tracks. No way could the police possibly tie him to anything. He was home and dry. Safe.

Bullshit!

It was not the police he needed to fear, Fai reminded himself, swallowing dryly. It was his father. The old man would not wait for everything to be proved in court. Or bother with any niceties like evidence. He was the great Alan Yip, Godfather of Asia's *kung fu* film industry. What applied to mere mortals did not apply to him. He would decide who was guilty, not a jury. Then once he had made his decision he would strike.

Strike to kill.

"YOU'RE SURE YOU can do it?"

"Relax, lady, I'm a professional."

"Afterwards you say nothing. Understood?"

"Just make sure to bring the money."

"You say nothing."

"I'll make sure to keep my mouth shut. Just you make sure to bring the money."

The line went dead.

The woman replaced the phone in the cradle then moved slowly across the deep-pile silk carpet, keeping her back straight and head up high, like a fashion model on the catwalk. She eased open the door that led to the kitchen, moved inside the kitchen and took down a porcelain cup from the shelf. She spooned coffee into the cup and switched on the kettle. As she waited for the water to boil she reflected on the call she had made. Should she have contacted that Triad thug? Yes. In cases of murder, even the slightest slip-up could bring fatal consequences. It was to ensure she avoided such consequences that she had made the call.

A red light on the kettle announced the water had boiled. She poured water over the coffee, picked up her porcelain cup and returned to the living room. To her dismay, she noticed that the storm had worsened: rain now hammered against the windows so loudly it seemed that someone was stood outside and banging the glass so hard that it might soon break. The harsh scream of the wind made her imagine a soul in torment. The noises unnerved her; she hated typhoons. They always reminded her of childhood days that she longed to forget. She switched on the radio, tuned to a classical music station, and then turned up the volume until it drowned out the swirling sounds outside.

Nerves repaired, she sat on the sofa and sipped her coffee. She glanced around the room. It was a spacious room: nicely decorated too. Done in a feminine style — pinks and whites and creams, silks and satins, soft furnishings — all classy and elegant. It should be. She had painstakingly copied the decoration from the home of a European countess which had featured in *Hong Kong Tatler*. More important than any countess, though, was the fact this room was unlike the room she had been brought up in.

She had spent her childhood years living in a stinking typhoon shelter in Yau Ma Tei, on board a tiny and leaky sampan shared by her mother, three sisters and a rapist stepfather. She had hated those years. Never mind. She had escaped them and come up in the world. This flat proved it. Only Chinese women who had succeeded in life could afford a luxury Mid-Levels apartment.

The apartment was not the only part of her new life which proved she had made it. There was also the relationship with her boss, film producer Alan Yip. On the surface, of course, it seemed nothing — the world was full of personal assistants who had love affairs with their rich and powerful employers. Hers was unique, though. In those other relationships the man was always in charge, the assistant merely a quick screw. With her, it was different: she had control. He knew it too, she reflected contentedly. Alan Yip knew she pulled the strings. That fact afforded her a great high. Greater than even the most passionate of lovemaking could ever have given her.

She had come far since those grim typhoon shelter days. She had powerful new friends now, had left old acquaintances trailing in the dust far behind her. At least she had left most of them behind her. She still remained in touch with a few. It was fortunate that she did. It had allowed her to move in those underworld circles where she could obtain that gangster's name.

Should she have contacted him? Would he be one of those fools who talked too much? No, she decided, gently resting her empty porcelain cup on the glass coffee table. His lips would stay sealed. He would do the job, take the money, cross the border and then lose himself in China. He wasn't stupid. He knew that ruthless people were employing him, knew about the strict rules of his employment. He knew he must never open his mouth about this job. If he did he would never open it again.

6

A BONE-JARRING BLAST of noise from the living room woke him as Ah Fah switched on the CD player. True to form, his daughter had the volume turned up to an ear-splitting level: then came the thump, thump, thump of her jumping up and down as she performed morning exercises. In case this was insufficient to give him brain damage, the phone helped by ringing.

After Wong's call last night, Chan had written his report, and then gone to bed to snatch a few hours rest. But he was still exhausted as he reached for the phone. He clapped it to his ear to be greeted by the husky voice of his longtime friend and police partner.

"We checked those ID records," Wong said.

"And?"

"Yip's son."

"You're sure?"

"Positive, boss."

"Does Lam know?"

"Not arrived here yet; want me to give him the good news when he gets in?"

"Leave Lam to me."

"How long will you be?"

"Depends on traffic," Chan said; "with luck, half an hour."

He put the phone in its cradle. A mosquito buzzed his head. He snapped at it with his hand but missed; what had happened to the reflexes he had once been so proud of? He switched on the radio. RTHK's newsreader had almost finished a report on the typhoon. It had not smashed headlong into Hong Kong, as experts had expected it to do. It had veered away and devastated the Philippines. In the end, despite the grim predictions, Hong Kong had suffered nothing more devastating than squally showers.

Next up was a report on the latest chickenpox epidemic. Health advisers urged those who had not contracted chickenpox to get vaccinated. Wearing surgical face masks in the street, as many people had begun to do, would not keep the virus at bay. The newsreader moved to the body in Mongkok. It had not been identified, he said.

Chan switched off the radio.

He dragged himself from bed and headed for the shower. As he tramped through the living room, he signalled for Ah Fah to lower the volume on her CD player. To his amazement, she obeyed. Then she flopped onto the sofa, sweating from her exertions.

"Sorry, dad, did I wake you?"

"Whatever gave you that idea?"

"You have to play western music loud. It's crap otherwise."

"Do you also have to demolish the ceiling doing aerobics?"

"Relax. I'll be more quiet tomorrow."

"*Tomorrow!*"

"I thought I would honour you by staying another night."

His eyes narrowed. "Have you and your mother rowed?"

From the way she reacted, he could have been forgiven for thinking he had just accused her of dancing naked in the street. "Absolutely and *definitely* not!" she sniffed haughtily, her over-the-top response confirming all his suspicions of a row. "Mum and I never argue. And even if we did, I couldn't have had one with her recently, could I?"

"Why not?"

"She's in Taiwan visiting granddad; she won't get back till ... What are you going to do in there?"

He had opened the bathroom door. "Buy a bag of rice. The man who lives in my shower tray sells it off cheaply on Mondays."

"Hilarious! I'm splitting my sides!"

"Well, ask a stupid question ..."

"Just clean the shower tray afterwards, inspector. And fix that lousy hot water tap too. Last night I almost scalded myself. Hire a plumber; it's easy. You just pick up the phone and punch a number."

He closed the bathroom door, and then took a calming breath. He loved his daughter dearly, of course. Always had. Yet sometimes he felt like grabbing Ah Fah by the neck and slowly …

He stared in the mirror: Buddha, he looked rough! His eyes were veined with red, the bags underneath them almost big enough to curl up and go to sleep in. Even worse, more of his precious hair was falling out — another year and it would be gone completely. Had the time finally come to swallow his pride and seek professional help? Should he try that herbal cures shop in Kennedy Town, the one Sergeant Ho from traffic section raved about? Ho swore it had helped his brother's hair grow back. Chan had never met this brother, or seen a picture of him, so had no way of knowing if the sergeant had told the truth. If he had and ... No, of course it wouldn't work. These wonder treatments were a trick, the people who administered them con-artists. He would let his head turn as smooth as a billiard ball before paying a single cent to the unscrupulous characters in that herbal cures shop.

He climbed into the shower unit and spent two minutes torturing himself under the cold water spray, jumping about and cursing almost as much as his daughter had last night. Torture over, he dried himself and returned to his bedroom to change. Ah Fah thumped on the door as he was thrusting his size nines into black Timberland loafers.

"Going jogging in Victoria Park," she announced.

"Take a key," he told her. "I'll be out when you get back … And close the door *gently* this time."

She slammed it. He finished changing and then went into the living room to check the weather. He gazed from the window: the sky had gone chicken-soup grey, rain drizzled down. But all the predictions of major typhoon damage had proved unfounded. A pity: he had hoped the storm would demolish the forty-storey office tower opposite his apartment. The tower was so ugly that he seldom stared from this window; it was too depressing. Yet when he and Mei had moved into their fourteenth-floor flat they could watch ships chug in and out of the harbour, could gaze across to Kowloon and the purple-blue New Territories beyond. The estate agent with the alligator smile had sold the flat on the strength of its postcard view.

"If only I had the money!" he had sighed, muddy brown eyes misting over dreamily. "I swear I would buy the place myself."

"You're sure?" Mei pressed him. "No office towers will be put up? The sea view's why we're interested."

The smiling estate agent laid a reassuring hand on her shoulder. "One hundred percent certain, dear lady!" His smile grew so broad that it threatened to explode from his face: "May Lord Buddha strike me dead if I'm lying! They're building a sports centre. Only four storeys high, with tennis courts on the roof — you'll keep your wonderful view."

They had bought it. Three months later, with the estate agent no longer smiling — he had just been jailed for fraud — construction teams had arrived to erect that office tower. Chan smiled wryly. It never ceased to amaze him how two supposedly intelligent people could have proved naive so often.

The doorbell rang. He thought it would be Ah Fah returning to announce she had forgotten her key. Instead it was Grandfather Chow, the sixty-year-old coin dealer who shared the flat across the corridor with his teenage grandson. Grandfather Chow stood in the doorway, looking as dignified and sincere as he always looked. But what was he doing with a football under his arm?

"I have come here to apologise to you, Ah Chan," the white-haired coin dealer announced, speaking with all his customary formality. "My grandson promised to return this ball to you after one week. Yet he has had it now for many months."

Of course! Chan understood it all now. Three months ago, Grandfather Chow had turned up seeking advice on how he could steer his only grandson away from street gangs. Chan had been rushing out to work, so had not had much time to talk, but he had suggested that he enrol the teenager in the Police Sports Club. Membership formalities would take about a week. But there was no reason why Ah Yat should not practice while he waited. Chan had handed over the ball, rushed off to work and completely forgotten about his promise to enrol the boy.

Grandfather Chow had not reminded him, of course; he was much too respectful of another person's dignity to do that. Even the slightest suggestion that Chan had broken his word would cause Chan to lose face. And for a Chinese person, especially one as old and traditional as Grandfather Chow nothing, not even mass murder, was as bad as losing face. That was why Chan couldn't mention the sports club now. To do so would imply the old man had been stupid not to remind him about his forgetfulness weeks ago — and the old man would lose face.

Instead, Chan said, "Thank you most kindly, grandfather. But my football days are long gone. Please keep the ball. Tell your grandson it is a gift."

"I ordered him to come here and apologise in person, but he refused."

"He's shy. Perhaps he thought I would be angry."

"Not shy, Ah Chan, disrespectful. It is the fault of the Americans and their hamburgers."

"Hamburgers?"

"American meat has many poisons that cause disruptive behaviour," the old man explained. "Since they began eating such food, Chinese children have grown stubborn with their elders. When our children ate noodles they were not so disrespectful. Your own daughter, I recall, was never stubborn with her elders."

Chan stifled a smile. He was about to say: "Are we talking about the same girl here? In an Olympics for stubbornness, my daughter would win gold, silver and bronze." But the coin dealer was such a serious and proper character that he would take the remarks the wrong way and think he was being called a fool. Chan merely said: "Wasn't she? It's so long since she was a child that I've forgotten. But keep the ball. Tell your grandson it's a gift."

"You do not require it yourself?"

"My football days are long gone."

"Yet you once played the game?"

"Long ago."

"And I have heard it said you were most exceptional."

Chan thought: I wonder who told you? Probably me after a bottle of rice wine. But you obviously haven't spoken to my ex-team mates. Two left feet and as fast as a crippled tortoise, was how one of them described me. And he was my best friend on the team. But no way could Chan say this. The old man was flattering him. It would be disrespectful not to accept the flattery. He said: "You are most kind, grandfather. And please assure your grandson I am not angry."

"Goodbye, Ah Chan."

"Goodbye, grandfather."

Chan closed the door. He chuckled as he grabbed his canvas jacket from the back of the sofa. So the problems affecting Hong Kong's youth were caused by hamburgers. Did the theory apply to adults? He must warn Sergeant Wong — Wong chewed three or four burgers a day.

He pulled on his grey canvas jacket, patting the left pocket to make sure it contained his phone and radio, then checked that the report he had written for Chief Superintendent Lam was in the right pocket. He opened the door and headed for the lift.

7

WHEN TOURISTS RETURN home from their holidays in Hong Kong there's a good chance they will bore friends to sleep with tales of profitable shopping expeditions.

Most expeditions take place on the crowded streets of Tsim Sha Tsui: the shopping pilgrim's Mecca. A place where sophisticated department stores, crammed full of expensive designer goods, rub shoulders with make-shift hawker stalls selling cheap baseball caps; where world-famous jewellery stores display golden bracelets worth an emperor's ransom and street touts offer to sell you, for one-tenth the price of the genuine article, a fake Rolex watch whose plastic parts ensure it breaks down after six months: a place that is brash and breezy, swarming and heaving: a place which can be extremely classy, yet at the same time, wonderfully tacky.

Nathan Road is the main route shopping pilgrims take. Starting at the harbour, it runs almost gun-barrel straight through Tsim Sha Tsui, then cuts a swathe through the shopping area of Jordan and working-class haunts of Yau Ma Tei, before halting some three kilometres away in one of the most crowded places on earth: Mongkok.

Along the route, as well as being accosted by touts selling fake watches, pilgrims will be assailed by tailors with offers of cheap made-to-measure suits. They will be tempted with offers of minced fish balls and pork dumplings by hawkers whose portable stoves send greasy fumes into the air.

True pilgrims will shrug off these mere side-shows and focus on what they are really there for: cheap electronic goods. Nathan Road is almost bursting at the seams with shops selling digital cameras, mini-disc players, Ipods, Nintendo and Xbox games, DVD players, the latest versions of digital radios — you name it, the Nathan Road stores sell it.

While bargains these days aren't what they used to be twenty years ago, they are still good. So good that pilgrims can allow ever-smiling sales people to charge them ten or even fifteen percent more than they would charge local Chinese shoppers, yet still emerge with a camera or DVD player costing a fraction what it costs in America or Europe. Which is why the pilgrims continue to plod down the street, smiling despite sauna-like humidity; why they cheerfully brush sweat off their reddened foreheads, casually flick away mosquitoes: they are happy; they are going to make some bargain buys.

The lean, angular figure in the yellow tee-shirt and black jeans, who strode down a busy Nathan Road at eight-fifteen this morning in the urgent manner of a man late for an important meeting, did not think about Ipods or DVDs: or about cheap baseball caps or imitation Rolex watches. He focused solely on the men he planned to kill.

His name was Liu Peng: a thirty-year-old assassin from China.

At first glance he looked nothing out of the ordinary, which would have pleased him because this was exactly how he wanted to look. He had always firmly believed that in his line of business, the true professional was the man who remained anonymous. Those who looked or behaved in a way that made them stand out from the crowd increased their risks of being arrested.

He stood five feet seven inches tall — about average for a Chinese man — and weighed one hundred and fifty pounds, which was also about the average. Dark wraparound glasses, a type similar to those worn by many other people walking down the road, shielded his dark, deep-set eyes from the glare of the sun — diamond hard even at such an early hour as this one. A grey baseball cap, lettered with the name of the sports manufacturer Nike, protected his head. Underneath the cap his hair was inky black. He had had his hair razored short in the harsh, military style three weeks ago, but it had grown slightly since then. Now it stood up stiffly like bristles on a brush. His face was lean and angular, like the rest of his body, and had been turned nut-brown by the sun. This deep tan almost succeeded in covering up the scars of childhood smallpox which pitted his face and which he had always felt made him look unsightly. From a distance, the smallpox scars were virtually invisible when he was as brown as this. When you drew nearer to him, though, you could still glimpse the craters in his skin.

He strode past a newspaper kiosk and turned on to Jordan Road, slowing momentarily as he passed the Jockey Club betting shop. Although it was hours before the first race, men crouched on the pavement by the shop, feverishly scanning newspapers for winning tips. Losers, Peng decided. You could see it in their weak, dispirited faces. They had already conceded defeat in life's battle. No way would they get rich — either here or anywhere. Even if they won today they would be back outside the betting shop tomorrow, and the next day and the day after that. They would return until they had lost everything.

Once, he might have felt twinges of sympathy; father had told him to pity those less fortunate. But pity lay buried in his past. Today he had no sympathy to spare for anyone. Life was often hard: sometimes cruel. You either measured up to all its tough challenges, or you fell by the wayside. It was that simple.

Besides, these gamblers were not only losers but fools. He did not suffer fools gladly; never had done. They got what they deserved. You should respect money, not fritter it away like these gambling idiots. When Peng had money he banked it. That was how you became rich. That was why he would soon be wealthy enough to quit this deadly business. But not yet, not until he had killed the *kung fu* film producer. Once he had done that, though, he would be rich enough; his new employers were paying him extremely well to eliminate movie boss Alan Yip.

Yet he would not quit the killing trade after disposing of Alan Yip — he must fulfil one more task before retiring. No one had paid him to carry out this last hit but he would still do it. In fact it was to eliminate this last target not to kill Yip that Peng had eagerly crossed over the border from China two days ago. This last target was the man responsible for the deaths of Peng's beloved sister and his father. Only when Peng had completed this final job would father and sister rest peacefully in the after-life. Only when their murderer had suffered as they had suffered would their spirits at last be appeased.

Peng swung left at the Chinese medicine shop. He brushed beads of sweat from his forehead, flicked a mosquito from his ear.

At that precise moment the bomb exploded.

"WHY ARE YOU scared?"

"I'm not," Fai said defensively. "Just …"

"What?"

"Supposing he finds out?"

"You *are* scared."

"My father isn't forgiving, Mister Tsang."

"Are you backing out of our deal?"

"No. It's just …"

"What?"

"Perhaps we should hold off; until his suspicions ease."

"No. We proceed as planned."

"He's hired detectives, Mister Tsang."

"We proceed *exactly* as planned; and don't call me again unless it's important next time."

The phone line went dead.

A tall, olive-skinned girl in a red silk dress, who was serving drinks to passengers in the first-class lounge, approached Fai.

"Are you feeling all right, sir?" A look of concern spread across her pretty, heart-shaped face. "You seem—"

"Where's the washroom?"

She pointed to a door. Fai strode briskly to the washroom, yanked open the door and entered a toilet cubicle. He bent down and threw up several times in the bowl.

He stood up and took deep breaths to try and calm himself. But his hands kept shaking. He left the cubicle and walked over to a washbasin. He splashed cold water on his face, took a few more deep breaths.

No good.

His hands still shook as he dried his face.

He glimpsed his reflection in the wall mirror. He had always been proud of his physical appearance. Justly so, too; the man who looks more like a film star than many of the stars themselves, was how a magazine writer had described him only last year. But all box-office glamour had vanished as completely as yesterday's dawn. His wide-set, raven-coloured eyes had not only lost their twinkle; they even possessed something of a haunted look this morning. The bags underneath his eyes seemed to be getting bigger and bigger; hardly surprising considering the fact he was finding it harder and harder to sleep properly.

Until about three months ago his skin had been a rich, tanned colour. It had given him the healthy, upbeat appearance of a man who had just come from a holiday on the beach. Today, though, his skin in some places had taken on the pale and greasy pallor of someone who had a serious illness. In other places it was blotched scarlet, a tell-tale sign of a heavy vodka drinker.

He turned away from the mirror. He left the washroom and returned to his seat in the lounge. The pretty drinks' girl approached him again.

"We take-off for Taiwan in another thirty … Is everything *really* all right, sir?"

"I'm fine," he said. "It's just pre-flight nerves."

8

OLD LU STOOD outside Chan's apartment block.

A teenage conscript with the Nationalists during China's civil war sixty years ago, Lu had gone crazy after being trapped for four days in a collapsed trench. These days he patrolled the pavement, grinning inanely at passers-by and playing the same Chinese opera tune over and over again on a battered fiddle. Chan gave him fifteen dollars, which should buy the old soldier a bowl of noodles. Lu saluted and flashed a grin that showed he had three teeth remaining.

Chan walked around the back of the apartment building to the car park, climbed into his ten-year-old Daihatsu and turned on the air-conditioning unit; the typhoon might have eased humidity levels slightly, but he still found the air too sticky for his liking. The police station lay less than three kilometres away, but traffic hassles usually made it a thirty-minute drive; without the air-con he would arrive soaking with sweat.

A monster traffic jam snared him a hundred metres from the Cross-Harbour Tunnel. He braked and switched the air-con to the super-cool level. He turned on the radio: pop star Gigi Leung was singing her latest hit. The congestion eased as he neared the Noon Day Gun typhoon shelter, home to leaking sampans and gleaming cabin cruisers. The gun itself would not be there much longer, though. Legislative Councillors wanted it dismantled because of its British colonial-era links and replaced by a statue of Chairman Mao.

Chan checked that the window was shut to keep out the shelter's smell of blocked drains and rotting vegetables. The smell was bad enough even on an ordinary day. On sticky ones like today, it became nauseating.

A glance at his watch showed he would be late for his appointment with Wong. And if he would be late for Wong he would also be late for Chief Superintendent Lam. He jabbed the accelerator and overtook a crowded double-decker bus bound for Kennedy Town. Lam hated unpunctuality.

BRANDISHING AK47 ASSAULT rifles, yelling at terrified bystanders to get the fuck out of their way, the three masked robbers charged out of the Dao Heng bank branch where they had just blown up the safe and jumped into a waiting Mercedes.

Car doors slammed.

The 3.2-litre, V6 engine roared as the getaway driver pressed down hard on the accelerator. In a whirl of exhaust fumes the sleek, silver-grey Mercedes sped up the road in the direction of Mongkok. A smell of cordite and burning rubber clogged the air. People shouted and screamed. They pointed at the bank where the robbery had taken place. The bank's alarm bell sounded. From somewhere in the distance came the wail of police sirens.

Peng strode briskly on. He had no time for mere side shows like this. He had seen them all before. He turned on to a street where hawkers sold tee-shirts and baseball caps. One elderly hawker reached out and seized his arm to get him to stop and examine the goods. Or perhaps he wanted Peng to explain about all the shooting. Peng brushed the man off as effortlessly as if he was swatting away another mosquito and continued imperiously on his journey. He had no time for fools like hawkers. No time to examine their trash. He had time to focus on one thing only.

Killing.

Should he go for long-range shots? Or tackle his targets from close range? Neither option would be easy. At least they would not be easy for other assassins. For him, they should pose no problems. He had handled much tougher assignments in the past. And he had always been successful too.

Yet it would be unwise to get overconfident. Overconfident men could sometimes turn into lazy men. Lazy men sometimes forgot details. Attention to detail in Peng's deadly business was crucial. It had been his key to success these past six years. He had outlasted all the others because he had paid attention to details, no matter how insignificant they might seem; had been painstakingly methodical in his approach to each and every hit; had never left anything to chance. Attention to detail had elevated him above his rivals. It had enabled him to survive for years in a business where one mistake meant the difference between life and death.

He crossed the road and entered the Urban Council Park, where po-faced old men hunkered on wooden benches while they watched youngsters play football on the park's concrete pitch. Other old men performed *tai chi* on the basketball court. As he completed his exercises, one skeletal-like geriatric gracefully waved a wooden sword high above his head. Father had been a *tai chi* devotee, Peng remembered. Each morning, even if rain lashed Beijing's streets, father had faithfully completed his exercises. He had behaved in that part of his life as he had in every other: he had been hard-working, conscientious.

And look how the bastards repaid him!

Father would be avenged, though, sister too. Both of them soon: in a few days they would sleep easy in the after-life.

Peng would make sure of it.

He strode over to a hawker selling drinks from an ice box by the park's exit, bought a can of Coca-Cola and took a drink. It was lukewarm, of course, not even the slightest bit chilled — these lousy hawkers were all crooks! But to make any complaint would draw attention to himself. So he said nothing; he threw the can in a rubbish bin and set off walking again. He turned right, then left, and landed in a street market. A crowd hovered by a seafood stall. The crowd parted to reveal the stall owner. A fat man in a grubby white tee-shirt and baggy blue shorts, he held a cage that contained a rat. The fat man placed the cage on the pavement and then gleefully poured boiling water over the rat. It died squealing in agony, much to his and the crowd's amusement.

The street resounded to the din of car horns, hawkers' sales pitches, the songs of a singer Peng had never heard before. A lorry crammed with chickens bound for restaurant cooking pots lumbered past. A reek of chicken shit, dirty cooking oil and petrol invaded the air. Few people seemed troubled by such swirling pollution. Dozens of them sat hunched over tables outside restaurants, happily swallowing diesel fumes with their congee and tea.

Peng moved past a cinema. Posters advertised Alan Yip's latest *kung fu* blockbuster. Peng knew about Yip's movies. In fact he was a fan — a big fan. He had particularly enjoyed the one he'd seen at a cinema in Shanghai last month. It was a shame Yip would never produce another *kung fu* classic as good as that one. Yet this was how it must be. Peng had been paid to do a job. Father had told him that when you pledged yourself to a task you never broke that pledge. A man who broke his word had no honour. Therefore Alan Yip must die.

And then?

Normally after a hit, he left the area as quickly as possible. However, this time would be different. Instead of taking the train or plane to China, he would stay in Hong Kong to finish that other task. No one had paid him to make this second hit, but he would still do it. And for the first time in his life, he would take pleasure in killing.

Despite what others in his elite military unit thought, he had never enjoyed carrying out any of his previous hits; he was no crazed psychopath. Killing was simply a job which he excelled at and a job which paid him well. So he did it: coldly, efficiently and professionally. This time would be different, though. Peng would smile as he squeezed the trigger. Savour the moment that the bullet shattered the second target's skull. The second target was not business. It was personal.

9

CHAN'S SMALL OFFICE rested in the older part of the police station. It contained a wooden desk that was almost as old as Confucius, two metal filing cabinets, a chair that had one shaky leg and an air-conditioning system which coughed and spluttered like a sixty-a-day smoker.

Wong sat in the chair with the shaky leg, scuffed size ten Nike jogging shoes resting on the aged desk, while he performed the seemingly impossible of eating a pork bun, slurping sweet milky coffee, smoking a cheroot and studying *Sing Tao*'s racing form — all at the same time. He glanced up cursorily as Chan opened the door.

"Don't trouble yourself getting up out of my comfortable chair, sergeant, I'll stand again — it's only my office, after all."

The sarcasm bounced off the ample frame of the man who had been Chan's close friend and colleague for twenty years. Wong's cheery grin revealed a gap in his top teeth. One of these days, Chan vowed silently, I'll wipe that smile off his face. I'll put drawing pins on the chair without telling him. Or cover it with a layer of super-glue. He won't be keen to jump into it after that.

Wong leisurely stubbed out the cheroot and put the newspaper flat on the desk; Chan spied the black circles that Wong always drew around the names of horses he planned to back that day. Gambling was a passion. That he almost invariably lost — the last time Chan could recall him winning anything at all was six years ago and even then it had only been a paltry fifty dollars — had never dimmed the sergeant's enthusiasm for the Happy Valley and Sha Tin race-tracks. Or altered his belief a big fifty-thousand dollar win was waiting just around the corner.

"From the amazing sunshine nature of your tone, Inspector Chan, sir, I'll lay five-to-four odds your meeting upstairs with that lump of bean curd that calls itself Chief Superintendent Lam didn't go too well."

He sounded different from last night, Chan noticed. In that rain-soaked Mongkok alley, Wong had been excited to the point of jumpiness. Feet up on the desk, he seemed calmness personified. It was often this way, though. At moments of high drama, Wong would charge around the crime scene like a man whose trousers had caught fire. When the drama had ended, and he could sit back and reflect, you would go a long way to encounter a more relaxed character. Chan had often wondered if his friend had an excitable identical twin, someone whom he sent out to cover for him on occasions like last night, while he stayed home in bed.

"For the first time in your life you win your bet," Chan said. "Every time I meet Lam I get the urge to strangle the lazy bastard. I'll strangle you too — unless you lift your feet from my desk."

"Have a heart, boss, I haven't finished eating yet."

Wong crammed the remains of the bun in his mouth. Eating was another passion with the fat, moon-faced sergeant. In fact as a youngster he had dreamed of running his own restaurant. After leaving school he had actually attended Hong Kong's top catering college. He had proved useless in the kitchen, though. It had taken only four days for teachers to discover that, far from being able to prepare the nine-course banquets they demanded from elite students, Wong struggled to boil a pan of rice.

The two sides had a chat, the upshot being that he quit for a job as a bakery assistant in Mongkok, only for problems to develop here too. A sweet tooth led him to eat too many cakes and pastries. The baker grew alarmed that if his new assistant consumed stocks at such a rate he would eat into profits — so he fired him.

Luckily, Wong then met an ex-schoolmate who had joined the police and who helped him join too.

Wong finished eating his pork bun. He looked around the office for somewhere to clean his hands.

"Don't even *think* of wiping them on that chair," Chan warned him. He tossed Wong a pack of paper tissues. And you've finished breakfast now — get your sweaty feet off my desk."

With a loud sigh, Wong lowered his feet to the floor and sat more upright. He looked bleary-eyed. Probably he had worked non-stop since the discovery of the body. To those who didn't know him well, the fat, moon-faced sergeant, with his feet up on the desk, reading of *Sing Tao*, munching of snacks throughout the day and refusal to take much seriously, often appeared lazy and uninterested in the job. But Chan knew his friend worked hard. Yes, he scanned the newspaper for that elusive big winner, though only when he had no work to do. Yes, he joked about the job. So what? Jokes relaxed you. Relaxed officers performed better.

It was Chan's considered opinion that if Wong had been less of a joker, more wary about his professional image and been born a fraction less clumsy, then he would be an inspector now. But in the past, whenever Chan had urged him to tone down his personality until he won promotion, Wong had insisted there was no need; he was happy as a sergeant.

As Chan moved closer, he detected the sour odour of beer. Wong must have visited one of the red-light bars that stayed open until the early hours before coming to the office. He spent a lot of his time in the Wan Chai bars these days. Not that Chan begrudged him. He could hardly do that, could he? Not when he himself had spent part of the early hours pouring wine down his own throat.

It was against rules to come to work smelling of the stuff, of course. Never mind the rules, though. While Hong Kong slept peacefully, Wong had been grafting away in that rat-infested alley; that gave him a right to relax however he saw fit. It was just that Chan liked Wong's wife, and he wished that Wong had gone home to her and ... *Aheya,* I'm getting as pious as the monks in Lantau's monastery, Chan thought. Who am I to sit in judgement? Let Wong and his wife sort out their own problems. Anyway, perhaps I'm imagining it. Perhaps no problems exist.

"Join the queue behind five hundred others at this station who want to strangle Lam," Wong said. "Anyway, what exactly did Chairman Mao's best friend say to you in there?"

"Apart from bawling me out for being fifty-nine seconds late and almost wetting himself when I mentioned the name Alan Yip, you mean? Nothing much — he just wants an arrest. And he wants it yesterday."

"You're definitely in charge, huh?"

Chan nodded.

Wong thoughtfully fingered the pencil-thin moustache one of the girls from the red-light bars had persuaded him to grow as an experiment; it would make him look more sophisticated, she had said. In Chan's opinion, the experiment had been a failure. It had turned Wong into a cross between Belgian detective Hercule Poirot and American funny man Oliver Hardy — with a bit of the villainous Fu Manchu lobbed in for good measure.

"You could avoid friction with Lam, you know," Wong said. "Just make him feel good about himself. Show him some respect now and again and try to keep your temper under wraps."

Chan sensed the beginning of another lecture. Not for the first time he wondered why despite — in theory at least — being boss, he had played meek husband to Wong's nagging wife for the best part of twenty years.

"I do show respect. Always have."

"Bollocks!"

"Don't be so diplomatic," Chan said. "There's no need to make such an effort to spare my feelings. Spit it out, Ah Wong, say what you really mean."

"You treat Lam like a prize jerk," Wong said. "All right, I agree — he is one. And I know that when you two worked together at the Anti Triad Bureau years back, you were the top man and he looked like he would be cleaning out the toilets for the rest of his career. But times have changed, Pete; Lam's the big boss here now. It's crazy to deliberately annoy him."

"Next time I'll send flowers and ask him to dinner," Chan said. "Now can we please change the subject, mother? There's no doubt those prints we took from that car belong to Alan Yip's son?"

"They're his," Wong said.

"Did we speak to anyone at the car hire firm?"

Wong nodded. "That Mercedes was hired to Szeto Yip."

"When?"

"Two weeks ago. He hired it for a month."

"What about Eddie's post mortem report?"

Wong shook his head: "Nothing yet."

"Has anyone informed our victim's father officially?"

Another shake of the head: "Not yet, boss."

Which meant Chan would have to deliver the grim news himself. He did not look forward to the prospect. He had never got used to that sombre part of the job. He checked his watch: almost twenty to eleven. He should leave for Kowloon immediately. The sooner he confronted Alan Yip the better it would be for both of them.

"In that case I'll go and see him now; unless you've got anything else to tell me."

"Your best pal was here an hour ago."

"Best pal?"

"Terry Duggan."

Chan stiffened: "Duggan?"

A British soldier posted to Hong Kong, Duggan had quit the army eighteen years ago and joined the police force. Many British detectives had gone home in recent years, but he had stayed; he enjoyed the lifestyle, he said. What he meant was that he would be nothing in Britain; no police force would tolerate his violence, no woman let him near her. Here, though, he could buy girls cheaply and throw his weight around.

"Wanted to know if he can work this case."

"No," Chan snapped.

"He's really keen to get involved."

"I don't work with thugs, Ah Wong."

Wong said slowly, "Shouldn't that be, you 'don't work with *western* thugs'?"

Chan frowned. He said tonelessly, "What are you trying to say?"

"Come on, boss, you know yourself that you've got a chip on your shoulder about—"

Chan interrupted.

"Don't give me all of that stupid Chinese-foreigner stuff again. When Lam was on the street he was a thug too, and I never liked any of his style either — and he's one hundred percent Chinese."

"It's weird too, considering you're half-*gweilo* yourself."

Chan shook his head. "What's weird is that for twenty years I've sat, or rather I've stood here, seeing as you always seem to be in my chair, and listened to your rubbish."

Wong grinned. "You're losing your temper. Know why?"

"Why?"

"Because you know I'm right. You've always had a thing about westerners. You're like one of those people who converts over to Buddhism, or a drunk who swears off the booze — they all feel they need to prove their new loyalty. So they criticise every other religion, or their friends who are still out boozing. *You* feel you have to prove you're a totally loyal Chinese, see. So—"

"I'm grateful for all the advice, Professor Freud, but I haven't time to hear more. I need to see Alan Yip."

"What do you want me to do while you're with him?"

"Dig up as much on our victim as possible," Chan said. "Your reporter friends might help — their files are often better than ours. I want names of all his friends at work and outside of work; names of girlfriends too — enemies if he had any."

"The complete works, huh?"

Chan nodded. "Get all you can on this Heavenly Ghosts cult too. How much do you know about it at the moment?"

Wong shrugged: "I know their leader's some crazy character who claims he can fly. I know it's banned in China, and I know the Communist Party big-shots over there are all wetting their pants about it — they're scared the cult might get so big it'll take over the country."

"They might have good reason to worry," Chan said. "Someone told me the cult caused that Shanghai gas outbreak."

Wong frowned. "China said it was all just a tragic accident."

"Because they didn't want to admit the cult was organised enough to cause it," Chan said. "Or so my source told me."

"Source?"

"Jack Spalding."

"*The* Jack Spalding?"

"Do you know any other Jack Spaldings living here?"

Instead of answering the question, Wong tossed back his head and then threw up his hands in a theatrical gesture. He closed his eyes and winced like a man in great pain.

"Are you practising for a part in Alan Yip's new film?" Chan queried tonelessly. "Or is it a problem with something you ate?"

Wong slowly opened his eyes. He sat up more straight. "Jack Spalding is my problem, boss. He—"

"I know, I know," Chan said. "He sometimes exaggerates a bit after a few beers."

Wong raised an eyebrow. "A *bit* is putting it mildly."

"Which is why I never took him too seriously at first," Chan said. "Yet you can't deny he's given us some good stuff before."

"He's given us a lot more junk."

"It might not be junk this time. Check your reporter friends at *Ming Pao* and *Sing Tao*. They might confirm what Jack told me."

Chan patted his jacket pockets. Satisfied that radio, phone and wallet were still in there, he headed for the door. He paused with one hand on the door frame and turned to face Wong.

"And for what it's worth, I'm *not* biased against westerners."

10

TWO MILES OF some of the world's most polluted water divides Hong Kong Island from Kowloon and the purple-green Chinese mainland that lies beyond. Three road and three railway tunnels link one side of Victoria Harbour to the other.

Chan chose to travel on the Star Ferry. Since childhood he had loathed going through any tunnels. He would board the ferry to Kowloon and then, once safely across the harbour, take a taxi to Alan Yip's office. He was about fifty metres from the ferry entrance when his mobile phone rang.

"You've locked me out," said his daughter Ah Fah.

"Don't you have a key?"

"Of course I have," she said sarcastically. "I just felt like standing by the door, looking an idiot in my running gear, while I rang you."

"I said take a key, Ah Fah."

"The word key never passed your lips."

"You weren't listening as usual."

"I'm listening now — how do I get in?"

"Go to the lobby and see the caretaker," Chan said. "He has a spare. And if you go out again, take the key. Are you going out?"

"I'm meeting university friends in Tsim Sha Tsui."

"Ah yes! I meant to ask you last night about university."

"Ask what?"

"I'll explain later. The line's breaking up. You forgot to recharge your mobile again. I'll see you tonight and …"

The line went dead.

He put the phone in his pocket. He passed through the ferry's turnstile and moved on to the gently rocking boat.

"HOW CAN I help this time, Mister Yip?"

"Double vodka and tonic."

The leggy Tawainese flight attendant reached obediently down to her trolley for the vodka and tonic bottles and a fresh glass. She slowly unscrewed the tops from the two bottles, poured first vodka then tonic into the tall glass, and then added a thin slice of fresh lemon. Why must he drink so much? They had barely been airborne an hour and this was already the third time she had served him. No wonder his voice had become slurred, his face so flushed. Yet he would be a handsome figure sober. Get rid of all the ugly blotched redness in his face, all that unsightly puffiness under his eyes … Yes he would be good-looking. A nicely attractive body too, about six foot tall and lean-framed. He wouldn't stay lean-framed for too much longer, though. Not if he kept drowning himself in alcohol like this.

"There you go, sir." She handed him the glass. "Enjoy your … Oh! I'm sorry. That was clumsy of me!"

His grey jacket had been resting on the arm of his first-class seat. She had just accidentally knocked the jacket to the floor while replacing the vodka and tonic bottles in her trolley. She bent down and retrieved the jacket for him.

"There you go, sir." She handed him the jacket: "Sorry about … Oh! something's fallen from the pocket ... No don't worry, sir, I'll get it for you."

It was a pamphlet the size of a paperback novel. The picture of a smiling grey-haired man, who was probably aged in his early sixties, adorned the front cover. A headline above the man's picture asked the question: 'what will you do when the world comes to an end tomorrow?' It supplied its readers with an answer: 'you can save yourself by joining the brotherhood of Heavenly Ghosts.' The flight attendant smiled to herself. Maybe this pamphlet explained all the vodka. After all, if the world was due to come crashing to an end tomorrow then you might as well enjoy yourself today. That way, you would be so drunk tomorrow that you would feel no pain when …

"Where did you get that?"

His sudden aggression surprised her.

"But — but it's yours."

"No."

"It fell from your jacket."

"Someone paid you to put it there."

"No need to shout, sir."

"Who paid you? Tell me."

"Your coat lay on the armrest. I knocked it down and—"

"Liar!"

"Calm down, Mister Yip, I'm trying to help."

She thrust out her hand which held the pamphlet, inviting him to take it. He shrank back from her as though she had some incurable disease.

"Take it away!" he yelled. "Take it away!"

CHARLES SUEN, THE balding sixty-year-old owner of Suen Investigations, a man whose staff secretly and disdainfully called him 'The Eagle' because of his dark, beady eyes, large hooked nose and the way he clawed as much work out of them as possible, frowned over half-moon spectacles as he read the report.

Early on in what had so far proved to be an extremely lucrative career, Charles 'The Eagle' Suen had realised how crucial it was to please his ultra-rich clients and keep them happy. Providing you kept them happy by giving them the results they wanted, they usually didn't mind paying you high fees. Keeping them happy also meant they would use your expensive services again. So Charles Suen had always done his level best to please important customers.

The problem was that this confidential report he now held in his hands would not please film producer Alan Yip. When Yip had finished reading the report's twenty-four pages, all neatly typed on pristine white paper, he would not be happy. In fact he would be furious. Charles Suen frowned more heavily as he laid the report flat on the top of his large, polished oak desk. He leaned over and jabbed a button on the intercom that linked him to his middle-aged secretary who sat in the office next door.

"Yes, Mister Suen?"

"Get me Kwong on the line," Suen said gruffly.

After about ten seconds, Suen's phone rang.

"You wanted to speak to me, sir?"

"I've just read your report," Suen said, speaking in the same gruff manner as he had to his secretary.

Sylvester Kwong, a clever but shy twenty-five-year-old, nervously cleared his throat. "And is there … I mean is there a slight problem somewhere?"

"There's a problem *everywhere*, young man!"

"Everywhere? But — but I don't understand, sir." Kwong sounded both puzzled and concerned. "I made sure to double-check everything. But if you want me to check it through all again, I'll—"

Suen interrupted.

"It's not a slight problem, either. It's a very serious problem. You say you've narrowed it to two suspects?"

"Yes."

"One is the financial director?"

"Yes, sir, but if there's a problem with him I can—"

"Not him, you fool! The problem is suspect two."

"Suspect two?"

"What do you think our important client will say when he gets this report, Kwong? How do you think he'll react when he reads the name of suspect number two written at the top of the page?"

Suen said haltingly, "Well, naturally … I mean, I don't expect him to be particularly pleased, Mister Suen. But—"

"Of course our client won't be *particularly* pleased. Have you any appointments this morning?"

"Yes sir; a meeting with Mr Hung from Bank of East Asia."

"Cancel it now," Suen said sharply. "Then meet me down in the executive car park in exactly fifteen minutes. We're driving to Alan Yip's film studios."

11

CHAN FELT AS though he had just stepped on to the set of a TV soap opera; one of those life-in-hospital dramas that had recently become so wildly popular. Many of his fellow passengers on the boat wore white surgical masks, presumably as protection against the chickenpox virus affecting Hong Kong — they must think that filtering air through the masks would keep them safe.

According to the experts, though, vaccination was the only useful preventative measure. Not that Chan needed to worry about chickenpox himself. He had caught it as a child in China and was now immune. Ah Fah too; she had contracted the virus as a three-year-old. Chan remembered the occasion well. He had been so terrified her chickenpox might develop into something more harmful that he had not slept for three days.

Dozens of tourists were also on board, though none of them wore masks. Judging from the cameras most of them carried, the tourists had come on board to take photographs: the eight-minute trip from Hong Kong to Kowloon offered a fantastic view of the harbour.

As the ferry pulled jerkily away from the pier, a stocky, blonde-haired woman in pink trousers, who was standing by the passenger rail at the side of the boat, gave a sudden shriek of delight. Then she started shooting pictures of the waterfront as though her life depended on capturing every detail of the scene. More camera-laden tourists joined her at the rail, all of them clicking away furiously.

The tourists would probably be back on board the ferry tonight. If not, they would miss something truly special; the waterfront was even more spectacular than it was during the day. The night-time view had never ceased to stun Chan. Not since his own first evening ferry trip two decades ago. He remembered it as clearly as though it were yesterday: the skyscrapers and their myriad of dazzling lights, the purple-black hills, the glow from the rich people's homes on the hillside, the Peak itself sparkling like a huge rare jewel — it had all seemed such a magical …

"Would you have the time, sir?"

The tourist who sat in front of him had swung around and asked a question. He was probably in his mid or late forties. A big, beer-truck of a man, with shoulders so broad they almost burst through his white tee-shirt, a face reddened by the sun and short, curly hair the colour of straw. Unlike most of the tourists, this one's wide-set, sea-green eyes were not hidden by a pair of dark glasses.

"Sorry," Chan said, "I was daydreaming." He checked his watch. "It's just gone twenty minutes after eleven."

The man nodded politely. "Much obliged to you, sir."

He nodded again, this time in the direction of the skyscrapers on the other side of the harbour in the metropolis of Kowloon. Sunlight bounced off the glass and steel walls of the skyscrapers turning them into huge diamonds.

"A really beautiful city isn't it?" the man said almost dreamily.

"Yes," Chan agreed. "Yes, it is."

"My wife and I will be real sorry to leave it all behind us." The man sounded genuinely sad. "That's Ellie stood over there." He nodded at the stocky, blonde-haired woman in pink trousers, who was still standing by the passenger rail at the side of the boat, still feverishly shooting her pictures. "We're over here to celebrate our twentieth wedding anniversary; we're staying at the Sheraton in Tsim Sha Tsui."

"It's a nice hotel."

"It sure is. And this city sure is really beautiful too." The tourist thrust out a large, meaty hand: "Bob Anderson from Louisville, Kentucky."

"Peter Chan."

"Live here, Mister Chan?"

"North Point; six stops on the underground railway from … I think your wife wants you."

The woman was waving animatedly at her husband, urging him to join her at the rail.

"Ellie must have jammed the camera again. She's always doing it. I'll have to go and help her. Will you excuse me, Mister Chan?"

"Of course and enjoy the rest of your holiday."

"You have a nice day too, Mister Chan."

Louisville? Surely that was where the boxer Muhammed Ali came from. A nice man, Mister Bob Anderson, Chan decided: friendly and polite. Intelligent too; a lot more intelligent than police sergeants called Wong, who made unfounded racism allegations. Chan wished that Wong had overheard that chat with Bob Anderson. Then he would have realised he had been stupid to make those accusations.

It's crazy, Chan thought. How can I be anti-western? — I'm half-*gweilo* myself, even if I only saw my English father once. His British blood still runs in my veins, though. I'm hardly likely to be anti-myself, am I? If I hate westerners as much as Wong claims I do, then why do I insist everyone calls me by the western name of Peter? Why have I got western friends like Eddie Gallacher and Jack Spalding? I'm not biased against westerners, it's the *gweilo* bullies like Terry Duggan who I've got no time for. That's why I barred him from getting involved this case.

Who killed movie mogul Alan Yip's son? When did the killer park the car in that alley? Eddie said Yip's son had been dead at least four days. Was the car parked there for the full four days? Why the army general's uniform? Had Yip's son been going to, or returning from, a fancy dress party? Did a guest kill him? Why? Not for money — his wallet had five thousand dollars. His ring and watch are worth thousands too. What about those other things? What was that Heavenly Ghosts' stuff doing there? Did a cult member kill him? Why?

Chan recalled his meeting in the Foreign Correspondents Club three months ago with Jack Spalding — had Jack spoken the truth? He had not taken Jack seriously when he'd bragged about knowing the true story of the fatal gas leak in Shanghai. Jack had drunk almost a bottle of Johnnie Walker black label and Chan knew about his friend's tendency to exaggerate when he was in his cups. In the past, a whisky-fuelled Jack had provided numerous allegedly red-hot tips which had ultimately proved useless. On the other hand some of his tips, even a few of those given when Jack had been the worse for wear from booze, *had* proved useful.

The shopping centre gas leak had left sixty-five people dead, most of them women and young children. In the official version, China claimed that an underground piping system had collapsed. Gas from this had filtered into the centre and mixed with chemicals from a paint store to create a cocktail of deadly fumes.

According to the Jack Spalding version, cult members had deliberately pumped killer gas into the centre. He had investigated the cult because he had been writing an exclusive feature for the *South China Morning Post*. Not only one but three people — all of them ultra-reliable types who had never let him down before — had told him the truth about the tragedy.

"Why?" Chan had asked. "Why poison women and children in a shopping centre?"

Spalding had stared at him as though the answer was obvious: "They're nutcases, your majesty! They hate everything about the modern world! The way they see it, everything modern is evil. Shopping is modern so … Yes, I will have another double whisky."

Chan had asked Jack for the names of the three 'ultra-reliable' people he had spoken to. Spalding had refused to give him them.

"That'll have to stay a state secret," he'd said, tapping his purple-blue nose. "A good reporter never reveals his sources."

The exposé he had claimed to be writing had not appeared in the paper. And since that whisky-fumed night three months ago, Jack had never mentioned the Shanghai tragedy. Chan had assumed the story was untrue, yet another case of his journalist friend exaggerating wildly when in his cups. But supposing that it *wasn't* untrue? Supposing …

The ferry docked with a jolt that shook him from his thoughts. He got up from his seat and followed other passengers off the boat and then out through the ferry exit. He emerged on to a crowded street. He dragged a paper tissue from his pocket, wiped his greasy face. Travelling on the Star Ferry, with a mild breeze drifting across Victoria Harbour, had kept him relatively cool. Now, he sweated profusely; despite twenty years in Hong Kong he'd never got used to this humidity. In the village by China's Yellow River, where he had been born, it had been cooler.

More annoying than the heat were the mosquitoes which dive-bombed his neck. He swatted one attacker away, then another, then stood and considered his options. It would be nice to travel in the mosquito-free, air-conditioned comfort of a taxi. But the queue snaked for a good twenty metres — he might wait half an hour. Better to walk five minutes to Nathan Road and hail a cab from one of the hotels there — the Sheraton, or Holiday Inn.

He crossed the busy highway. A tall, bespectacled young man approached him. The young man was well dressed and looked more like a college student than the street tout that he actually was. He asked if Chan wanted to buy a fake Rolex. Chan ignored him and kept walking. A few right and left turns and he found himself on Nathan Road outside Chungking Mansions, the tower block full of Indian restaurants and budget hotels. Keen-eyed Indian tailors patrolled the pavement, thrusting clothing price lists into the hands of passers-by and dragging the more prosperous-looking tourists into their shops. They left Chan alone. They knew a pauper when they saw one.

He decided to head for the Holiday Inn's taxi rank. No need, though. A cab was coming down the road. He waved it down.

"Where to, chief?" the driver asked

"Kowloon Tong: Oriental Action Movies."

12

RUBBER BURNED AGAINST asphalt.

The new town of Sha Tin flashed into view on the right. Apartment block windows winked in soft, pink-yellow moonlight. On the car radio, pop star Gigi Leung was crooning her latest hit. The driver of the Mercedes threw another nervous glance in his rear-view mirror, and then jabbed the accelerator harder. The lights of Sha Tin became a silvery-orange blur that grew smaller and smaller as the Mercedes sped faster down Tolo Highway.

Tolo Highway joins Kowloon's teeming concrete jungle to the Chinese border some forty-odd kilometres away, cutting a swathe through what the tourist guides, keen to create a mysterious aura for the place, call 'The Land Between'. This is the New Territories, a sprawl of farming villages, container terminal depots and new towns crammed with high-rise apartment blocks, which all motorists must drive through before reaching China.

During daytime, Tolo Highway is clogged with traffic. Lorries trundle up to the Chinese border loaded with cargo, some of it legal and some illegal; taxis ferry passengers between villages and towns; tour buses transport visitors to 'The Land Between'. Petrol fumes shimmer in polluted air, horns blare as drivers become frustrated by long jams in steamy heat. Curses are exchanged, fists raised in anger.

At night, it is different. The monster traffic jams disappear. On some stretches of Tolo Highway, far away from the bright lights and the apartment blocks, swaddled by a thick, velvety blackness, you rarely encounter another car. At night, on such deserted stretches of the highway, it is often possible to feel that you are the only person living on the planet. Which was how the driver of the Mercedes felt right now.

Alone and afraid.

He threw another anxious glance in the rear-view mirror. No one was behind him. What had happened to that security detail? The one he had been promised when he had called HQ on the radio five minutes ago? They had assured him a security team was speeding down the highway, on its way to catch him up and help.

What had happened to it?

Should he slow down and pull to the side of the road to wait? No. It was too risky. Supposing it was not the security team that pulled up behind him but Fung and his team of hired assassins? It was safer to keep going. The driver pressed down harder on the accelerator. The Mercedes' speedometer needle moved past the eighty-five-miles-an-hour mark. Up above him, the crescent-shaped moon nudged behind a bank of clouds; the sky darkened.

Then the bomb detonated and everything turned a brilliant shade of white.

The driver jabbed the brakes. The car screeched to a halt. The driver's door burst open and he leaped out, dragging a Colt .45 automatic from his shoulder holster: he fired twice, his attackers who had exploded the bomb shot back. Bullets rattled the Mercedes' silver skin. The bullets ruptured the fuel tank. There was a strong smell of gasoline. A dull click as though a cigarette lighter had failed to ignite.

The car burst into flames.

Before the flames could reach the driver, he leaped high into the air, somersaulted over the blazing car and landed safely about five metres away. The film director yelled, "Cut!" A six-strong team of workers armed with fire extinguishers jogged on to the film set. They sprayed foam over the car, killing the flames. The smell of burning rubber and plastic replaced that of gasoline. Black-out curtains on the huge indoor set, which had been drawn to simulate night-time, were pulled back. Light flooded in.

"Wow!" exclaimed the tall and extremely thin young man who had been given the job of escorting Chan to Alan Yip's office, but who had insisted they pause here to watch this blockbuster being shot. "Fantastic, huh — made you feel you were sitting right there in that car yourself, huh? And the explosion … Wow! Then the crazy somersault at the end — brilliant! We use acrobats from the state circus in China to do that leaping stuff, you know." The guide bobbed up and down on the balls of his feet like an athlete. "And once the boss has dug into his box of tricks and edited all those shots that driver won't only jump two metres, he'll jump twenty! Do seven or eight somersaults too!"

"I need to see your boss," Chan reminded him, "urgently."

The tall young man raised both hands in a gesture which urged Chan to relax. "The office is just around the corner. But I knew you wouldn't want to miss seeing an Alan Yip film being shot — it's what everyone wants when they come here. Of course, they're always surprised not to see people from the Ming Dynasty wandering around — no good guys in flowing silk robes battling evil landlords, I mean. People sort of expect that from a *kung fu* film, don't they? But the boss, he's changing all of that with his brilliant special effects. He's hauling the *kung fu* film into the twenty-first … Anyway, what did you think about the shot yourself?"

Chan did not reply. He had no time to think about *kung fu* films. He was too busy wondering how to tell Alan Yip his son had been murdered. Should he work slowly up to the announcement, or would it be better to disclose the truth immediately? How would Yip react? Chan considered how he himself would behave if a policeman arrived at his door to announce that Ah Fah had been murdered. He would be heart-broken, of course. It'll be like that with Yip too, Chan decided. No matter how I deliver the news to him, he'll still be devastated.

Once he had said farewell to his guide, then walked down the long corridor to Yip's office, a corridor lined on either side with pictures of the movie boss in various poses: director Alan Yip, posing behind a camera; producer Alan Yip, putting the final touches to a film in the editing room; victorious Alan Yip, belly straining against the seams of his dinner jacket as he swaggered forward to collect another award; then entered the film producer's office, he realised he wouldn't need to deliver any news. Yip already knew his son was dead. A police station snitch must have leaked the information, hoping to earn a big pay-back.

One glance at the movie mogul told Chan Yip knew the worst. Normally, the film producer was a loud-mouthed braggart. When Chan and his partner Sergeant Wong had entered this same office eighteen months ago to investigate the murder of a Yip employee — a murder which had ultimately proved to be suicide — Yip had sprung up from his big swivel chair.

"Park your arses and give your brains a rest!" he had boomed. "Cigar? They're the best. Rolled between the legs of Havana's finest whores — heh, heh, heh! Or so my supplier says. But I wouldn't be surprised if he has his own grandmother do the job — heh, heh, heh! Always give myself the best. Know why? Alan Yip's worked hard to get where he is, that's why. Sprang from nothing and just look at him now. Runs the biggest film company in Asia — and that includes all those Indian jerks over in Bollywood."

This morning, there was none of this swaggering bluster. Yip looked as shattered as any loving father who had lost a son would look. He sat slumped in his big swivel chair, nodding zombie-like as his assistant, a tall and pencil-slim woman called Miss Yeung, ushered Chan over to the desk. Yip's fat, round face was ashen. Redness around his eyes showed he'd been weeping.

"Coffee?" Miss Yeung enquired politely in a soft voice as she directed Chan to a chair in front of the desk.

"Thank you," Chan said.

She looked to be in her early thirties and stood about five feet seven tall, which was four inches above the average for Chinese women. Her dusky complexion and dark, jewel-like eyes gave her the appearance more of someone who had been born in Thailand or the Philippines rather than in China. She wore a peach-coloured business suit, whose extreme simplicity meant that it had probably cost a small fortune, and used the same Chanel perfume as Chan's estranged wife Mei liked to use. A heart-shaped golden pendant hung on a slim gold chain around her neck. Her ebony-coloured hair had been cut in fashionable layers, ending just above her shoulders.

"Milk and sugar, inspector?"

"Just black."

The half-inch scar on the side of her face — she had covered it up with a generous layer of make-up but it still showed — meant you could not call her beautiful. Yet something elevated her out of the mere ordinary. As Chan sat down he tried to work out what that something was. At first he thought it might be her imposing stature — she was extremely tall for a Chinese woman — and the elegant way she walked, or rather glided around the room, almost like a fashion model on the catwalk. On second thoughts, he decided, it was those dark, jewel-like eyes. They gleamed with intelligence.

She headed towards the coffee machine. As she passed Yip's chair, she stopped to rest a manicured hand on his shoulders. The film producer reached up with one of his hands and gently touched her painted fingernails with his fingertips. Chan glimpsed the loving expression on Miss Yeung's face — *personal* assistant described her job perfectly. More than a business relationship united this pair.

Still touching her hand, Yip asked in a hoarse, faltering voice: "You're sure about this, Chan? The body in that car … There's no … There's no mistake … It's definitely my son?"

"I'm sorry," Chan said. "But I'm afraid there's no mistake."

"You're absolutely sure?" Yip persisted, clinging to one last, desperate hope. "There's no chance that … No chance that you've made a mistake?"

"I'm sorry," Chan said. "The fingerprints of the man who died match those on identity card records for your son Szeto."

Yip's fat face turned so white that for a moment Chan thought he might faint. The moment passed. The film boss grabbed several deep breaths and regained control of his emotions. With tender loving care, he gently removed Miss Yeung's manicured hand from his shoulder.

Miss Yeung walked over to the coffee machine.

"When did you last see Szeto, Mister Yip?" Chan asked.

"Five days ago," Yip replied. "He didn't live at home with me and my other son — he had his own flat."

"In the same Mid-Levels block as me," Miss Yeung said from her place by the coffee machine. "I live up on the fourteenth floor, Szeto lived on the thirteenth."

"So you last saw your son on Tuesday?" Chan said.

Yip nodded. "He called here on his way to the fancy dress party."

"Organised by the Chamber of Commerce to raise money for charity," Miss Yeung said. "Normally they hold the party in the Excelsior Hotel, but this year it was staged at the Mandarin."

Which would explain that army general's uniform, Chan thought. The uniform Szeto was wearing when we found him. He must have attended the party in the uniform. Always assuming he ever got to the party, of course. He might have been killed before arriving.

"Did you see Szeto after Tuesday, Miss Yeung?"

"Me?" She seemed surprised by the question.

"You lived in his apartment block," Chan pointed out.

"But on a different floor, inspector; you don't usually run into anyone at the block unless they're on the same floor."

"You never saw him?"

"Not after Tuesday."

She returned from the coffee machine and placed cups of steaming coffee before both men. Chan sipped at his drink. Yip left his untouched on the table beside a half-empty bottle of brandy — he must be using alcohol to help numb his feelings. As well as the brandy bottle and coffee cup, a newspaper also lay on the table. Chan spied a headline beginning, 'Multi-million-dollar deal …', but couldn't read any more because Yip, had scrawled in black pen across the page, obscuring the rest of the headline as well as the story and photograph below. In fact he had dragged his pen so savagely across the photograph that he had actually torn the paper there.

Chan was puzzling over which newspaper it was — it lay folded in such a way that he couldn't glimpse the title, but judging from the style of certain headlines it looked like it was the *Hong Kong Economic Journal* — when Yip snatched the newspaper up and stored it under the desk.

"I'll need to talk to as many of Szeto's colleagues as I can," Chan said. "So perhaps—"

"*I don't want fucking talk!*"

Alan Yip no longer sat hunched in the chair like a broken man. Now he leaned forward, jabbing his finger aggressively.

"I want a fucking arrest! And if you know what's good for you, Chan, you'll get me one — quickly!"

The outburst stunned Chan. Why had Yip's attitude changed so suddenly? That heartbroken look of a moment ago had vanished as completely as yesterday's dawn. This was the old Alan Yip, the loud-mouthed bully Chan remembered from their previous encounter. He had misjudged the situation, he decided. Yip's grief about his son's death was not as severe as he had at first assumed it was.

"I want to build a picture of his personality and movements," Chan started to explain reasonably. "It'll—"

"No need," Yip snapped. "I *know* who killed Szeto."

13

PENG CAREFULLY SNAPPED the magazine into his sniper's rifle. In a moment he would squeeze the trigger. His target stood one hundred metres away. At such distance a 7.5mm bullet would blow the man's brain apart.

Peng clipped the telescopic sight on to the rifle.

He flicked off the safety.

Everything was ready.

He moved to the window, silent as a cat in his rubber-soled shoes. He raised the gun to his shoulder, screwed his right eye over the telescopic sight; swung the barrel gently to the right, until the cross in the rifle's telescopic sight rested on the head of a man who had just begun to emerge from a restaurant opposite the hotel. Peng breathed more slowly to steady his firing arm, tongue lolling childlike from his mouth, the way it always did when he concentrated. As he imagined how the target's head would explode when a bullet slammed into his skull, he experienced the adrenaline rush of a big-game hunter.

Then he paused.

Should he move from a head shot to the stomach? No, it was best to target the head. His elite army unit instructors in China had always urged him to go for the body, because the body's bigger target meant that there was a greater chance of making a hit. But there was also more chance of the target surviving a body hit — so

Peng always aimed for the head. You needed to be good to hit the head of a moving target from this range, of course. But he was good. In fact he was very good. He had never missed a head shot at one hundred metres. Never ...

What was that?

Floorboards had just creaked in the hotel's corridor. His trigger finger relaxed. He held his breath for a moment, strained his ears for other sounds. Nothing. Relax, he told himself, it was just a gust of wind. He licked his lips, took another deep breath. The target's head still lay trapped in the rifle's telescopic sights.

Peng squeezed the trigger.

"IT WAS THE cult bastards!" Film boss Alan Yip spat out the words. "That's why you found all that stuff under Szeto's body."

Chan cursed silently. When would they stop these information leaks at the police station? An informant must have told Yip about those cult leaflets.

"Wanted to let me know, see … They wanted to give Alan Yip a message … To tell him they would—"

"It's time to take your tablets!" Miss Yeung announced brightly. She unscrewed the top from a glass bottle and eased out two cylindrical white pills. "Doctor Fung said every three hours," she reminded her boss rather primly.

Yip slapped her hand away, dashing the bottle and the two pills to the floor.

"I'm not taking them, you stupid bitch!"

Stupid bitch!

The outburst left Chan stunned. What had happened to all that love? To all that tenderness Yip had expressed only a few moments ago when he had reached up and caressed Miss Yeung's fingertips. Am I wrong about their relationship being more than just business? Chan wondered. No, I don't think I'm not wrong; in fact I'm sure they're having an affair. But in this area of life, as in all others, Alan Yip is obviously the master.

Miss Yeung obediently bent down to retrieve bottle and tablets.

"Leave them alone," Yip snapped.

She obeyed him again and moved into the background. Yes, Yip is the master, Chan thought. A cruel, bullying master too — or am I being unfair on him? Has the pain of his son's death, mixed with too much brandy, made him act out of character today? No. He feels nothing for his lover. She's not a person as far as he's concerned, just another one of his many possessions, something to be discarded at whim.

"You mentioned threats," Chan said.

Yip nodded: "In China. Eight months ago."

"Mister Yip is famous there," gushed Miss Yeung. "His films are the most popular in all of China — everyone knows his name over there."

She had recovered amazingly quickly from Yip's rebuke. So quickly that Chan grew angry at her as well as at Yip — did she have no pride? Apparently not: once again she gazed lovingly and admiringly at her employer.

"Everyone knows Alan Yip's name *everywhere*." Yip corrected her.

"Who threatened you in China?" Chan asked.

"I was shooting my latest film," Yip said. "In Shaanxi, in some tiny village stinking of pig shit by the Yellow River — one of those places where the men wash about once a month."

Chan stiffened. He himself had been born in a Yellow River village. While he had not returned there for twenty-seven years, he still regarded that village as home. It always angered him when so-called Hong Kong sophisticates like Yip scorned mainlanders for their backwardness.

"I employed part-time technicians," Yip went on, "to work on the film's special effects."

"Mister Yip is world famous for the special effects in his films." Miss Yeung beamed with pride. "He's won a large number of top international awards."

"I learnt that some technicians belonged to this cult," Yip said.

"The Heavenly Ghosts?" Chan said.

Yip nodded. "Alan Yip's home is Hong Kong now, Chan, but he was born fifty-two years ago in Chengdu. And he's still a fierce China patriot. He'll do anything for China, willingly make any sacrifice."

Yip sipped his coffee. "Do you know the Chinese leadership has outlawed this cult?"

"Yes."

"Know why?"

"They see it as a threat."

"They're right. It is a threat. It's becoming so big it could take over China. So Alan Yip did his duty."

Chan frowned: "Duty?"

Yip sipped more coffee then shoved the cup to one side. He unscrewed the metal top from the brandy bottle. He seemed to be recovering quickly from the pain of his son's death. Or am I judging him too harshly? Chan wondered. He might lack affection for his assistant but that was genuine grief I saw for his son when I came in. Talking about the cult has angered him, though. Anger can often override grief — one strong emotion driving out another.

"My duty as a China patriot, of course" — Yip half-filled his glass with brandy. He added tonelessly. "I reported all of these technicians to the proper authorities. They were shot."

"Then the cult made death threats?"

Yip drank half the glass of brandy in one swallow. He wiped his lips with a tissue. He said, "But I didn't take too much notice. I was wrong, though. Yes, I was definitely wrong …" His top lip quivered. "Now my son ... Paid the price … For my mistake … My …"

He sobbed

Miss Yeung reached over and rested a hand gently on his shoulder. Chan waited patiently for Yip to recover. Had the film boss got it right? Had the cult killed his son? It could have recruited a hit-man from across the border; killers came cheap in China. If this was what had happened, the assassin would have fled back across the Chinese border after carrying out the hit. He could be anywhere now: Guangzhou, Shanghai …

"So?" Yip demanded aggressively — his tears had quickly vanished, the bully had returned — "Members of that cult are in Hong Kong. Arrest the murdering bastards!"

"It's not easy," Chan said. "I need hard evidence before—"

"You have evidence — I've supplied it! This isn't some flea-ridden street-sleeper you're speaking to, Chan. This is Alan Yip!"

"All possibilities have to be considered, Mister Yip," Chan said reasonably. "Perhaps this cult hired an assassin from China, or perhaps from here in Hong Kong. They might have persuaded one of your son's enemies to kill him, or even bribed a friend."

And perhaps the murder has nothing at all to do with the cult, he wanted to add. Yet he didn't say this — such utterances would only annoy Yip and prove counterproductive. Instead he said,

"That's why I need to form a detailed picture of your son. Why I need to speak to those who knew him best."

"Then you should meet my other son, Fai. My two boys were always incredibly close. They …"

Yip continued to speak. But while Chan still listened to the movie boss, he now no longer looked at him. A movement by Miss Yeung had grabbed his attention. Her shoulders had stiffened; only slightly, yet enough for Chan to wonder what was the reason for her sudden tension. His gaze travelled to her face. So far this face had assumed two expressions: admiration and affection for Yip. A new look hovered there — disbelief. She caught him staring. The disbelieving look quickly vanished.

"But Fai left for Taiwan this morning," Yip said. "He's on a business trip. He won't return until tomorrow."

Chan said, "Perhaps I could see him then?"

"Fai doesn't know anything yet. I need to speak to him first … Need to tell him about Szeto … To tell him how …"

Chan nodded understandingly. "We'll wait until you've done that, of course. In the meantime, it would help me if you could provide names of Szeto's friends."

"There's someone working in my publicity unit called Wan," Yip said. "Or is ..." He shook his head. "It's no good. My brain is too crammed full of thoughts of Szeto to be able to think about anyone else. I can't remember the man's name."

He reached for the glass at his side. He raised the glass to his lips, drained the brandy then replaced the glass on the desk. His body language suddenly changed again. He no longer looked or acted like a weary and grief-stricken father. His face grew hard and aggressive.

Once again he was the tough, bullying film tycoon.

"But Miss Yeung here will be able to tell you. There's nothing about Alan Yip's family that my super-efficient assistant doesn't know — isn't that so, Ah Yeung?"

His voice had changed as dramatically as his body language. He sounded angry and bitter. He shot his assistant a look of what could only be described as pure hatred. Chan gazed at her too. Years of interviewing people had made Chan sensitive to changes in voices and expressions. Despite Miss Yeung's attempts to hide her feelings, he sensed such changes occurring now: the faintly smug smile, triumphant tilt of the head, glint of steel in her eyes — they sent a message. Put all these things together and you gained an impression of a woman who had just tasted power — a woman who had enjoyed the taste. I got it wrong, he thought, she isn't some weak creature in thrall to her powerful employer. Their relationship is much more complex than that.

She opened a leather-bound filofax, and then proceeded to read from it in a level and emotionless voice, the sort that she probably used to announce the minutes of a board meeting. She gave Chan the names and addresses of two of the dead man's colleagues.

"Did Szeto have a girlfriend?"

Chan had addressed Yip. But Miss Yeung jumped in.

"He'd broken up with her. Until three weeks ago he'd been seeing a dancer from a Wan Chai bar — they lived together at Szeto's flat. She's from Manila, twenty years old, first name Giselle. She dances at a Lockhart Road place called The Wild Cat Club."

Chan was stunned by the amount of detail. How did she acquire such information — spy on the family?

"You're sure?"

"One hundred percent," she replied firmly. "I *never* make a mistake on any family matters." She drew nearer to her boss, rested a manicured hand on his broad shoulders. In a voice softer than any she had used so far with Yip; a sultry voice, the sort a lover uses, she said, "Isn't that so, Ah Yip?"

It was the first time she had called him anything but 'mister'. She started to knead his shoulders, the way that a masseur does to ease tension. Yip submitted, but it was clear from his look of barely restrained fury that he was far from relaxed.

"No, you're *never* wrong about any family matters," he said acidly. "Like I told you, Inspector Chan, he continued, his voice turning increasingly toxic. "Miss Yeung knows everything about Alan Yip's family."

14

"BANG!" PENG SAID. "You're dead, whoever you are, or would be dead if I hadn't removed all the bullets from the magazine."

He moved over to the double bed, put down the rifle and gazed at it affectionately, almost lovingly. The French FR-F2 sniper's rifle was a good weapon, even though it would not normally be his first choice for most jobs — whenever he could, he preferred to use the American-made Barrett Light Fifty. The five-foot long Barrett was accurate up to a mile and despatched a half-inch calibre bullet at two thousand miles an hour — its high muzzle velocity made it close to cannon power, capable of piercing armour plating.

Its bulkiness made it impractical for this job in Hong Kong, so Peng had chosen the French FR-F2. A 7.5mm weapon, it weighed only twelve pounds compared to the Barrett's thirty-five, and at forty-four inches it was a foot shorter than the Barrett.

Peng reached underneath the bed for the black leather attaché case he had placed there. He lifted the case up, placed it on the bed beside the rifle; he slipped locks on the case, flipped open the lid. Then he picked up the rifle and began to slowly, methodically dismantle it. With tender loving care, he first placed the stock, then the magazine and telescopic sights into the individual slots reserved for them in the foam-rubber lined case. He closed the case then frowned. There was a smudge of dust on the lid. He pulled a handkerchief from his pocket and used it to brush away the dust, then spent the next two minutes buffing the leather.

Only when the leather was as shiny as new did he finally place the case back underneath the bed. He had always been a perfectionist; it was an obsession with him; even when it came to something which many people would consider insignificant, like a few specks of dust on an attaché case. He hated untidiness like the plague, despised anything that lacked mathematical precision. He was so much a perfectionist, so keen on exactness, that rivals in his elite military unit called him 'Mister Symmetry'. Never when he was within earshot, though — they all valued their health too much.

And they were stupid to jeer. Attention to detail was the main reason why he was here in Hong Kong. It had kept him alive these past five years in a business where one tiny mistake could mean the difference between life and death. That was why he was devoting so much time to the details surrounding his next hit, the assassination of film-maker Alan Yip.

Peng had still not decided how to kill the film-maker. It might be safer to operate at close quarters, in which case he would use the snub-nosed Makarov pistol he had also smuggled past China's border guards. If the job had to be done from a distance then a shot from this room with the FR-F2 rifle, like that practice one he had taken five minutes ago, would be best. A long-range hit should be routine. Yip ate regularly at that place across the road. It would simply be a matter of waiting until the film-maker's limousine pulled up, Yip stepped out on the pavement …

"Bang, you're dead!"

It should not be too difficult. Peng had successfully carried out tougher hits. This year he had killed Muslim separatists in China's north-western province of Xinjiang, as well as supporters of Tibet's exiled Dalai Lama. No one got rich working for the state, though, you needed to secretly subsidise your state work with freelance business. That was why he had agreed to kill Alan Yip. The state would be furious if it ever found out, of course. It viewed Peng's latest employers as a bunch of dangerous terrorists. Fuck the state! Loyalty got you nowhere. Those Party bastards only respected strength. That Chairman Mao joke explained it all. Mao had asked two cadres how they would get a cat to eat pepper.

"Easy," said the first. "Stuff the pepper in its mouth and ram the pepper down with a chopstick."

"Wrong," Mao replied, shaking his fat ugly head. "Using force is undemocratic."

"Starve the cat for days," suggested the second cadre. "Then wrap the pepper in a piece of meat — the cat will be so hungry it'll swallow the meat whole."

Mao shook his head again. "A good Party comrade never uses trickery."

"So how do we do it?" the two bemused cadres asked.

"Rub your pepper into the cat's arse," Mao replied, as though the answer was obvious. "When the pepper burns, the cat will willingly lick it off. What's more, it'll be happy it was *allowed* to lick it off."

That was it. That was how you dominated the Party. Be good and honourable like father and they treated you worse than garbage. Squeeze their balls in a vice and they said: "Thank you for guiding me on the path to true enlightenment, comrade." So Peng had learned to be one of the biggest ball-breakers around. Yet if father had lived it could have been different. Father had despised violence, had encouraged his son to follow him in the ways of learning. If he was still alive today, Peng thought, I might be teaching mathematics at his university. It's what he wanted for me, and I always tried to follow his wishes. Not out of fear, though; he never struck me even once. I always did it for love.

He had only ever truly cared for two people in this world: his father and his sister. Following the death of Peng's mother, while he was still only a baby, he had clung to his sister. She had become his new mother, feeding him, washing him, sitting by his bed whenever he fell ill, wiping away his tears when he cried; until that fateful night when she ... Peng winced as he experienced a sudden stabbing pain in his side. Twenty-five years on! And still the memory of that freezing January night remained hard to bear. He took deep breaths. Slowly, the pain in his side receded.

After his sister's death, Peng and his father had moved from Chengdu to Beijing. His father had become head professor at the university's mathematics department. A man who had the ability to make even the dullest learning fun, students had adored him, Party officials had respected him.

Until the protests in Tiananmen Square.

The professor had supported the students when they launched democracy protests in Tiananmen Square. Although he had avoided a prison sentence after the army crushed the protests, he had been sacked from his university post. Peng had watched impotently as the same Party officials who had once been eager to praise his father now lined up to abuse him. The professor had lost his confidence, his love of life; he had become a recluse.

And then?

An accident while cleaning a gun, according to the grim-faced headmaster; but Peng had known the headmaster was lying. Sauntering out of the classroom as if nothing had happened, he had gone to his secret hiding place in the woods and wept.

Everything changed from that moment.

The outward-going schoolboy became an introverted teenager who blamed China's rulers for destroying his father. Adopted by an uncle with the Ministry of Security, Peng attended a school for the sons of Party officials. He did well. Teachers recommended him for the elite military unit that he joined after graduating. But he never forgot how his father had died.

That was why he had really agreed to kill Alan Yip. He had been fooling himself pretending he had taken the job for the money. He had agreed to eliminate Yip because it allowed him to side with China's enemies and take revenge on the Party officials responsible for father's death. Yip was a friend of Party chiefs — they would be furious when he died. They would be scared, too, wondering if they were going to be the next in line for a bullet.

After Alan Yip?

I avenge my sister, Peng thought. And allow both her and father to sleep peacefully in the after-life, knowing that her murderer has finally faced justice.

Last year, clearing out some of father's belongings from the attic, Peng had found a diary. In the diary's yellowing pages, written in heart-wrenching detail, was the full story of how Peng's sister had died; Peng had wept as he turned the pages. Then he had dropped to his knees and sworn on his sister's and his father's ashes not to rest until he found the murderer and killed him.

It had taken six months, because the murderer no longer lived in China, but in Hong Kong. Finally, though, Peng had found him. Now he would fulfil the vow to his dead sister — he would take revenge; a fitting revenge; the *perfect* revenge. One worthy of the man elite military unit rivals had scornfully branded Mister Symmetry. It must be so precise — the hungry ghosts in the after-life would accept nothing less. Only if he gave them true perfection would they let father and sister rest peacefully.

Peng remembered the exact moment he had learnt of his sister's death: thirty-six minutes past nine on January the fourth. He had been in bed, while father talked to security officials in the living room. The murmuring of adult voices had ceased, the bedroom door had swung open and father had entered. Peng had glanced up and seen tears in father's eyes, and Peng had felt a stabbing pain in his chest. Because even before father spoke Peng had known what had happened.

He had known it all.

He gazed at the clock on the hotel room's wall; the calendar part showed it was January the third; the time ten to one in the afternoon. In precisely thirty-two hours and forty-six minutes he would take revenge on his sister's killer — the perfect revenge. At thirty-six minutes after nine tomorrow evening, at the same time that his beloved sister had been so cruelly murdered twenty-five years ago, Detective Inspector Peter Chan would die.

15

AT A KIOSK outside the film studios Chan bought a copy of the *Hong Kong Economic Journal.* He found the article that he was looking for on page three of the business news section. Under the headline: *HK firm in China army deal* was the picture of a smiling businessman whose company had won a huge military contract. Chan tore out the page, folded it and put it in his pocket. He tossed the rest of the newspaper in a rubbish bin.

He flagged down a cab.

"Tsim Sha Tsui," he told the driver, "Star Ferry pier."

As they headed towards the harbour, Chan used his mobile phone to call the police station.

"Ah Wong? I want a background check done on John Tsang."

"*The* John Tsang?"

"Particularly his links with Alan Yip."

"Any particular reason?"

"Just a hunch; I'll explain later. Check out Yip's personal assistant, too. Her name's Yeung … Yes, Yeung. First names are Kam Sau. And check out last week's charity party the Chamber of Commerce held at the Mandarin — our victim was a guest."

"Anything else you need?"

"Not now, I'll call you if I do. Otherwise, I'll see you tonight."

"*Tonight?* What are you doing the rest of the day?"

"Yip swears blind the cult killed his son," Chan said. "I'm going to Lantau to check the cult out. Call me if anything comes up."

He switched off the phone. He checked his watch: almost one. On a normal day, since his daughter had started pressing him to watch his health, he usually ate lunch at this hour.

He had no time for luxuries like lunch today, though. He needed to travel to Lantau. But not yet. First he needed to meet up with his reporter friend, Jack Spalding. Jack had boasted of writing an exposé of the cult. It had never appeared in print, but Jack must still have the information he'd based the exposé on. Jack was not at his desk in the *South China Morning Post*'s office tapping out news stories. Surprise, surprise, he was in the Foreign Correspondent's Club knocking back beer. Yes, he said, when Chan reached him, he had the information that Chan needed.

"I'll be half an hour," Chan said. "Don't go away."

MISS YEUNG SAT alone in the office; five minutes ago Alan Yip had gone to the conference room with the private detectives he had hired.

Her phone rang. She picked it up.

"Miss Yeung speaking," she said brightly into the receiver. "How can I—"

"We need to talk, lady."

She stiffened at the sound of the Triad thug's voice.

"You know the rules," she hissed angrily. "You were told *never* to phone me on this number during the day. It's too dangerous. Call my home tonight after seven."

"Fuck your rules! We need to talk now."

Miss Yeung's mouth suddenly felt dry.

"Why?" she asked anxiously. "What's wrong?"

"I need more money."

"No," she said. "You've already been paid enough."

"I want more." The thug paused for a second. Then he said aggressively, "And you'd better give it to me."

I've acted foolishly, Miss Yeung thought. I've misjudged him. I expected him to act like a professional. I thought that he would do the job and then head across the border and lose himself in China just like I ordered him to.

"Don't make threats," she said. "People who do that often find themselves in trouble."

"I can go to the cops, lady. And if I do—"

"How much do you want?"

"Another ten thousand."

"All right," she conceded after a pause, "another ten thousand. She paused again. "But you only get the extra money *after* the job's been done."

"I want it now."

"Half now," she said, "half after."

"All right," he said. "Meet me tonight at seven; the usual place."

The line went dead. I should never have hired him, she thought. I should have realised he would try to double-cross me; all typhoon-shelter trash like him are greedy. I should have known he would cause problems.

No matter. She could overcome such problems.

She got up from her chair, walked slowly across the deep-pile carpet until she stood by the steel filing cabinet beside the wall. She unlocked the cabinet, tugged open its middle drawer. She lifted a pile of manila folders from the drawer. Underneath the folders lay a snub-nosed Beretta semi-automatic. This would solve her problems with the Triad thug.

SPALDING HAILED HIM in a loud, rasping voice that could have ripped the top off a can of Foster's at thirty paces.

"Over here, your highness! Over here!"

In case Chan was the only person in a five-mile radius who hadn't heard him, Spalding waved his People's Liberation Army cap in the air, a general urging troops into battle. Chan walked across to the oval-shaped bar. Spalding got up and surrendered his stool with an exaggerated, almost courtly flourish.

"Park your arse, your majesty!"

He was so small that, stood like this, he barely managed to peer over the top of the bar. Painfully skinny, too: it never ceased to amaze Chan how, despite swallowing beer like a dehydrated fish and wolfing down food enough for a man twenty times his size, Jack remained as light as a Happy Valley jockey.

"So how are we this sunny day, your lordship?" Spalding said. "A wee bit on the warm side, don't you agree?" He chucked his Chinese army cap on the bar. "Jeez! It's hotter than a dingo's arse out there!"

Chan sat down and wiped his sweaty brow. "I'm fine, Jack."

"Don't look it," Spalding said. "In fact you *look* bloody awful. Two cold beers for me and my weary comrade," he instructed the elderly barman, "and another double Johnnie Walker black label for your favourite uncle."

He was dressed as elegantly as ever: tartan waistcoat, baggy khaki shorts, lime-green shirt; orange bow-tie. The clothing sent the loud-and-clear message — this man is different. Jack was fifty-six. But a life-long love affair with the whisky bottle had ravaged his complexion so much that he looked closer to seventy. A purple-blue nose, which Chan always expected to explode at any moment, dominated a weasel-like face, while grey weasel-like eyes peered out from spectacles with lenses as thick as the bottom of a soy-sauce bottle. But Jack never let trifles like that bother him, he was one of those optimists who never let anything bother them — he thought he ruled the world.

They had been friends for twenty years. They had met for the first time here, in this bar, three weeks after Chan's arrival in Hong Kong. Spalding had taken the newcomer under his wing. Twenty years ago, Jack had known everyone who was worth knowing. He had freelanced for top American magazines like *Time* and *Newsweek*. But the glory days had gone. Now he worked for the local *South China Morning Post*.

"And make sure those beers are *ice-cold* … No, of course I don't want ice in the bloody whisky. It spoils the taste."

The barman poured the beer. Chan waited for it to settle. He raised the frosted glass, pressed it against his sweaty face and let it cool him, then took a long, thirst-quenching gulp. Ah! that was good. The Carlsberg was so cold that it stung the back of his throat.

Spalding raised his glass of whisky high in a toast: "To drunkards everywhere!" He drained the whisky in one swallow then smacked his lips: "So, Mister Chairman. What do you want Uncle Jack to tell you about these crackpots?"

"Everything you can."

"Where do I start?"

"My teacher in China always said the beginning was best."

16

"PLEASE FORGIVE MY intrusion, sir."

Charles 'The Eagle' Suen shot film-maker Alan Yip a look that was an uncomfortable mixture of sympathy and obsequiousness. "Had I the slightest inkling … Well, naturally I would never have bothered you by—"

Yip cut him off.

"Save your grovelling for someone who's fooled by it. My boy is dead, Suen, and there's nothing that either you or I can do about it."

Charles Suen blushed crimson.

"I assure you, Mister Yip," he protested, shifting uneasily on his chair "the condolences I have just expressed are entirely sincere. I'm also a father with a son myself, sir, and—"

"But I *can* do something about this other matter." Yip leaned his bulky frame across the polished mahogany desk until he was so close that he could have reached out and slapped Suen in the face. He fixed Suen with a level stare. He said aggressively, "You claim that you now have proof."

Suen shifted more uneasily on his chair. "Not quite *absolute* proof, sir," he said hesitantly. "What I mean is we …"

An icy look halted him in mid-sentence.

"I hope you haven't come here to waste my time, Suen."

The detective agency boss shook his balding head: "Certainly not, sir. I have information of the utmost importance to convey." He turned to the tall young man in steel-rimmed spectacles, who sat stiffly beside him, staring down intently at the slim manila folder that he cradled in his hands. In a much firmer voice than that he had used when addressing the film producer, Suen said: "Tell Mister Yip what your team has discovered, Kwong."

Sylvester Kwong nervously cleared his throat. He said tentatively, "We've narrowed it down to two men, sir."

Yip's dark eyes narrowed: "Who?"

"One is your financial secretary."

"And the other?"

Kwong hesitated.

"Well?" Yip demanded aggressively. "Who is the other man?

"The other man is your son, sir."

Yip stiffened: "Fai?"

"We've checked and double-checked everything, sir," Sylvester Kwong said, his nervousness causing him to speak more quickly than he normally did. "And … Well, one of these men … What I mean, sir, is—"

"One of these two men *must* be guilty," Charles Suen cut in. "It can't possibly be anyone else."

Then Suen sat back and awaited the inevitable explosion. He expected Yip to start screaming threats. To furiously hurl objects round the room. To his surprise, Yip remained eerily calm. The film boss said nothing for a while, simply stared down at his polished desk as he digested the information.

Then Yip suddenly broke out of his calm state.

He said aggressively, "So which one of them is it, Suen?"

"As Kwong just explained, sir, our—"

"Is it Fai?" Yip shot a fierce look at the detective agency boss. "Well is it? Is my own son the lousy cheating bastard who's been swindling me out of millions?"

"As Kwong said, sir, we've no absolute—"

"So why come here?" Yip raged. "Why waste my valuable time with your pointless bullshit?"

"We can get it, though," Suen said hurriedly. "Proof, I mean. Yes, yes …" He nudged his assistant. "Outline your plan."

"We want to tap their phones, sir," Kwong explained. "Not only here at work. I also would like permission from you to place devices at your home."

"Do it," Yip said abruptly. "Do it now." He waved a hand curtly to the door as a signal that he was dismissing the two men. "My assistant will handle the rest of …" He paused when he saw that neither man had got up to leave. "Is there something else on your mind?" he asked Suen testily.

"I'm afraid so, sir," Charles Suen began tentatively. "Only … I'm not too sure if—"

"Say what you came here to say," Yip snapped.

"We believe your son Fai," Suen said. "Always assuming, of course, that it ultimately transpires that he is in fact your guilty—"

"Spit it out, Suen!"

"We believe your son Fai has a partner."

Yip's eyes narrowed dangerously: "Who?"

Charles Suen hesitated.

"A name," Yip demanded. "I want a name."

"The owner of China Enterprises."

A muscle twitched at Yip's jaw: "John Tsang?"

"Yes."

"I'll kill him!" Yip shouted.

PENG AWOKE AT a quarter to two.

He always slept for thirty minutes before a job. It improved his focus. He rose from the bed, walked over to the table by the wall where he had arranged all his equipment. He picked up the black leather shoulder holster, pulled it on and then adjusted it until it fit snugly. He picked up the 9mm Makarov semi-automatic, felt its reassuring weight. He removed the snub-nosed pistol's seven-shot maazine and tested the Makarov's firing mechanism.

Satisfied everything was in perfect working order, he replaced the magazine in the pistol, made sure that the safety was on, and then put the Makarov in the leather shoulder holster. He slipped into his canvas jacket, stood back and examined himself in the hotel room's mirror. Would anyone detect a gun under the jacket? No. Both the gun and shoulder holster were invisible.

He picked up the Makarov's bulbous silencer and examined it for imperfections. Satisfied that none existed, he put the silencer in the left pocket of his jacket. He took a thin strip of copper wire about four inches long from the table and added this to the left pocket, then lifted up a photograph and put it in the right pocket.

He picked up the phone and punched a number.

A man answered almost immediately: "Police station."

"Inspector Peter Chan, please."

"One moment, sir."

After about five seconds, another man came on the line.

"I'm Sergeant Wong. Inspector Chan is out. Can I help?"

"I need him personally. When will he be back?"

"Not until tonight."

"I'll call back tomorrow."

Peng switched off the phone. Chan would be away from his apartment for the whole day. Good. That meant the first part of the plan could go ahead. Peng would sow fear in Chan, before ensuring the murderer met a suitably painful end. Father and sister would soon be sleeping peacefully in the after-life. He checked his watch. Twelve minutes before two. Everything was going perfectly. Peter Chan had thirty-one hours and forty-eight minutes to live.

17

SPALDING RAISED A finger to his lips then glanced furtively from side to side; he had always been big on melodrama. Satisfied no Secret Police officers lurked underneath the beer taps, waiting to jump out and arrest him, he grabbed his army cap and beer and motioned for Chan to follow him to a corner table where they could talk without being overheard.

Not that such top-level security was really necessary. Only two other people sat in the club, a fat middle-aged westerner with a goatee beard and his young Filipina girlfriend. Both of them were so drunk that they would have trouble remembering their own names, let alone anything Chan and Spalding discussed.

"It was formed over in Sichuan Province five years ago, your majesty," Spalding began quickly once they had sat down, only to pause equally as quickly for a drink of his beer, half of which he swallowed in a single gulp. "By an ex-Communist Party hack, a bloke called Ho Lee-young. Our friend Ho had this vision, see, that if the world didn't quickly mend its wicked ways then it would meet a sorry end — the usual hell-fire stuff that your friendly guru comes out with."

The door in the corner burst open and two men carrying beer crates stumbled in. They hauled the heavy crates to the bar and left them there for the old barman to unstack. Chan hoped the barman would be sensible enough not to try — the effort might kill him.

"But the jury is still out on whether he had his mystical vision after downing a few bottles of Johnnie Walker, or smoking *ganga* cigarettes all day," Spalding continued. "Personally, I favour him getting monumentally pissed. I know the feeling well — I've often felt like starting up my own cult after eight bottles of Foster's. Just imagine it! Free booze for life and all the women you can screw!" He chuckled. "Jeez! That would really be something now, wouldn't it?"

"Save your fantasies for later, Jack. Get back to the story."

"All right, all right, keep your hair on — what's left of it."

Spalding ran mottled fingers through his own steel-grey hair, whose unruliness indicated that he remained ignorant of the comb's invention. He drained his beer and then signalled over to the bar for two more even though Chan's glass was still half empty.

"Well, when our friend sobered up next morning, I reckon he probably just wanted to forget about it and get back to the day job of counting tractor parts, or whatever other exciting job he did down there in Chengdu," Spalding said. "But a bunch of screwballs are banging on his front door, begging to join a quest for spiritual enlightenment. So he takes the plunge and forms a cult. Grows his hair too, of course; I mean you can't be a *proper* guru these days without long hair, can you?"

"He's a con man?"

Spalding gave a snort of laughter. "We're talking about a joker who claims he can fly! Now he may have long hair, but he's not got wings on his dick or a jet engine on his arse. So—"

"Point taken," Chan said irritably, "get on with the story."

Spalding stroked stubble on his pointed chin. Either he had decided to grow a beard, or what was more likely, had forgotten to shave again.

"Yes, he's a con man. In fact half the stuff he comes out with he swiped from those Boxer jokers who fought the Brits a hundred years ago. But he's a bloody *clever* con man. I mean, it might still be true some jokers in China haven't got two grains of rice to rub together, but some jokers in the big cities like Shanghai are loaded with cash now. And some mad bastards have handed it to him."

"He's rich?"

"He could certainly afford to stand me and you a few rounds," Spalding said. "But whether …"

He broke off as the barman arrived at their table with the fresh beer. Spalding swallowed most of his in a few gulps.

"Where's our friendly guru now, Jack?"

Spalding shrugged. "If I knew that I wouldn't be sitting in here swapping stories with you. I'd be sitting in the office knocking out tomorrow's front-page splash. For a year he's been hiding. As to exactly *where* he's hiding, your guess is as good as your Uncle Jack's. There's thirty million Chinese in that crazy cult of his, so he's not exactly short of friends. Maybe he's shacked up with some Sheila — giving her private spiritual enlightenment. Or maybe he took his money to Las Vegas to blow it on the tables." Spalding wiped beer foam from his lips. "One thing's for sure, I bet he wishes he stuck to screwing and gambling when he had the chance."

Chan frowned. "What are you talking about?"

"Politics of course," Spalding replied, as though the answer was obvious. "Those big-shots over in China didn't outlaw Ho's crazy cult because he prattled on about spiritual enlightenment." Spalding shook his head. "They couldn't give a toss about a nutcase claiming he can fly, or screwing himself silly — providing that was *all* he did. But the mad bastard started thinking he was God — it happens to these gurus. Think about it, your majesty. Millions of people are jumping around saying you can do no wrong. They say it loud and long enough and you start believing."

Spalding paused for a drink of beer. Then he said, "It was definitely a political crackdown. Ho got too big for his boots. He wasn't content with just ruling his own cult — he wanted to rule China. He might have managed it too, if the Party bureaucrats hadn't driven him underground. In fact he might still manage it. That cult of his is thirty million strong, don't forget. It's become a genuine political force. The bastards are well organised, too. Don't be fooled by all of that anti-modern crap they churn out — it's not stopped them using mobile phones and websites, and any other technology they can get their paws on to tout their message round town. Even though Ho's in hiding, his mob can still cause a hell of a lot of trouble. In fact they already have."

"You mean the Shanghai gas attack?"

Spalding nodded.

"Why did you never write your article about the cult, Jack?"

"I did, but it got spiked."

"Why?"

"My editor got scared that it would upset the Party big-shots in China." Spalding drained his beer. He said philosophically, "You see, Pete, to stay in power the Party needs stability — it needs the punters in China to think that it's all-powerful and that the cult's a pile of junk. Your Uncle Jack revealing the cult was actually powerful and crazy enough, to leak poison gas into a shopping mall would have scared seven tones of crap out of everyone and that would have weakened the Party's hold. So my story got spiked." He shrugged. "Not that it surprised me. There's as much chance of our editor daring to upset China as there is of me screwing Naomi Campbell tonight … Another beer, your lordship?"

Chan shook his head. "I have to catch the Lantau ferry."

"Meeting friend Ho's mob at their temple, huh?"

"I'm curious," Chan said. "Why did the cult site their temple in a backwater like Lantau?"

"Nothing curious about it."

"But if they're keen to convert people, surely it makes sense to build it where more people are living — why not Hong Kong?"

"A backwater was exactly what they wanted," Spalding said. "After all the trouble they'd had in China, being outlawed and all that, they wanted to keep a low profile here. They thought if they made too big a song and dance about things, China would pressure the jokers in the Hong Kong Government to outlaw them here too. Anyway, when you get to Lantau, watch out for those sharks."

"Sharks?"

"Those cult jokers aren't spiritual enlightenment and goodness to all men," Spalding said. "Underneath those stupid white bed sheets that they all wear are some tough political operators. The danger is a soft bastard like you … Well we've been mates for years … So I just thought I'd …"

His voice trailed off. He's embarrassed, Chan thought. Despite being a self-proclaimed cynic, Jack has admitted liking someone. Why is it hard for a man to show his feelings to another man? Or rather why is it hard for *some* men? Ah Wong doesn't see expressing his feelings as a weakness. He's Chinese, though. Is the difficulty of expressing softer feelings a western problem? It would explain why the letters sent every month by my English father, until they stopped arriving nine months ago, were so formal and absent of warmth.

Does the problem affect me? Is that why I never wrote back? Mei urged me to write before it was too late. It probably is now — he must be dead. I did write back, though, dozens of times. But I never posted the letters. Was that the English part of my character showing, the part of me that's scared of showing emotion? I only ever saw my father once, but his English blood still flows through me. So perhaps it's no big surprise that I act like him sometimes.

"Sure you can't have just a *small* one for the road?" Spalding said.

Chan stood up: "Another time." He leaned over, squeezed his friend's bony shoulders. "And don't worry, mother, I'm a big boy now. I'll make sure those sharks don't bite."

18

WHEN CHAN HAD asked film-maker Alan Yip if he could question his son, Fai, Yip had replied that Fai had gone to Taiwan on a business trip. To the extent that Fai was now in Taiwan's capital city of Taipei, Alan Yip had spoken the truth. But Fai did not sit in some air-conditioned, oak-pannelled company boardroom, discussing merger deals with a group of smartly dressed executives. He strode hurriedly down a steamy Taipei street, trying to escape from a killer.

He had spotted his would-be assassin ten minutes ago: the squat, shaven-headed man in the red tee-shirt standing by the wall of the Hyatt Hotel on Song Shou Road. The shaven-headed man had quickly turned away when he had caught Fai staring at him, but not quickly enough. For one brief telling instant, Fai's gaze had met his. In that instant Fai had known who the shaven-headed man was and why he was there.

It had something to do with the look in the shaven-headed man's eyes, the look almost of a hunter sizing up his next prey. But what had really warned Fai that the shaven-headed man planned to murder him was the pain which had pierced his chest the moment that their two gazes had met. The same fierce, stabbing pain that Fai had always felt, since as far back into his lousy childhood as he could bear to remember, whenever he confronted danger.

In an effort to lose the shaven-headed man, Fai had immediately turned off Song Shou Road. Then he had swung left and right, and then left and left again — taken so many turnings in the last ten minutes that he no longer knew where he was. He knew where he needed to be, though — he needed to reach the bus stop. That bus stop over there by the herbal medicine store, about fifty metres away.

Reaching it was his only chance.

He wanted to glance over his shoulder. Had all his crazy twisting and turning in the past ten minutes succeeded in throwing off the assassin? One quick glance behind would … No. Looking back, even for a moment, could prove fatal. If I haven't managed to throw him off, Fai thought, and he is still shadowing me, then if I glance behind he'll realise that I've spotted him — if he hasn't realised it already. I'll put him on his guard. When I make my dash for the bus, he'll be ready to rush forward and intercept me.

Fai kept looking straight ahead, his gaze fixed firmly on the bus stop and on the bus that had begun to appear over the brow of the hill about a hundred and fifty metres away. He grabbed a deep breath. Not long to go now, he told himself. When the bus arrives at the stop, I make a run for it. Not too early, though, I have to make sure I don't rush for the bus too soon. I need to stay calm — it's vital that I wait until the very last moment. That way I give him no chance of cutting me off. By the time he realises what's happening, it will be too late for him to do anything about it. I'll be inside the bus and heading up the road away from him.

The bus pulled into the stop.

With a loud hiss, the door slid open; four passengers got out, five began to climb in. Fai grabbed another deep breath. Patience, he told himself, wait until the very last possible moment. Let the old woman with the plastic shopping bag get on the bus first, and then those four kids standing behind her. Then give the driver five seconds to check his wing mirror, another five to slip the bus back into gear, remove the handbrake …

Go now! Go now!

Fuck! He had left it too late. The bus was pulling away from the stop much faster than he had expected. He might not get on board. He lunged for the handle on the entrance door, managed to grab it with his right hand. He ran alongside the bus for a few metres, tried to half-jump, half-pull himself on board.

He couldn't do it.

"Slow down!" he yelled.

No good. The bus was going faster. No way could he keep up. And now the door was closing too. In a moment it would be over. He didn't have much time. Only enough for one last appeal to the driver, for one final desperate shout. Then he would have to release his grip on the door. Otherwise his arm would be torn from its socket.

"Please!" he screamed. "Please!"

CHAN SURVEYED THE harbour scene.

Ahead of him cargo boats lay at anchor, their crews waiting for permission to offload cargo into Kwai Chung's container terminal. On his right, green-and-white Star Ferries criss-crossed the two mile-wide channel that divides Hong Kong from Kowloon and the Chinese mainland which lies beyond Kowloon. Sampans and fishing junks bound for the typhoon shelter in Yau Ma Tei weaved between the ferries, some of the sampan captains at times steering their tiny craft so close that they were almost swamped by the ferries' bow waves.

Chan glanced to his left. One Star Ferry was drawing away from Hong Kong's pier while another ferry was pulling in. Chan's attention was grabbed more by a lone pollution-control boat which struggled to remove rubbish from the sludge-coloured water. The pollution-control boat was close enough for him to distinguish the mechanical scoop fixed to its bow, which made it resemble a floating bulldozer. The captain could press a button to lower this scoop into the water and then snatch up cans, bottles and any other rubbish which was floating in the water. But he would be wasting his time pressing that or any other button. The real pollution problem lay *underneath* the waves. Hundreds of gallons of chemical waste churned out by factories in Kwun Tong and Kwai Chung and thousands of tonnes of pig shit pumped daily into the harbour by New Territories' farmers.

The sun nosed from behind a cotton wool cloud. Chan pulled on a pair of sunshades to shield his eyes from the diamond-hard glare. At least it wasn't sticky out here, though. In fact that dull breeze which had just begun to drift across the harbour made it feel pleasantly cool.

No lousy mosquitoes dive-bombed him either. He was on board a ferry. But not a green-and-white Star Ferry bound for Kowloon. His bigger, triple-deck boat, headed for Lantau Island an hour away. It was on a rural part of Lantau where the Heavenly Ghosts cult had sited their headquarters.

He reclined further in his chair, closed his eyes to try and concentrate better on the case. Had film-maker Alan Yip got it right — was that cult responsible for the murder of his son Szeto? Before being outlawed by the Chinese state last year, the cult's leaders had made a big show of protesting that theirs was a purely peaceful organisation. But if Jack Spalding's claim about that Shanghai poison gas incident was true, then it was obvious that some cult members were not averse to …

His phone buzzed. He sat up straight, opened his eyes.

"That you, boss?"

"What is it, Ah Wong?"

"Got stuff to tell you."

"What sort of stuff?"

"Really important stuff," Wong answered, "stuff that could blow our murder case wide open."

19

THE DOOR Of the bus burst open and a breathless Fai staggered on board. With a loud hiss, the door slid shut. Had the driver taken pity on him and stepped on the brakes? Had the Taipei traffic slowed the bus? Fai did not know or care. Being safely inside the bus was all that mattered.

"You daft bastard!" the driver swore. "What …"

The fifty-dollar bill that Fai stuffed into his greasy hand, together with an instruction to keep the change, halted the swarthy-skinned driver in mid-complaint. Fai collapsed onto the front seat, beside an old woman in a flowered Mao pyjama suit. He oozed sweat. His heart pounded so hard that he thought it would punch a hole in his chest.

"You ought to act your age," the old woman admonished him. She shook her head at his stupidity. "You'll do yourself a serious injury if you ever try that again."

He smiled foolishly at her. "Urgent appointment," he gasped between deep breaths, "can't afford to be late."

He gazed through the side window. The squat, shaven-headed figure in the red tee-shirt was nowhere. Did I lose him with all my twisting and turning? Fai wondered. Yes, perhaps I did. But the danger isn't over yet. These people always work in teams. Others might be waiting at the hotel. In fact they'll *definitely* be waiting there. I need to get away from the hotel as soon as possible.

He called the hotel on his mobile phone. "This is Mister Yip," he told the receptionist who answered him almost immediately. "I'm staying on floor seven in suite number twenty-three."

"How can I help, sir?" she asked politely.

"I'm returning to Hong Kong early. I haven't time to go back to the hotel. Can you have my bags packed for me and sent on to the airport?"

"We'll see to it immediately, sir"

He replaced the phone in his pocket. He gazed past the driver and out through the windscreen. There were surprisingly few cars on the road — Taipei's traffic congestion was normally as bad as that in Hong Kong. The driver swung the bus on to a wide, tree-lined highway; they seemed to be heading away from the centre of the city. Fai waited until they had travelled for about half a kilometre down this highway. Then he stood up and motioned to the driver.

"Stop here," Fai told the driver.

He got out, crossed the road and walked for about a hundred metres in the opposite direction to that which the bus had travelled. At the first set of traffic lights he came to, he swung left on to a street that was full of fashion boutiques, shoe shops and jewellery stores. Thankfully, there was also a bar. Fai went inside.

"Double vodka," he instructed the elderly barman.

He drank it quickly, standing at the counter, and then immediately ordered another. As he waited for the elderly barman to pour this one, Fai reflected on his narrow escape and silently cursed himself for his stupidity and greed. It had been stupid to ever get involved with Tsang. In fact it had been complete madness. Now he would be always on the run, always looking over his shoulder. His enemies would never rest. Not until they had …

"Your vodka, sir."

He went to a table near the door. By the time he had sat down the first double he'd tossed back so quickly had begun to have an effect on his nerves; as the alcohol reached his bloodstream, he grew calmer. His heart beat slowed. The dry, sour taste of fear left his mouth. He swallowed some of his new drink. As he grew calmer he began to think more positively. Did I overreact? he wondered. Maybe the man in the red tee-shirt wasn't following me. I never saw him through the windows of the bus. Why? Was it because he was never there? Supposing no one sent an assassin after me because no one suspects me of anything?

He swallowed more of his vodka, continued to grow calmer. I overreacted, he thought, just like I did on the plane coming over here. I shouldn't have screamed at that flight attendant. She never put any Heavenly Ghosts' junk in my pocket. The Yeung bitch did it. She's trying to scare me. She won't succeed in scaring me, though, because … Hold on! He gulped the remains of his vodka. He suddenly felt nervous again. In fact he felt scared. If the Yeung bitch knew enough about the cult link to scare him by shoving that Heavenly Ghosts' stuff in his pocket, then perhaps she also knew enough about the deal with Tsang to ... Fai yanked the mobile from his pocket. He punched out a number.

"China Enterprises," a woman said. "How can I help?"

"Get me John Tsang," Fai said, "urgently."

PENG SWEATED AS he picked his way through the crowd.

He wanted to remove his canvas jacket to make himself cooler. But this would mean revealing the shoulder holster that lay beneath the jacket and the snub-nosed Makarov 9mm semi-automatic which rested in the holster.

He kept the jacket on.

He swung left at the Bank of East Asia branch and turned on to Hennessy Road — he crossed the busy road, moving between two trams which clanked to opposite sides of Hong Kong Island, one heading to Kennedy Town the other bound for Shau Kei Wan. At a stall by a seafood restaurant, a hawker was selling cold drinks. Peng bought a Coke, swallowed it in three gulps and then tossed the empty can into the hawker's bin.

He resumed walking. He turned right on to Shell Street. The bad eggs smell from the harbour was worse here than it had been on Hennessy Road. It hung heavy in the sticky air, unable to escape, penned in by all the high buildings.

The apartment block that Peng wanted stood thirty metres down the street. A Filipina child-minder, probably in her early twenties, and the Chinese toddler in her charge were exiting from the main lobby. Peng politely held the door open for them and stood aside; the pretty Filipina smiled her thanks.

Peng moved into the lobby. The clock on the wall showed it was five minutes past three. No residents were in the lobby, just an elderly security guard-caretaker who sat behind his desk, talking loudly on the phone; to his bookmaker judging from the names of the racehorses that he mentioned. Or perhaps he was chatting to a horse race-loving friend. Whoever it was on the other end of the line, the old man was too busy talking to them to pay attention to the stranger who had just entered the block.

Peng pressed the lift button. The metal doors slid open with a hiss. The lift was empty. He stepped inside, pressed the button for the fourteenth floor, got out here, turned right and walked down the corridor his rubber-soled shoes making a soft click-clack on the floor tiles. He halted at the fourth flat that he came to. He bent down, examined the lock on the metal security grille which guarded the wooden entrance door. The grille's lock was an older type; it should not provide much difficulty.

In a moment, Peng would pick that lock. He would open the door of the flat and move inside. Then he would put into operation the first stage of his plan; a plan which would slowly but inevitably destroy Inspector Peter Chan.

Everything was going perfectly.

20

"WE'VE GOT THE ballistic and post-mortem reports, boss."

"Did ballistics identify the murder weapon?"

"Colt .38," Wong replied. "And Eddie Gallacher's post-mortem report confirms that our victim was killed four days ago. Eddie reckons … You still there, Pete?"

"I'm here."

"Sounds like you're speaking from Outer Mongolia."

"I'm on the ferry," Chan explained. "I'll speak up a bit — is that any better?"

"A little bit."

"Good. Now listen carefully, Ah Wong. I want a check done on all locally-registered owners of .38 calibre Colts."

"Already got someone doing it," Wong said, "Do you reckon it'll work, though? Supposing our killer's from China — checking local .38 owners won't help us much if he is."

"It will if he's from Hong Kong. What did we get on prints?"

"Only our victim's showed on that Mercedes."

"What about his wallet?"

"Same story," Wong said. "And on those leaflets he was lying on top of too."

"We found no one else's prints anywhere?"

"Not apart from those belonging to people working at the car hire firm," Wong said. "You don't suspect any of them, do you?"

"No," Chan said. "But you'd still better get someone to check they all have an alibi."

"Will do, boss. What happens to all these reports now? Want me to give them to your friend Lam?"

"Lam? Why would he need them?"

"I forgot to mention, boss, the top floor have decided to go public with our victim's identity. They're holding a press conference this afternoon. Lam's been put in charge. I figured it might help him if … Does he get these reports or doesn't he?"

"All right," Chan said. "Give him the reports. Now tell me what your friends …"

His next words were drowned out by a helicopter passing overhead. He removed the phone from his ear and watched the chopper head off to Macau. Or was it taking holidaymakers to the tennis ranch on Lantau? When the helicopter was far enough away, he put the phone back to his ear.

"What's that you say, Pete?"

"I was going to ask about your reporter friends," Chan said. "What did they tell you about the cult?"

"Hold on, I made a few notes."

Chan heard the sound of a drawer being yanked open, and then of paper rustling as Wong turned pages in his notebook.

"Formed five years ago," Wong began officiously. "As a protest against the modern world … Outlawed by China fifteen months ago — but they can still operate here ... Hong Kong headquarters is—"

"Is over on Lantau," Chan interrupted impatiently. "Yes, yes, I've already got all this, Ah Wong. What I *really* want to know is if your friends support any of that stuff I heard from Jack Spalding. Have they heard any rumours the cult was responsible for those deaths in Shanghai?"

"My friend who works at *Sing Tao* has," Wong answered. "The rumours aren't only about Shanghai either — the word is this cult had some Party big-shots in Sichuan bumped off in October. These big-shots put other cult members behind bars, see."

"Who's your friend's source?"

"An officer with Shanghai Security Bureau."

"What's the officer's name?"

"My friend wouldn't say. But he claims he's reliable."

Which meant Alan Yip might have got it right, Chan reflected. If the cult was not averse to becoming involved in revenge killings in Sichuan, then its leaders could have hired a hit-man to murder Yip's son in a revenge attack in Hong Kong.

"What about that John Tsang background I asked you for?"

"Still working on it," Wong replied. "Don't worry, though, it'll be ready when you get back. But you still haven't said what part Tsang plays in all this."

"He might not play any part."

"So why the background check?"

"Because when I saw Yip at his film studios he did something that made me … Let me read the Tsang stuff first, Ah Wong, then I'll be in a better position to explain."

Chan put the phone in his pocket. A glance at his watch showed it was five past three. In fifteen minutes more the ferry would dock; it was making steady progress along Lantau's coast. He glanced over to his right, at a scattering of white-washed holiday apartments set against a backdrop of rolling green-brown hills. The sight of the hills made him feel more serene.

He had always possessed a fondness for Lantau. Perhaps it was the love of wide-open spaces and rural surroundings that growing up in a village by China's Yellow River had bequeathed to him. Despite being almost twice the size of Hong Kong, Lantau had for years been home to fewer than a hundred thousand people. Many more lived there now, of course, because the opening of Lantau's new airport a few years ago and a new high-speed railway link with Hong Kong, had encouraged developers to build apartment blocks. Quiet spots still existed, though. The Heavenly Ghosts had sited their temple in one of these spots.

Twenty years ago, Chan had wanted to live on Lantau: to enjoy its wide-open spaces, and commute to work on the ferries. His wife had axed the plan.

"I'm an urban girl, Peter."

"But we'll breathe clean air."

"I'm a Hong Konger."

"We'll escape the noise. Go for walks."

"I don't *want* to escape — petrol fumes and overcrowding are in my blood! Don't you understand? I'm one of those millions of crazy people who *like* noise and hassle — it makes life exciting. You go to dull old Lantau and you go without me, Peter."

The argument had ended there. No way could he have gone to Lantau without Mei; he couldn't have gone anywhere without her. He would never have dreamed, in those early days together, that their marriage would collapse as spectacularly as it had done. The ties binding them had been strong. And Ah Fah's birth, two years into their marriage, had made them even stronger.

But the birth of a son or daughter always strengthened the bond between a child's parents. Unless, of course, you were Mister Peter Collins from The Laurels, High Barnet, Hertfordshire: if you were Mister Peter Collins, then as soon as your only son was born, you took your ugly English face back to your big house at The Laurels, High Barnet, Hertfordshire and stayed there and never saw your son again. Now was no time to dwell on the past, though, Chan reminded himself. He must focus on the present. Lantau's ferry pier loomed ahead. The Heavenly Ghosts awaited him.

"I TOLD YOU not to phone me unless it was important," said an annoyed John Tsang.

"It *is* important," Fai protested. "The Yeung bitch — she must know everything. That's why … That man in the street … He tried to kill me … Half an hour ago … He—"

"Control yourself!" John Tsang snapped. "You're drunk again. You're imagining it all."

"No, I swear I—"

"How could she know anything?" Tsang cut in aggressively. "You claim you took all the precautions I told you to take."

"I did."

"So how could she know anything?"

"Because that night … Night that I spoke to Szeto, I mean … She lives in his apartment block and … My father had asked her to pass a message to Szeto … She was standing outside Szeto's flat when I opened the door … *She could have heard everything that I'd told him!*"

"Why didn't you tell me before?"

"I did tell you," Fai protested. "I told you the same night when I spoke to Szeto. I said I'd confessed everything to him. And then, after talking to me, Szeto rushed off to see you. And you managed to calm him down and—"

"I'm not talking about Szeto! I mean the woman. Why didn't you tell me last time that she was standing outside the door?"

"Because at first … Well, I thought she hadn't heard me. But — but now I think maybe she did and … What do *you* think, Mister Tsang?"

Tsang did not answer him for a moment. Then he said, "I think you have a problem."

"That's why I called. To ask what we do."

"*We* do nothing."

"Nothing? I don't understand."

"I said *you* have a problem. One I expect you to deal with."

"But — but how? What do I do?"

"What anyone does who has a problem; eliminate it."

21

PENG PULLED THE four-inch-long piece of copper wire from his jacket pocket. He placed the wire into the security grille's lock then moved the wire around until he heard a dull click. With his free left hand, he slid the security grille open.

He examined the lock on the wooden entrance door: even more flimsy than the one the security grille. Again, it should cause him no problems. He pulled a bank credit card from his pocket, gently shaking his head at the absurdity; it never ceased to amaze him that something as simple as a credit card could be so devastating.

He slipped the plastic card into the thin gap that existed between the entrance door and the door frame, and then slid the card down until it rested against the door's flimsy bolt. With a quick twist of the card, he snapped the bolt back from the groove it rested in and opened the door. Eighty seconds. That was all it had taken him to break both of the locks. When would the people who made these apartment blocks provide some real security for tenants?

He nudged open the door and stepped inside the flat. It was a small, untidy affair: not exactly overflowing with furniture. There was a brown leather sofa and matching armchair, a coffee table, a TV cabinet with TV, a hi-fi system and a bookcase. Two unwashed wine glasses and an empty wine bottle stood on the coffee table. Newspapers and magazines lay scattered on the floor and armchair. Apart from the entrance door, four other doors led from the living room. Peng checked these doors methodically, one by one, to see what lay behind them. The two doors furthest from the entrance opened on to bedrooms, the other two doors led to the kitchen and bathroom.

He returned from the bathroom to the living room.

A photograph on top of the TV cabinet drew his attention. He walked over to examine it. It was a family shot: husband, wife and teenage daughter; all three smiling. The woman and girl — he did not know either of them. The man's face was burned into his memory. Peng reached into his shoulder holster and removed the snub-nosed Makarov, then took its bulbous blue-black silencer from his jacket pocket. He screwed the silencer onto the pistol barrel. He pressed the Makarov against the picture.

"Bang!" he said. "You're dead, Chan!"

Not yet, though, Peng thought. If he dies now he escapes my perfect vengeance. And only if revenge is perfect will my sister rest easy in the after-life, secure in the knowledge that her brutal murderer has suffered the same fate as herself. So no, he doesn't die now. For his punishment to match his crime, he dies on the exact same day and at the exact same time as my beautiful sister died. The same way too — slow and in agony. First, I make him suffer like she suffered. Make him know fear and pain like the pain father and I endured. Then, and only then, do I finally finish him off with a bullet. Not a bullet in the head, either. Chan gets it in the guts. That way he dies hard, just like my sister.

Peng reached into his jacket pocket and pulled out a photograph. A black-and-white shot of a teenager wearing school uniform, hair in pigtails, braces on teeth: his murdered sister. He would leave the picture of her here: it would spark Chan's fear. Especially when Chan read the message on the back of the picture that told him the precise time he was going to die. He would know then what fate awaited him — that he had only one more day to live. He would run, of course, cowards like him always ran. But no way would he escape. His fate was sealed. Chan would die.

Not yet, though, Peng reminded himself. First I have to allow his fear to fester. I have to keep him constantly looking over his shoulder, have to get him to experience real fear, real terror. Then, and only then, do …

What was that?

Someone was outside: a key turning in the lock. How could that be? The sergeant at the police station had said Chan would be away from his home all day. Peng opened the nearest bedroom door and moved inside, closing the door gently behind him. Not completely, though. He left a crack, which while narrow enough to prevent him from being seen, still allowed him to view the entrance door.

With a clang, the security grille slid free.

The wooden door banged open and a tall girl with spiked hair clomped into the flat. The girl was probably eighteen or nineteen. She wore a blood-red tee-shirt with a picture of a foreign rock star on the front and a pair of camouflaged army trousers. She slammed the door shut and then glanced around the living room. She threw her arms up and shook her head, as though she could not believe what she saw in the room.

"Jesus! What a state!"

She continued to shake her head ruefully as she viewed the mess in the flat: the newspapers and magazines on the floor, the unwashed glasses on the coffee table.

"Dad, you ought to be ashamed of yourself! I don't know how I put up with you. I ought to turn around right now and leave."

Yet you could tell from her smile, the smile that a parent bestows on a wayward yet lovable child, that there was no way she was going to leave. She was obviously fond of Chan. In fact it was more than that. She obviously loved him. She …

Loved him!

What right does Chan have? Peng thought. What right has a brutal murderer to be loved by her — by anyone? And why should his daughter, the same age now as my sister was when Chan killed her, be alive today? Why should she strut around this room? What right has she to be smiling like that while my sister died screaming in agony?

She passed from his view and moved into the kitchen. He heard cupboard doors banging open and shut, heard her exclaim, "I don't believe it! It's even worse in here! How come I didn't notice any of this mess last night?"

She returned to the living room where he could view her through the crack in the door again. View her more closely this time. Too closely. She was coming this way, heading for this bedroom.

Peng flicked off the safety on the Makarov.

But she did not enter his bedroom. She chose the other one. He heard more doors bang open and shut, heard her singing. After about half a minute, she re-emerged into the living room. A large pink towel was in her hands, a pair of shorts had replaced the camouflaged army pants. She kicked the bathroom door open and went inside.

Peng eased open the bedroom door and stepped into the living room. He held the Makarov in one hand, his sister's picture in the other. Five minutes ago he had planned to pin this picture to the wall. It would have sparked Chan's fear, would have shown him that he could never be safe — not even here in his own home. And the message on the photograph would have warned of the fate that awaited him; would have made him aware of the painful death he was destined to endure. Then the girl had walked into the flat — and changed everything.

There was a better revenge. It lay behind that bathroom door, in the shape of Chan's daughter. Before Chan died, his only daughter would die. Chan would discover what it felt like to lose a loved one. Peng pointed the gun at the bathroom door.

Prepared to fire.

22

CHAN PASSED THROUGH a wooden gate which led to a garden where two men were kneeling down and planting flowers. They both wore long, flowing white robes; the type of thing Chinese peasants had worn three hundred-odd years ago. Why did these cults always make their followers dress so weirdly? Did they *want* people to think they were all crazy?

The men glanced up. They eyed him suspiciously.

"Police," Chan said officiously. "Here to see Brother Li."

Neither man spoke. One of them returned to his planting. The other, with the briefest of nods, indicated a single-storey, white-washed building with an orange tiled roof that stood about twenty metres away. Chan walked over to the building and pushed open its double glass entrance doors.

A receptionist, probably aged in her early twenties, sat behind a desk, tapping industriously at her computer keyboard. She looked up when Chan entered. She had long silken black hair, tied back in a pony tail with a red ribbon, and an olive-tinted face. She wore the same sort of white robe as the gardeners outside, but to better effect. While they had both looked ridiculous, she appeared stylish.

Chan glanced around the room. Its walls were all white-washed and bare, apart from a large framed head-and-shoulders photograph of a grey-haired man who smiled down serenely.

"Grand Master Ho," the girl announced, when she caught Chan gazing at the portrait. She had an attractive, purring voice, the sort of voice that might lull you to sleep if you listened to it for long enough. Her nut-brown eyes glowed warmly. "The founder and spiritual leader of our group — you are Inspector Chan, yes?"

Chan said that he was.

"Brother Li is expecting you." She pointed at a door behind her. "But he is in his room meditating right now." She indicated a chair. "Perhaps you would care to sit down for a moment." Her right hand disappeared below the desk and reappeared with a magazine. "Perhaps you would also care to read this. So many people fail to understand the good works Grand Master Ho aims to do — this will help you discover the truth."

Chan would much rather have flipped through the file he had spied on her desk, the one with 'personal' stamped on the cover in red letters. But no way would she willingly hand the file over. And ordering her to do so would mean him getting heavy-handed. It would be unwise to become confrontational so early on. It would probably make her defensive and less willing to volunteer any information.

He accepted the magazine. It was a professional-looking product. Featured on its glossy cover was a picture of the same grey-haired figure who gazed down from the wall. In this photograph his eyes were shut while he meditated in the lotus position. Chan thought the picture made the grey-haired man look like a modern-day Lord Buddha.

The magazine's inside pages contained the sort of slick promotional material which any large company might produce to win over new customers. Lots of relaxing shots of white-robed figures in well-maintained gardens like the one outside, and of the grey-haired man in various poses: hands on the heads of followers; accepting flower garlands from smiling children; old people sitting at his feet, gazing up devotedly.

Beneath the pictures were articles which scorned claims by the Chinese state that the cult brainwashed all its followers, or forced them to worship its leader, or turned Party officials into cult members to discover state secrets. According to the authors of the articles, the cult simply wished to bring harmony to an evil world that seemed hell-bent on self-destruction. And if everyone would just obey the teachings of the great and good Grand Master Ho, this was what it would succeed in doing.

"As you can see," the pretty receptionist purred, "we are so wrongly accused. Our enemies say that we kidnap people. But as you can clearly observe, we do not participate in any illegal activities. People join our family willingly because … Oh, there's no need for you to return the magazine. Please keep it."

Chan folded it up and put it in his pocket. The girl smiled again, showing dimples and even, pearly-white teeth. He was being softened up for the man next door, Chan realised. This cult would not be the first big organisation to realise the advantages of putting a pretty girl on its reception desk. Have her smile sweetly and speak in that purring voice — soon you would be eating out of her hand.

"We offer the people *hope,* Inspector Chan — their only hope." Her voice had suddenly become infused with passion. "China's economic freedoms may have enabled a greedy few to enrich themselves, but millions more have lost all hope. They have lost jobs and self-respect, have become destitute and suicidal. Master Ho offers them their only hope. Their lives will not be improved by China becoming a global financial centre, or by the actions of greedy businessmen. Their only chance of salvation is through a purer life of meditation and prayer."

She paused, and gazed at Chan as if she expected him to comment on her speech. When he said nothing, she rose from her chair.

"This way, please. Brother Li is ready to receive you."

"HE'S BEEN ROBBING you blind!"

"We can't prove it."

"I heard them," Miss Yeung said, "him and Szeto."

Film producer Alan Yip shook his head: "You might have misheard them. We need to wait for more proof."

"If we wait it'll be too late. We need—"

"I said we wait."

They were in his office at the film studios. He sat at his desk. Miss Yeung stood about ten feet away from him, one hand resting on the coffee machine. Yip leaned forward in his executive swivel chair. He gazed levelly at her.

"I'm in charge. And don't you ever forget it."

She smiled sweetly. "Of course you're in charge, darling."

"And I say we wait." He eyed her challengingly. "Understood?"

She nodded. "I understand you," she said calmly. "But you need to understand something too, Ah Yip."

"And what's that?"

"You must resolve this problem now, not later. And I know the way to do it."

He frowned. "What are you talking about?"

"That police inspector."

"Chan? What about him?"

"We use him," said Miss Yeung. "It shouldn't be difficult. Some words whispered in his ear. Words about how Fai—"

"No."

"You must resolve this, Ah Yip."

"In my own time and own way."

"Do it my way and we solve your other problem."

He stiffened: "*Other* problem? What do you mean?"

She did not answer him for a moment. Then she said, "I know what happened that night, Ah Yip."

He sat more upright. He eyed her coldly. "What night?"

She smiled at him, but without showing her teeth this time. She left her place by the coffee machine and walked across the deep-pile carpet until she stood beside his desk.

"But I'll protect you, my darling." She rested a manicured hand on his shoulder. "I won't tell anyone what happened that night."

He shoved her hand away. "*Nothing* happened."

"All right, darling, all right; whatever you say."

"We do this my way. I'm in charge. Understood?"

"Of course."

"We wait for more proof."

"Of course."

She replaced her hand on his shoulder. He stiffened, but this time he did not try to push her hand away. She began to expertly knead his muscles with her long, slender fingers. She lowered her head until her lips were almost touching Yip's ear.

"We'll do whatever you say we do, my darling," she whispered into his ear. "After all, you're in charge."

23

THIS ROOM WAS much like the other room next door; whitewashed walls that were bare apart from a framed picture of the serene-looking, grey-haired Grand Master Ho; a polished desk complete with computer, telephone and notebooks. One thing was notably different from that room next door, though: the air-conditioning was turned up so high in here that Chan felt he was standing inside a huge fridge.

"Welcome to Siberia!"

The man sitting behind the desk shot Chan an ingratiating smile which revealed two gold teeth in his top row. The man struggled to his feet and waddled across the room, right hand extended in a greeting. Chan had met some strange-looking characters over the years, but few had looked as strange as this one. The man was almost a dwarf and seemed to have no neck. And he was so fat that Chan would not have been surprised to see him suddenly explode the seams of his double-breasted grey jacket which was far too tight — unlike the receptionist and the gardeners outside he wore no white robe.

"I'm Brother Li."

Chan shook hands: it was like grasping a damp sponge.

"So *terribly* sorry about the air-con level," Li said. "I do beg your pardon ... Yes, I apologise sincerely ... But this *awful* humidity! ... Well, I find it *unbearable!* I much prefer a cool environment ... Yes, yes, I do."

He spoke quickly, almost stumbling over the words. His voice was high-pitched, almost a squeak.

"It's a hangover from my home life, I suppose. Mother *always* insisted on running the air-conditioner at full blast … Said it was very good for the brain and ... Well, she was always *awfully* keen to stimulate my brain because …" Li halted his runaway voice in its tracks for a moment. He gestured at a chair by his desk. Then speaking more slowly, though only just, he said, "I'm sorry, I'm forgetting my manners — mother would never forgive me. Please, sit down, inspector."

Chan sat down.

Li loosened his tie and unfastened the top button of his white shirt. He did have a neck, Chan noticed. A purplish-red colour, it seemed to have been attached by mistake to Li's waxy-pale face. Dun-coloured eyes gazed out beneath a flat, wide forehead which did not seem to indicate any great degree of intelligence. Why had he been put in charge? Chan had expected to encounter an imposing figure — leaders of cults like this usually possessed personal magnetism. That was how they managed to secure the devotion of their followers despite talking nonsense. Li seemed as inspiring as a bowl of cold noodles. Why had the cult's bosses put him in control of their Hong Kong operation?

A likely answer came when Li said, "Tragically, mother died last year … I felt so *alone*! Oh yes, I had money: a great deal of it. But as Grand Master Ho always reminds us, money is worthless paper. I read about him ... His good works … Realised my shallow life was leading nowhere. So—"

"You gave him your millions and started a new life?"

"But — but how did you know? And I've never been happier, inspector … Yes, I feel such inner *calm!*"

Chan thought: It doesn't look it. But *why* are you agitated? Is it because Alan Yip spoke the truth about your cult murdering his son Szeto? Or am I jumping to conclusions? Your edginess might have nothing to do with Yip's son; it could just be part of your personal make-up.

Li was obviously strung as tight as piano wire; you only had to spend twenty seconds listening to the twittering about his mother to realise that. And the way that he had handed over his cash in exchange for this job indicated instability. But whether it was guilt about Yip's son or problems in his psychological make-up, Li was *definitely* shaky. Even if those pale fleshy hands had not fluttered through the air like a pair of large moths whenever he spoke, the mass of stubbed-out cigarettes would have betrayed his nervousness to Chan. The butts were all of varying lengths, tell-tale signs of a worried man — one cigarette had burned out in the ashtray practically unsmoked.

Chan drummed his fingers on the side of the chair while he considered what tactics to adopt. Sometimes he found it best to engage in a bit of small talk before getting down to business. It often relaxed people and made them more friendly disposed — willing to provide information. His instincts told him that this would be the wrong approach here. He should try to break Li quickly.

"I'm investigating a murder," Chan said without ceremony. "A man's body was discovered in Mongkok last night."

Li clicked his tongue, nodded his fat head. "I read all about it in *Oriental Daily* — terrible, don't you agree? But as Grand Master Ho tells us, all the evils of this modern world will inevitably produce destruction."

"The victim was Alan Yip's son."

Chan searched for tell-tale signs of guilt: a blanching of Li's face, a stiffening of the jaw, tenseness in the shoulders; anything that might betray the fact he knew the victim's identity, even though it had not yet been officially released. While Li's nervous state persisted, Chan glimpsed no guilt indicators. Li seemed to be genuinely ignorant of the victim's identity.

"Alan Yip the film producer?"

"Yes."

"Mother would never have believed it." Li shook his head half in sorrow, half in shock at life's sinfulness. "No one's safe. No, no, they're not. But as Grand Master Ho says, the modern—"

"Alan Yip says your followers killed him."

"We must return to a purer life. Yes — yes, we …"

Li stopped twittering as the enormity of Chan's last words sank in. He stared aghast at the inspector, eyes widening in disbelief.

"*We* killed him?"

"Yes."

"It's a lie, an outrageous *monstrous* lie!"

One pale, fleshy hand fluttered over Li's bald head before coming to rest shakily on a tuft of hair which sprouted from his right earlobe. According to Chinese custom, such hair brought its owner good luck — Li gave the hair a tug. He grabbed a gold case from the desk, pulled out a cigarette and lit it. But he took only a brief pull before stubbing the cigarette out.

"There's no truth in what you say — none at all. Why would we want to kill Alan Yip's son?"

Chan mentioned the threats that Yip had said the cult had made.

"No — no, it's a lie, a *monstrous* lie!"

Li trembled with indignation. Or was it fear? Should I drag him to the police station? Chan wondered. No. I've no hard evidence. Despite what officers like Terry Duggan think, you can't arrest someone just because they get nervous — you require proof. Without it a lawyer would bury me. I need to be patient. *Bat yan sing gam*, grandfather used to say; a wise man who waits sees lead turn to gold. Better to follow his advice and wait for some hard evidence before taking a tougher line. How do I get hard evidence? Is it in the 'personal' file I saw on the reception desk? In that case all I need do is order the girl to hand it over. But supposing the file contains nothing useful? I'll have played my hand too early. Li and his friends will be more on their guard. There's another way of checking that file without making them defensive, though.

"Have you a wash-room, Mister Li?"

"You go back through Sister Kwan's office, then down the corridor," Li said. "It's the first door on the left."

Chan got up from his chair and headed for the washroom. Once inside the washroom, he reached into his jacket pocket and took out his mobile phone and the magazine which the receptionist had given him. The temple's phone number was listed on page two of the magazine.

Chan rang the number.

"Sister Kwan," the receptionist answered almost immediately in her purring voice. "Can I help you?"

"I hope so, sister." Chan hoped that his disguised voice would be good enough to fool her. "I've arrived from Hong Kong and I'm at the bus stop beside the school. But I'm having trouble finding your temple."

"It's not far. You—"

"I'm *hopeless* at directions." Chan gave a bashful chuckle. "Always get lost. So I … Well, could you come down here and guide me?"

"I'm extremely busy."

"Only I've a big donation to—"

"Give me five minutes."

He heard her door open and shut, then her feet pattering down the corridor. He returned to her office, moved to her desk. He picked up the file marked personal and examined its contents. Nothing special: just gas and electric bills. He glanced at the computer screen to see what she had been typing. A letter to the phone company, complaining it had overcharged last month.

A notebook lay on the desk. He flipped through it: phone numbers, pages of shorthand and a caricature of Li. She was an accomplished cartoonist. And judging from how she had depicted Li, as half-man half-whale, no great fan of her boss. Chan tugged at the drawer beneath the desk: locked. He was about to try and break the lock with his penknife, when a click on the phone on Miss Yeung's desk told him Li had picked up the phone next door.

He moved closer to the door until he could hear Li speaking.

"He's here now!" Li said in a frightened voice. "Asking about … Well, I need *help!* … No, no, he doesn't suspect me — not yet … But supposing … Well, if that's your advice … Yes, I'll ... But are you *sure* it will be all right? … Supposing …"

Chan heard footsteps in the corridor. He checked his watch. The girl had only been gone three minutes. Had she realised that he had tricked her and turned back before the bus stop? Had she sent one of the gardeners there?

He pushed open the door to Li's room.

"Look, I must go … Yes, yes, I'll call later." Li put the phone in its cradle. "A brother," he said, in a voice only slightly calmer than the one that Chan had heard him using a moment ago. "He needed assistance." Li tugged at the lucky hair on his ear. "In a responsible role like mine I'm always being asked for help." He smiled nervously. "Some days the phone rings non-stop … Yes, yes, it does."

Chan nodded. "I can see you're a busy man. That's why I won't keep you a moment longer than is necessary. I've only one more question. Where were you four nights ago?"

Li stiffened. "But — but why do you want to know?"

"Nothing sinister," Chan said soothingly; "it's normal practice to ask everyone to account for their whereabouts."

"Normal … Oh, yes I see." Li relaxed slightly. "Yes — yes, of course. Well, I would have been here."

"Doing what?"

"Meditating, or reading. Or writing down my thoughts — Grand Master Ho says we should always write down our thoughts. It helps improve our lives, you see. It …"

The phone rang. Li snatched up the receiver.

"Brother Li … What? … Look, this isn't the right time … No it's impossible … Call later and … I said *later*."

He replaced the phone.

"Are you all right?" Chan asked.

"These reporters are so *intolerably* annoying," Li said. "You tell them you don't want to be interviewed, but they still refuse to listen." He tried to make a joke of it. "They're almost as stubborn as my ex-wife — but not quite." His attempt at a smile was painful to watch. Sweat shone on his upper lip, but he made no effort to wipe it off; perhaps he was scared his hand would shake too much. "Now then: what else can I do for you, inspector?"

"I think we'll call a halt for the moment," Chan said. "If I need your help again, I'll be in touch. Thanks for … Are you *sure* you're all right? You look pale."

"I might have a touch of flu coming on," Li said. "It's terribly inconvenient, but not life-threatening."

24

THE JET CLIMBED higher into the sky. Buildings in Taipei grew smaller and harder for the Boeing 747's passengers to see, until there were no buildings for them to see at all, only grey-white clouds. Fai turned away from the window and settled more comfortably in his business-class seat.

He breathed a sigh of relief.

He was safe.

A few hours from now and the plane would land in Macau. From there he would board a jet cat for the one-hour journey across the South China Sea to Hong Kong. Once home in Hong Kong he could sit back and relax. He would be able to recharge his batteries and ... Hold on! This sort of thinking was foolish. Of course he couldn't relax. If his enemies could strike at him in Taiwan, then what would prevent them from also striking at him in Hong Kong? Nothing, he realised, swallowing dryly. I'll never be safe. Not until I deal one and for all with that Yeung bitch. But I wouldn't have to deal with her. I wouldn't have to deal with anyone if I hadn't got greedy.

Once again he cursed himself for having agreed to a business pact with John Tsang, and then for foolishly telling his brother all about it. I was more than foolish, he thought. I was crazy. If I'd kept quiet about everything Szeto would never have gone charging off to see Tsang. Szeto would probably still be alive today. What happened at the late-night encounter between the two of them?

When I quizzed him about it, Tsang claimed that he had managed to buy Szeto off. He was lying, though; no way would he have been able to buy off Sezto. My brother would never have accepted Tsang's money. Not a single cent. All the stuff that Szeto got so involved in before his death, all those crazy meetings that he attended, all the crazy stuff that he'd begun to read and talk about ... it all made my brother way too self-righteous to take anything that even remotely resembled a bribe. How did Tsang manage it? What did he do, or say, that made Szeto turn full circle and agree to do what Tsang wanted?

"A drink, sir?"

A flight attendant stood over him.

"Vodka and tonic," Fai said. "*Double* vodka."

She searched her trolley for the bottles.

Something strange took place at that encounter between Tsang and Szeto, Fai thought. It must have done, because after that night Szeto acted even more intense and disturbed. So what happened? What ...

"Enjoy your drink, sir."

The attendant handed him the glass, then moved down the aisle. Fai sipped at his drink and then screwed up his face with distaste: she had forgotten to add the tonic water. He stood up, moved down the aisle to where she was busy serving another passenger. He tapped her shoulder.

"Excuse me, but ..."

"Are you all right, sir?"

"Yes, yes, I'm fine."

"You've gone all pale. Are—"

"Yes, yes, I ... My mistake ... Everything's fine."

He did not bother to ask for tonic water. He no longer wanted it. All that he wanted to do was to get away from that passenger she was serving: as quickly as possible.

He sweated as he returned to his place. His heart thumped as though he had run a five-mile race. He fell into his seat, rather than sat on it. He swallowed his neat vodka in two quick gulps. But his heart still pounded heavily. The killer in Taiwan: the squat, shaven-headed man whom he thought he had escaped from.

He was on the plane.

SHANGHAI SIZZLED.

A fireball sun blazed from a cloudless turquoise sky, scorching office buildings and warehouses which lined the waterfront. The pedestrians tramping along the Bund had discarded jackets and ties to try and keep cool, but they still oozed sweat. On the Huangpu, ferry boats and cargo ships glistened like huge silver ingots while the river itself, normally a turgid grey-brown colour, today flowed pearl-white.

Businessman John Tsang knew this weather well. On another blisteringly hot day, thirty years ago, he had fallen passionately in love. An on a scorching afternoon, fifteen years ago, his lover had tragically died when ... No, that last bit isn't true, Tsang thought, turning abruptly away from the window of his hotel. My lover didn't die.

She was murdered!

He stared at the picture on his bedside table. A framed black-and-white shot of a serene-faced woman in her early twenties: the greatest love of his life. He had never loved anyone — either before or after her tragic death — in the same intense, possessive, madly passionate way that he had loved this woman. And now she was dead; murdered by Alan Yip.

But finally Alan Yip was going to face justice: he would pay for his crime. Tsang would make sure of it. He would destroy Yip the same way that Yip had destroyed her: slowly, piece by tiny piece, until finally, a blow would be delivered to finish Yip for good.

Tsang had devised a plan to bring Yip to justice. It was a complicated, high-risk plan. He had formed alliances with groups and individuals whom he would normally steer clear of, had made some dangerous and illegal deals — even been responsible for a man's death. But all the risk and complexity, even that man's tragic death ... Yes, it had been worth it, because the plan was going to succeed. Alan Yip, the man who had cruelly destroyed the love of Tsang's life, would finally himself be destroyed. Providing that young fool

Fai kept his nerve. I should have expected it to be this way, though, Tsang thought. Fai's a coward. Not a bit like my own son. My son was courageous; as brave as a lion. His bravery will all have been for nothing, though, if Fai abandons our deal. My son will have died in vain. The plan to destroy Alan Yip will fail. A murderer will escape justice.

That's why I can't let it happen. Under no circumstances can I allow Fai to back out of our deal. Nothing and no one is going to interfere with the plan to destroy Alan Yip. Anyone who does will pay a heavy price. As that coward Fai is about to discover.

25

"HOW COME YOU didn't drag Li to the station?"

"What I heard him say on the phone isn't enough, Ah Wong. We need more proof."

"But you reckon Li's definitely hiding *something,* huh?"

Chan signalled to the waiter to hurry up with their beers. It was six-fifteen. They sat in a Sichuan restaurant near the ferry pier. Chan had arrived on the boat from Lantau fifteen minutes ago.

"The cult had a firm motive to kill Szeto," Chan said. "It wanted revenge against his father for what Alan Yip did in China."

"Got a proven track record too," Wong pointed out. "My reporter friend from *Sing Tao* said it ordered the deaths of Party big-shots in Chengdu."

"It also has enough money to hire a hit-man," Chan said. "And so far all the forensic evidence suggests that a hit-man could be our killer. We only found Szeto's prints on the car and his belongings. A professional wouldn't leave any prints behind."

Wong nodded as he mused over what Chan had told him. Then Wong said, "So if everything's so straightforward, how come you think the cult isn't responsible?"

"Did I say I thought that?"

"You don't have to say it; you've got that look on your face."

"Look?"

"The look you have when you're not totally convinced."

"Did you bring that background?" Chan asked.

Wong looked surprised: "Background?"

"The John Tsang stuff."

"Ah, yes! The Tsang files."

"Well?"

"Well, I'm … Hey! Watch your arm, boss! You almost knocked the tray out of his hand!"

The elderly waiter Chan had told to bring their beer hovered by his shoulder. The waiter leaned over and placed two *Tsingtaos* on the table. Beads of perspiration coated the sides of the chunky green bottles. Good. That meant the beer would be icy cold.

"Why are you interested in Tsang anyway?" Wong asked.

Chan poured his *Tsingtao,* waited until the creamy foam at the top of his glass had thinned out, and then took a long, thirst-quenching gulp. Ah! that was good: so cool and refreshing! He wiped his lips. Then told Wong about his meeting with film producer Alan Yip, and how Yip had defaced John Tsang's picture in the newspaper.

"So?" Wong said when Chan had finished.

"Doesn't it seem strange?"

"Not really. Yip just doesn't like him."

"It was a lot more than that," Chan insisted. "He didn't only draw a stupid beard or glasses on Tsang's picture. What he did was done in a frenzy. He scrawled across that picture so hard he even ripped the paper."

"Like I say, he doesn't like him."

"Then, when he knew I could see what he'd done, he went and stored the newspaper out of sight."

"He was embarrassed."

"I'd just told him his son was dead."

"So?"

"A man in his position would be too busy thinking about his son to get embarrassed about childish scrawl in a newspaper — if it *was* childish scrawl. He wouldn't care about anyone seeing what he'd done. All he would care about would be his dead son. Yet Yip still had presence of mind to hide that newspaper."

Wong's expression showed he remained unconvinced: "Don't you think you're reading too much into it?"

"Then there was the look on his face."

"What look?"

"When he knew I'd seen what he'd done. It was only there for a split second, but there was definitely something unusual about it; a hint of guilt in it — or maybe even of fear."

Wong shook his head. "I still think he was just embarrassed."

"It was more than that," Chan said. "Anyway, the stuff in that file on Tsang should help clear things up." He held out his hand. "Let me have it."

Wong looked sheepish. "We have a slight problem."

"What sort of problem?"

Wong shifted in his chair. "When I got your message saying you wanted to meet … I was keen to make sure, see … Make sure I wasn't late, I mean … I left the office really quick and—"

"And you forgot," Chan said. "You've left all that background in the office."

"Everything will be all right, though," Wong said. "I've arranged with Terry Duggan to …"

Wong's explanation was halted by the arrival of the silver-haired waiter with their food; spicy soup-noodles, fried green beans with chilli, onion cakes and sliced pork with a small jug of chilli sauce.

Wong eyed the dishes disdainfully.

"Something wrong?" Chan queried.

"I still don't understand why you eat this Sichuan junk," Wong said. "It's the worst Chinese food around. In fact calling it food should be a crime. They put so much chilli on the food that you can't ever taste anything else."

"I can see you hate it," Chan said. "It's obvious from the way you're cramming your bowl that every morsel is poison."

Wong shrugged his flabby shoulders. "A hungry man will eat the floorboards if he must, boss. But I would much rather we'd gone someplace else." He shook his head, puzzled. "I'll never understand this side of you. I mean, you eat all of this chilli-sauce junk, yet you turn up your nose at good honest Cantonese cooking! And it's the best food in the world. Especially the genuine Cantonese stuff those food-hygiene pricks won't let us eat in Hong Kong any more. That's why I like to cross the border every so often and give myself a nice treat. There's a great place over in Shenzhen." Wong closed his eyes, licked thick lips. His voice took on a dreamy tone "Braised side of dog, stewed snake, a few gently barbecued rats — all washed down with a healthy glass of snake bile." He smacked his lips. "Wonderful!"

"Do you drink the snake bile before or after?"

"Before or after what?"

"Vomiting on the floor."

Wong's eyes flickered open. He gazed pityingly at Chan. "There's no hope for you," he said sadly. "I'll never get you to appreciate good food."

"Forget your stomach for a second," Chan said. "What were you going to say about Duggan?"

Wong rested his chopsticks on the table. He wiped his lips with a napkin. He said, "When I realised I'd forgotten the Tsang background, I rang the station and asked Duggan to bring it over here. But maybe …"

Wong's moon-shaped face assumed the appearance of a man anxious that he wouldn't be overheard. He looked to his left and then to his right, then threw a glance over his shoulder.

Chan raised an eyebrow. "If you're worried about the agents from China's Secret Police, they're hiding in the bin by the door."

"What I've got to say is no joke," Wong said, suddenly looking serious. "I did some hard thinking while you were in Lantau and … Well, I reckon all of this could be Triad-linked — this case, I mean. Because … Don't groan, boss! I know you think I'm screwed-up about Triads, but … Supposing Yip's kid got in debt with Triad money-lenders? He refuses to repay the loan, so …"

Chan groaned more loudly. He should have known that sooner or later Wong would bring Triads into it. His fat sergeant friend was fascinated by the working of the Chinese criminal gangs.

"They tried to persuade you to join the 14K as a kid, didn't they, Ah Wong?"

Wong grinned. "Remember me telling you, huh?"

"Only five hundred times — or is it six hundred?"

"Be fair! It's only four hundred. And sometimes I wish I'd taken the bait. I'd be worth millions now."

"Or serving twenty years in Stanley prison." Chan drank some beer then wiped foam from his lips. "There's no Triad connection. The answer …"

The ring of Wong's mobile phone interrupted him.

"Sergeant Wong … Oh it's you, Ah Lau … What? … No, of course I haven't forgotten … Half an hour? … No problems."

Wong replaced the phone in his pocket

"Trouble?" Chan queried.

Wong sighed. "There will be if I'm not home in thirty minutes. I forgot that Ah Lau's having dinner with some friends tonight — I'm supposed to be looking after the kids."

"Better get back quickly," Chan said. "We need to meet early tomorrow, though. How about *dim sum* at the Causeway Bay place we went to last week?"

"Overlooking Victoria Park?"

Chan nodded: "Seven-thirty?"

"I'll be there."

26

PALE, WATERY EVENING sunlight washed over the typhoon shelter's sludge-coloured depths and over the fleet of fishing junks and sampans bobbing at anchor. Families who lived in the typhoon shelter had hung out washing to dry. Shirts, socks and underwear festooned the decks of sampans and fluttered from masts of fishing junks.

On one sampan, tattooed young men played *mah-jong* and drank beer; on another they gutted fish, and then tossed blood-red entrails into the polluted water. On other boats, old women in Mao pyjama suits and wide-brimmed hats squatted beside woks and cooked dinner. Or cradled babies left in their care by the babies' mothers, the old women's daughters, who were working in the factories of Lai Chi Kok.

With a shudder, Alan Yip's assistant turned away.

How could anyone tolerate the awful squalor? Apart from the stomach-churning stink of rotting food and raw sewage, there was monstrous overcrowding. A sampan measured barely six metres long yet often served as the home for a family of ten. She had spent her childhood on one and had hated every minute of every day: the dirt and the squalor and overcrowding, the men with their lust-filled eyes, greasy hair and yellow teeth — she had hated everything she could see around her. And when darkness had fallen and she could no longer see the squalor there had still been no relief.

Miss Yeung had feared the night.

She would lie wide awake, tense with apprehension, dreading the moment when it would happen. The moment when she would feel the roughness of her stepfather's hands as he slammed her against the floor; the foulness of his hot breath; the stink of his sweat as he jabbed harder and closer; the burning pain that seemed as though it would never end; his pig-like grunts until finally, his animal lust sated for another night, he left her alone to the pain which pressed her body against her like a hot iron.

She had feared and hated it all.

So why return to a place which stirred up so many unwelcome memories? That gangster, of course — he had refused to meet her anywhere else. But she had wasted time coming here because the coward had failed to turn up. He had taken that money she had already paid him and run without doing the job. She should have expected it, though; should have known that such a small-time hoodlum would prove treacherous.

Perhaps it wasn't treachery or cowardice which had made him stay away. Perhaps he had simply got drunk and was sleeping it off: all the men in this area were drunkards. Her stepfather had been the biggest drunkard of them all. He would never threaten her again, though; she had made sure of it. Just as she would make sure — even without the Triad thug's help — that no man ever threatened her in the future.

A tragic accident, the police had decided after recovering her stepfather's bloated body from the harbour — he had got drunk and fallen overboard, banging his head on the boat before hitting the water. It was true, he *had* been drunk — whenever had he not been? But he had not got that gash by banging his head against the boat. Determined to ward him off this time, she had brought a claw hammer down on his skull, cracking it like an eggshell.

She turned around and stared again at the typhoon shelter. It was strange, she thought, as her gaze came to rest on the spot where the nightmare had ended twenty years ago. She had expected to feel only relief that he was finally dead. And it was true that she had felt *some* relief. But the dominant emotion that had coursed through her veins, as she watched his carcass sink beneath the inky-black waters, had been something else: power.

It was the first time that she had experienced such an exhilarating feeling — it would not be the last. After her stepfather's death, her mother had been unable to cope, so Miss Yeung had been sent to a children's home in Mongkok. Compared to the sampan, it had been a holiday camp. The other children, mainly boys, had been smaller and she'd bullied them mercilessly — overdue payment for pain suffered at the hands of the male race.

It was not only the exercise of power that she had developed a fondness for at the home. She had also acquired a taste for learning — an eagerness to cram her brain with knowledge. So when, aged seventeen, she had left the home to find a job, she had been an intelligent young woman; unafraid of hard work, confident that she would be a success.

To her dismay, she had soon discovered that it was a man's world. Brains and hard work would never take a woman to the top. To succeed she must use her body. Male employers desired a woman's body, not her brains or office skills. Under all the glitzy jewellery and expensive after-shave, and Armani suits and sham boardroom sophistication of big-shot businessmen lurked the same lustful yearnings that she had encountered in those sweaty bastards from the typhoon shelter. She could cope, though. She was tough and clever. Ah Yip had only begun to realize just how clever.

Although she had allowed Ah Yip to possess her body she had taken something far more important from him in return — his life. It had not happened overnight, of course. It had taken her years of skilled manoeuvring to gain control over him. But as their relationship had grown more intimate she had discovered more and more of his secrets — she knew them all now.

There was nothing he could hide from her. She knew everything about him and his business. With her supreme knowledge had come power. She was now so powerful that she only had to snap her fingers and Alan Yip's mighty film-making empire would come crashing to the floor — just like that! But she suddenly found herself confronting a threat which could bring an end to all this exhilarating power. That was why she had come here to meet the Triad thug.

He had been too scared to turn up, but that was no problem. The more she thought about it, the more she realised that she didn't need his help. All she needed to do was to change her plan. When she returned home she would call that policeman. She would use Inspector Chan as a weapon to destroy Fai.

AFTER WONG LEFT him, Chan ate alone for ten minutes. He had almost finished his meal when the restaurant door opened and a tall, blonde-haired man with swimming-pool blue eyes and a long, thin face burned red by the sun entered. He strode jauntily over to Chan's table.

"Evening, Ace. How goes it?"

"It was going fine," Chan said coldly, "until you showed up."

Sergeant Terry Duggan shrugged off the insult, pretending that Chan's attitude was all part of a game, and that Chan really liked him. He grinned, displaying a set of large and slightly crooked teeth: "Wonderful to see you too!" He slapped two manila files on the table. "Here's all the stuff Wong wanted. Where's the fat man hiding himself, anyway?"

Chan stowed the two files under the table. He said flatly, "If you think bringing this stuff is a way of you getting involved in the case, think again. Pigs have more chance of flying."

Duggan chuckled. "Don't like me, do you?"

"No."

"In fact, not liking me is an understatement — you wouldn't piss on me if I was on fire."

"I wouldn't call us blood brothers."

"Yet I respect you, Ace. More than I respect any other officer."

"Save your breath. I'm immune to flattery."

"It's true," Duggan insisted, his joking of a moment ago suddenly replaced by earnestness. "Perhaps it's because we're so alike — neither of us insiders, I mean. The top-floor looks down on you because you're from China. And as for me … When the Brits ran things I never really fitted in — accent's the wrong sort, see. I'm a northerner from Liverpool. Those London pricks all looked down on me. So I never got promoted."

"Accent had nothing to do with it," Chan said bluntly. "They were scared promotion might make you even more violent — they didn't want all their suspects leaving the station with broken arms."

Duggan's chest swelled, his cheeks filled with air. He seemed about to indignantly protest. At the last moment, he relaxed. He blew air from his cheeks and shrugged. He said nonchalantly, "So I don't shy from physical stuff — but sometimes you need to get tough. And I don't get hard on them just because they're Chinese." He shook his head. "I'm not racist — I like Asians. When I worked in Macau, before joining the cops, my best friend was Asian. In fact he was Chinese — I like you Chinese best of all, see."

"You like Chinese women," Chan said, "*young* women."

Duggan stiffened. "That's a cheap shot."

"It's also the truth."

Duggan clenched a fist. For a moment Chan thought he might throw a punch. Then Duggan relaxed. He gave another shrug.

"So I enjoy a recreational screw in Mongkok — where's the harm? You've got it wrong about me being a cradle-snatcher, though. Those rumours are bullshit. And even if I was a cradle-snatcher *you* could still sleep easy." He grinned. "I'd never go near your daughter — for lots of reasons."

"Watch your mouth!"

"She isn't demure and petite like the rest of you Chinese. She—"

"Why do you keep saying *you Chinese?*" Chan snapped. "I'm only half-Chinese. You should know that by now. You've been calling me *jap jung* behind my back for years."

Duggan threw up his arms: "Jesus! What's your problem?"

"We don't like each other. Never have."

"You've got a chip on your fucking shoulder as big as Everest. You're *obsessed* about being a fucking Eurasian! It's not me who's the racist, pal, it's you."

"Shut your mouth!"

"And you've got it all wrong on another score too. Other people might have called you a *jap jung,* but not me."

"You've done the favour that Ah Wong asked you to do him," Chan said. "Now do me one and disappear."

Duggan opened his mouth to say something, thought better of it and remained silent. He merely stared at Chan, slowly shaking his head. He shrugged, turned around and walked unhurriedly to the door. At the door he turned around again and blew a kiss. Chan pretended not to notice.

Chan paid his bill and left. He had planned to take a taxi to Wan Chai, but the long queue meant he might have to wait thirty minutes. He headed to the tram stop at Des Voeux Road, a two-minute walk away. As he waited at the stop for the tram to arrive he reflected on Duggan's words. Am I a racist? Not only Duggan says so; Ah Wong made more or less the same claim this morning. Surely they're both wrong. Surely only westerners can … Rubbish! Chinese people are some of the most racist types around. They think being descendants of Confucius gives them a right to look down on everyone. What about Eurasians like me? Do I look down on everyone?

If he had not been so focused on providing himself with an answer, he might have sensed the danger. Assassin Liu Peng had been following him from the moment when Chan had stepped off the Lantau ferry an hour ago. As the tram approached the stop, Peng stepped up behind Chan and placed both hands in the small of his back.

He shoved him on the tram line.

27

FOR A MOMENT he thought he was dreaming.

This could not be happening to him. This could not be his body falling through the air and heading for the tram line — it must be a nightmare. In a moment, a second even, he would wake up at home in his bed. Shaking and covered all over with sweat, but safe and alive.

He hit the ground hard.

This was no nightmare. That huge block of solid metal heading down the tram line was heading directly for him. There was no escape for him, no way out. In a few seconds the tram would run over him and crush him.

The sound of the tram roared in his ears, a deafening, mind-numbing thunder of raw engine power and metal scraping on metal. He could hear the sound of a woman screaming too. Or was it a man? Yes, a man. Not just any man, either; the scream came from his own throat. A sharp and piercing scream.

Get away! Get away!

He rolled to his right. Hot air exploded against his spine as the tram went past him. He closed his eyes, curled up into a ball. The tram howled like a wounded animal as the driver slammed on the brakes. The howl grew louder as the brakes bit harder. Sparks flew up from the tram line. A smell of burning oil filled the air.

Then the awful pressure on his ears eased. The tram stopped howling. Now it merely groaned, still an animal in pain, but one coming to terms with that pain. The tram's slowing, Chan thought. In fact it's stopped now. It's come to a complete halt.

I'm safe.

"Is he okay down there?" a man yelled — maybe the driver. "Did we hit him?"

"I'm trying to find out."

Chan felt an arm press against his shoulder. Someone turned him roughly over on to his back. A blurred shape loomed above him. Man or woman? Man, judging from the strength of that grip on his shoulder. Slowly, Chan realised that the man was asking him if he was all right.

"Yes, yes, I'm fine."

Another man joined the first man. Together, the two of them half-pulled, half-pushed Chan to his feet. The crowd of passengers stood back to give them room. He heard the passengers muttering.

"Why did he do it?"

"Stupid bastard!"

"Is he drunk?"

"I'm the driver," said one of the men who had helped him up. "You'd better wait while we call the police and get an ambulance — why did you want to kill yourself?"

Shakily, Chan reached into his jacket pocket and pulled out his ID card. He showed it to the guard. "It's all right, I'm a police inspector. It was all an accident. You can restart the tram."

"You still need an ambulance."

"I'm all right. You can restart the tram."

"I'll have to report to head office. What happened?"

"I was daydreaming and got too close to the line," Chan said. "When the tram pulled in and people pushed forward, someone in the crowd must have slipped and fell against me. I was near the edge and lost my balance. I'm all right now, though."

"Sure you don't need a doctor?"

"I'm fine."

"You've had a shock. You should go home and rest."

"That's what I plan to do."

He did not go home. After the driver had restarted the tram and set off for Shau Kei Wan, Chan entered the first bar that he came to and swallowed a double brandy. Then he set off for Wan Chai, taking deep breaths as he walked. As the fresh air and effects of the brandy kicked in, he grew calmer. One more thing would complete his rejuvenation. About half-way to Lockhart Road, he pulled his mobile phone from his pocket: he needed to talk to his daughter. He would not say what had happened, of course; it would scare Ah Fah. He still needed to listen to her voice, though. Just to hear her would make him feel better. She wasn't in her room at university; the answer machine was on. He left a message on the machine then tried to reach her on her mobile number.

No answer.

FAI STARED INTO the washroom mirror.

Coward! he hissed at his reflection. Coward!

It was true. He was a coward. A fool too; he had got everything wrong. No one on this flight wanted to kill him. There would be no bullet in the back when the plane landed at Macau in half an hour's time. No knife thrust in the ribs as he walked through the airport terminal. That man who was sitting further down the aisle from him, the man he had been convinced had tried to kill him in Taipei — it wasn't him!

The more that Fai had gazed at the man in the last thirty minutes, the more that he had come to realise his mistake. This character was considerably bigger and older than the shaven-headed hit-man in Taipei. It could not possibly be him.

Fool! Fai hissed into the mirror. Fool!

It's fear, he thought. Fear is making me as jumpy as a scalded cat; making me imagine all sorts of crazy things. That's why it will be a good idea to go gambling in Macau. It might help me forget my fears — at least for a few hours. Going gambling has often helped me before when I've been really stressed. I'll head for the Macau casinos. Then hit the roulette wheel and blackjack tables and lose myself in a few hours of ...

Hold on! This is crazy. I've got no time to go gambling in Macau. I have business to sort out in Hong Kong: life-threatening business. I got it wrong about the hit-man boarding the plane, but I was right about that Yeung bitch — she knows all about me and Tsang. She wants to bury me. If I don't act quickly, she will. I don't go gambling when we land in Macau. I sort out my Hong Kong problem.

ALAN YIP GRIPPED the phone receiver more tightly.

"You're sure about this, Suen?"

"Yes sir."

"How come you're suddenly so certain? This morning you said you needed to tap all of my phones before you would have your definitive proof."

"The fact is, sir ... One of my operatives ... Well, he made a slight miscalculation with your financial accounts."

"You mean he made a *mistake*."

"Not really a mistake, Mister Yip," detective agency boss Charles 'The Eagle' Suen said defensively. More a case of—"

"I don't like it when people I pay money to screw up, Suen."

"We've remedied the situation, sir. We—"

"There's no need for phone taps?"

"No. My team has gone over all the records again. And we're absolutely positive this time that we have our man."

"Fai?"

"I'm afraid so, sir. What do you want us to do now? Hello? ... Are you still there, Mister Yip?"

There was no answer. Alan Yip had broken the phone by hurling it against the wall.

28

BY THE TIME Chan reached Wan Chai he had got his nerves mostly under control. But he remained concerned about his daughter. Had she fallen ill? Was that why she had failed to answer either of her two telephones?

Should I ring the university administration people and ask them to check her room to make sure she's all right? he wondered. No. Ah Fah would never forgive me for making her look like a baby. I'm overreacting again. There's probably a rational explanation for why she hasn't answered the phone in her room: she's out with friends. As for her mobile, she must have forgotten to recharge the batteries; she's done it before — she would forget her head if it wasn't screwed on. Her mobile even went dead when I spoke to her this morning. I won't phone the university yet. I'll call her room when I get home. She'll probably have returned by then.

Mosquitoes were on the warpath. He felt one nip his cheek as he rounded the corner of Johnstone Road and swatted another from his ear while crossing Hennessy Road; sticky evenings like this always brought the tiny blood-suckers out in force. A jet roared overhead, heading for the airport on Lantau Island. He looked up to see it slice through a purple-green sky, glanced back down just in time to dodge a hawker selling fish balls, and then swung left on to Lockhart Road.

The US Fleet was in port on a goodwill visit. Groups of navy policemen in starched white uniforms patrolled the area. Shaven-headed sailors in various stages of drunkenness crowded outside bars, chatting to hookers in tight jeans who giggled obediently at lousy jokes which they'd already heard a thousand times before. Tame stuff, though, compared to other Asian red-light areas. Wan Chai was a shadow of what it had been during the Vietnam War when American troops had packed bars; Manila and Bangkok's steamy exploits now made it resemble a Buddhist nuns' convention.

A sultry, long-legged Filipina who lounged against the wall outside Popeye's Bar smiled. "Why you no come inside, darling?" she purred, stretching out the syllables of the last word. A pink tongue flickered across red gloss lips. Painted nails caressed the seams of skin-tight faded denims. "It's so very nice, darling, so very relaxing."

Chan smiled back. "I'm relaxed already, but thanks for the offer."

"But you look so *hot!* I help cool you down, darling. Take care of you *personally!*"

He gazed more closely at her. For a moment she reminded him of his daughter. Perhaps it was the age; this girl couldn't be more than eighteen. She smiled again. Would she smile as sweetly ten years on? He doubted it: too worn out from booze and cheap dope and from servicing greasy types like the middle-aged western pair who had slouched up to her shoulder. Balding heads leaked sweat, beer guts bulged. Tourists, judging from those baggy shorts and sandals they both wore; respectable characters at home probably, maybe even with teenage daughters of their own: church-going pillars of the community, perhaps. Here, far from the prying eyes of neighbours and families, they became baby-snatchers. The threat of catching Aids had scared away some sex tourists, but not nearly enough, Chan reflected bitterly.

From within the confines of the bar came the alluring throb of disco music and tinkle of girlish laughter. The tourists decided not to hang around ogling the teenager; better lay on offer inside. They pushed roughly past, almost knocking her to the floor. On another occasion Chan would have dragged them back and made them apologise. Tonight he had no time for any hassles. After making sure that the girl was unhurt he continued down the road to The Wild Cat Club.

Two shaven-headed sailors retched up by the door. He walked around them and pulled back the green velvet curtain that masked the club's entrance. A thick fog of cigarette smoke made him gasp for breath. Swatting away the grey-brown mist, he saw that the place was crammed with American sailors. He threaded his way past them and over to the bar. A Thai bargirl in an orange wet-look swimsuit and white, thigh-length PVC boots asked him what he wanted. As he had with the girl in the street, Chan spoke English to her; dancers in here had a limited grasp of Cantonese. He had to shout to make himself heard above the din of the music.

"I need to speak to Giselle."

With a flick of jelled black hair the bargirl gestured to her right, where two dancers occupied a small circular stage behind the bar, pouting and grinding to a thumping disco beat. A Filipina in white stockings, suspender belt and stilettos leaned over and touched the dance floor. At the same time she stuck out her tongue and waggled it at a group of sailors, one of whom was tearing off his tee-shirt and threatening to clamber on the stage and join her; his three friends hauled him back. The second dancer, a pencil-slim Chinese girl whose bronzed body glistened with oil, reached for-ward and grabbed the Filipina's hips. She thrust hard and rhythmically against the Filipina's raised buttocks, tossing back her long silky hair as she writhed in mock ecstasy.

The bargirl with jelled hair touched Chan's arm. "Buy me a drink, darling."

"If you pass my message to Giselle."

"I promise. Go on, darling — just a small drink."

Normally, he avoided red-light bars and their teenage dancers as he would a plague of mosquitoes. If you were allowed to just sit and drink the wildly expensive beer in peace these places might be barely tolerable. But the young dancers, mainly Thais and Filipinas with a few mainland Chinese thrown in for good measure, always wanted to talk in order to wangle more cash out of you. And their juvenile conversation would tax a four-year-old's patience.

He shouldn't be hard on the kids, though. Most of them came from poor homes and supported large families back in Thailand or the Philippines. And they weren't all the hard-nosed gold-diggers that they often appeared to be in here. Anyone encountering them outside the bars could attest to that. Chan knew some bargirls who were so shy that they had become tongue-tied when he had met them in the street.

In the bars, though, it was different; it had to be. Girls survived by persuading customers to buy them drinks. The more drinks customers bought them, the more money the girls made. They were desperate for cash to send home to give their families a half-decent life. So desperate that even the shy kids forced themselves to act like street-hardened professionals.

Chan paid two hundred dollars, enough for a good meal in many local restaurants. In here it bought him a Coke in a glass the size of an egg cup. The dancers started a new routine, wrapping their legs around a pole that was fixed between the floor and the ceiling. They slid their crotches up and down the pole and flicked their tongues across its shiny metal.

It was an act staged a dozen times a night in every Wan Chai red-light bar. On the occasions when Chan had seen it, all it had ever aroused in him was the thought that it must be uncomfortable rubbing your bare legs against a piece of cold steel. The sailors seemed to like it, though; they whooped and hollered, beat their chests like gorillas and chucked ten-dollar bills on stage.

"How about you buy me one more drink, darling?"

He paid another two hundred dollars.

The dancers jabbed their tongues out one last time, and then left the stage to a chorus of loud cheering and wolf whistles. The American sailor who had earlier taken off his tee-shirt now tried to leap the bar to grab the Filipina in the suspender belt. The woman in charge of dancers in this bar was built like a sumo wrestler; she easily shoved him back. The bargirl with jelled hair called out to the Filipina dancer then pointed to Chan. The Filipina dancer strutted the few metres over to him on her stilettos, hips swaying catwalk-model style.

"I'm Giselle Maria." She eyed him with a mixture of suspicion and insolence. "What's all this about, mister?"

“We need to talk. It’s about your boyfriend.”
She scowled. “I’m busy.”
Chan showed his police ID card. “Get unbusy. I’ll wait outside.”

29

WHEN SHE EMERGED ten minutes later she had undergone a transformation that amazed Chan. She wore a red tee-shirt, faded denims, jogging shoes and a battered grey cap lettered with the name of the Chicago Cubs.

Minus stiletto heels, she stood four inches smaller. And though her ID card said she was twenty-two, she looked three years younger. She looked refreshingly normal, too: a girl you could imagine living in the flat upstairs and working behind the counter of the local Hang Seng Bank. Nothing like the hardened professional who ten minutes ago had engaged in frenzied simulated love-making, then strutted around stage jabbing her crotch at a bunch of slobbering sailors.

Perhaps she sensed his thoughts, because she suddenly smiled at him. "It's only a job, mister." She pronounced it mees-ter, stressing the first syllable. "Just cause I act that way back in there don't mean I *am* that way — I always wanted to be a photographic model."

Chan became defensive. "I didn't say you were that way."

Her dark eyes danced. "Your face did, though. It ... Hey! Why are you smiling?"

"Because you sound just like my daughter; let's walk."

They strolled down Lockhart Road where two sailors on a trawl of local bars, shocked to see a middle-aged Chinese man and young Filipina together, hurled obscene suggestions.

"Got many daughters?"

Chan wiped his sweaty face: "Only one."

"Me, I got *seven* sisters," she declared with pride. "All of them younger than me. How old's your daughter?"

"Eighteen."

"Married?

"No."

"Must have a boyfriend, is he handsome?"

"It's your boyfriend we need to talk about, Giselle." He took a deep breath. As gently as he could he said, "I don't know how to say this to make it easier, but—"

"You're gonna tell me Szeto's dead. You don't need to because I know — I heard it on the radio."

He was stunned. He had expected her to be heartbroken, or at the very least shocked. To his surprise, she didn't seem to be even slightly upset.

"Don't look at me like that, pal!"

"I'm sorry, I—"

"I'm no hard-hearted bitch! Sure I'm upset for what happened to him. When I heard the news, I cried and felt sick inside. But staying home crying for Szeto … It won't pay my rent." She shrugged. "Besides, we split up weeks ago. And even when we were together … Sure, he loved me. Leastways in his own crazy way he did. But I never really loved him. I felt more sorry for him than anything."

She halted outside the Country Club red-light bar and adjusted her baseball cap. The sodium glow of a streetlamp turned her heart-shaped face golden-brown and made her mink-coloured eyes smolder. She was pretty. If life hadn't dealt her a bum rap, and if she had not been born in a poor rice-farming village in the Philippines, she might have become that photographer's model.

They resumed walking.

"How did you two meet?" Chan asked.

She brushed strands of raven-coloured silken hair from one cheek. "He came into the bar last year with friends. The usual rich-kid pricks — red-faced from beer and full of schoolboy jokes. Sure that because you're a Filipina, you'll go down on them for a lousy hundred bucks." Her voice rose in a flash of anger. "Who do those pricks think they are? I'm smart as them — smarter!" She glared at Chan, daring him to dispute this.

"I'm sure you are."

"You bet your bun I am! I went to university, had a white-collar job at home. But I can make fifty times as much here so … Yeah, I know. You've been shot the same sort of line a dozen times before. Me, I'm different — don't gamble, don't booze. I'm here for the cash. Another year and I'll have enough to put my sisters through college. Then I'm off home."

"What happened that first night?"

"What first night?"

"The first night with Szeto."

"He tried to calm those jerks down. Then he apologized to me. Working in a bar you see so many men that you get to trust your instincts. I figured he was a decent guy. So when he asked me for my number …"

"You gave it to him?"

She nodded. "Things sort of took off. But like I say, I never really loved him."

On the other side of the road, outside an Indonesian restaurant, navy policemen struggled with two drunken sailors. A hooker who was even drunker than the sailors scratched the steamy air and screamed abuse at the navy cops.

"You said you felt sorry for him."

"Yeah, I did."

"Why?"

She shrugged. "Maybe … Well, there always seemed to be this sort of inner sadness about him. I mean … Like even when he was bouncing around, grinning and looking happy, I sensed the sadness kind of bubbling away under the surface — know what I mean?"

"I think so."

She removed her cap and wiped sweat from her forehead.

"Mama always said I was too soft to make it in this business," she sighed. "I guess mama was right. A hard-hearted bitch would have jumped at those chances to marry Szeto. And if I'd married him, I might have got that money I need to put my sisters through college. But Giselle Maria Santiago is romantic — couldn't never marry a guy she don't love. Not even if it means missing a chance of getting rich. Sounds real crazy, huh?"

"It doesn't sound crazy."

She laughed. "That last bit shocked you, huh? Didn't know Szeto asked me to marry him, huh?"

"No."

"Asked me just about every other week — wanted me to quit my job. But me, I'm a girl who likes her independence. Supposing I *had* quit and then he'd gone off the idea of getting married and dumped me — where would Giselle Maria be then, huh?"

In the same position as a lot of other poor kids, Chan thought: no job, no money — within weeks she could turn suicidal. He had seen it happen. A big-shot businessman fell for a bargirl, told her he loved her and would marry her. But the only person these big-shots loved was themselves. There was more chance of Chairman Mao coming back to life as a Buddhist nun than there was of a big-shot marrying a bargirl.

They crossed Hennessy Road, avoiding the crowded trams that clanked to Kennedy Town and Shau Kei Wan. On the pavement, groups of hawkers were frying noodles, bean curd and meat balls. A stomach-churning smell of dirty cooking oil and garlic arose from their portable stoves and hovered in the petrol-soaked air. To Chan's surprise, one of the older hawkers shot Giselle a toothless grin then asked her what she would like to eat. She smiled back, shook her head and said she wasn't hungry.

"It's all because of Szeto," she explained. "The toothless old guy knows me because Szeto bought stuff from him — the old guy sells Shanghai food, see. Leastways he *claims* it's Shanghai food, it seems the same old Hong Kong garbage to me. But Szeto, he was crazy about the stuff. Said he got the taste from his father. Szeto's old man was born in Shanghai, see."

"Szeto told you that?"

She nodded.

"He said his father was born in Shanghai?"

"Yeah."

"What did Szeto tell you about a group called the Heavenly Ghosts?"

"Who?"

Chan repeated the name.

She shook her head.

"He never mentioned being threatened by them?"

"Nope."

"Never behaved as though he was scared of someone?"

"Not scared. But he sure acted weird."

"Weird?"

"That's partly why we broke up. I mean … Well, Szeto always was a little bit *deep,* if you know what I mean … Sometimes wanted to talk about some really strange things."

"What sorts of things?"

"Deep sorts."

"Such as?"

She gave a loud sigh. "Such as what the meaning of life is, and why we're all put on this earth, and where the world's heading … I forget most of the rest — I wasn't really interested. Me, I'm a girl who would rather talk fashion."

"So you split up?"

"Not because of that. Like I told you, I felt sorry for the guy. I could have put up with him a bit longer — if the meaning of life was as far as it went. But he got weirder and weirder. I mean, just before we broke up he was asking really *scary* questions."

"What sorts of questions?"

"About mama; wanted to know if I was close to her — *really* close; asked me what I would do if someone killed a person I was really close to; kept asking the same thing over and over. And when I finally tell him I don't know, he gets angry. Says if I had *really* loved mama I would have killed that person who'd hurt her and ... I mean it's not what a girl wants to hear, huh? So I called it a day and … Your phone's ringing; you gonna answer it?"

He dragged the mobile from his pocket.

"You need to get back," Terry Duggan said. "It's urgent."

"Listen, Duggan," Chan said tersely. "I'm busy now, so—"

"You need to get back to your flat. It's your daughter."

Chan stiffened: "Ah Fah? What's happened?"

"Get back. Get back quickly."

30

BEFORE THE TAXI had come to a stop Chan was shoving open the passenger door, then jumping on to the pavement and sprinting for his home a hundred metres away — he made it there in less than twenty seconds. He skidded to a halt in front of his apartment block, kicked open the main double doors and half-charged, half-fell into the lobby.

The noise jolted the old caretaker-security guard awake.

"Hey! What … Oh! it's only you, chief. For a moment I thought … Hey! What's wrong? You're sweating and—"

"Is she all right?" Chan gasped.

"Who?"

"If anyone's hurt Ah Fah, I'll—"

"Oh, you mean your daughter?"

"Is she all right?"

"Don't know, chief, I just … No good battering the lift button — the doors won't open any quicker."

"Come on, come on," Chan snapped; "get it working."

"It's out of order. An engineer's coming, but …"

Chan was no longer listening. He was wrenching open the door leading to the stairs. Charging up the stairs two, sometimes three at a time, ignoring the strain on his lungs and pain in his chest, his whole being focused on one thing only; the safety of his daughter. At the fourteenth floor he kicked open the door and staggered on to the corridor — his flat was second on the left. He yanked at the metal security grille guarding the wooden entrance door.

Locked.

"Duggan!" he shouted, as he fumbled in his jacket pocket for the key. "Duggan; it's Peter Chan!"

No reply.

He pulled the key from his jacket pocket, placed the key in the lock and turned it, then jerked back the metal security grille guarding the door. He tried the knob on the wooden entrance door — the door was unlocked. He twisted the knob and then pushed hard at the door. So hard that he lost his balance and crashed face down on the living room floor.

"Duggan!" he yelled as he struggled to pick himself up. "Where's my daughter? Where's Ah Fah?"

"Relax, dad! I'm here!"

He glanced up from the floor. The voice had come from the direction of the bathroom. Ah Fah's voice. She was alive. She was leaving the bathroom and walking across the wooden tiled floor towards him, a concerned look on her face.

"Relax, dad, everything's fine."

"That's right, Ace," Duggan said. "Everything's fine."

"We were in the bathroom cleaning up the cut on your Sergeant Duggan's face," Ah Fah said. "It's really nasty. Need some stitches, I reckon."

"But are *you* hurt, Ah Fah? Did anyone—"

"I'm fine, dad." She held out a hand. "Let's get you up from that floor." She helped him to the sofa. "Sit down and relax — you look shattered."

"Ran here the whole way," he panted. "From where the driver dropped me ... Scared that you …" He stabbed an accusing finger at Duggan. His voice rose angrily. "This bastard—"

"I told the *truth!*"

"You said a killer—"

"You never let me finish."

"You said he was after Ah Fah."

"You cut the line. You should have let me finish."

"If it was true and I *had* waited—"

"Calm down, dad! Everything's fine."

Ah Fah put her hands on his shoulders and squeezed. "How about I make some of my industrial-strength coffee with lots of sugar? Sugar's good for shock."

Without waiting for answer, she clomped off to the kitchen.

When the kitchen door closed behind her Duggan said tersely, "I told you the truth — she *was* in danger. She's acting relaxed now, but that's only because she never came face to face with him. The danger hasn't really hit her yet. But Christ knows what would have happened if I hadn't stopped him."

"Stopped who?"

"How the fuck do I know! — I never saw him before."

"What makes you sure he wanted to hurt Ah Fah?"

"He was holding a semi-automatic. It seemed obvious that he'd not come to play tiddlywinks. You ought to have more faith in my judgement, Chan; your hating my guts doesn't stop me being a good cop."

"You're sure?" Chan pressed him. "He definitely had a gun?"

Duggan pointed to the welt on his face. "He slugged me with it. Then legged it downstairs; I chased him, but he was too quick and … Well, I was groggy from that belt on the head so …"

Chan nodded. "It's not your fault." He took a deep breath. Then he said, "I seem to have screwed things up in a big way tonight — I'm sorry, Duggan. Sorry about how I acted towards you when I charged in here, I mean."

"Our man ran off in the direction of Fortress Hill MTR station," Duggan said. "I radioed the uniformed boys with details. But so far they've drawn a blank."

"The important thing is you stopped him harming Ah Fah,"

"Might not be her he wanted to harm."

Chan frowned. "What do you mean?"

"It's *your* flat."

That's true, Chan thought. And it's more likely that he wanted me. Why? Is he an ex-criminal with a grudge? Someone I helped jail years ago?

"What did he look like?"

"Thirty to thirty-five," Duggan replied. "Slim, but not skinny — still a fair bit of muscle; five foot eight or thereabouts."

"Any distinguishing features?"

"None I could make out. Mind you, I only grabbed a quick look at him before he slugged me. He said something when he ran down your stairway, though."

"What?"

"Don't know exactly. My Chinese is garbage at the best of times. And that echo on your stairway's such a bitch it was hard to hear him clearly. I managed to make out the last bit, though; because he didn't just speak it he shouted it. When he was at the bottom of the stairs he shouted: 'Liu Yan'".

"Liu Yan?"

Duggan nodded. "Mean anything? Maybe you arrested a Liu Yan before and … Hey! Are you okay?"

Chan struggled to suppress a shudder. "I'm fine."

"Don't look it."

"It's probably the delayed effects of what happened with Ah Fah. You're sure the name was Liu Yan?"

Duggan nodded. "Recognise it?"

"No. I'll check the files, though. Maybe you're right, maybe I arrested a Liu Yan before."

"It's a woman's name, isn't it?"

"Yes."

"Why yell out a woman's name?"

"Your guess is as good as mine."

"Reckon he's this Liu Yan's boyfriend?"

"It's possible."

"Could be a hooker you arrested," Duggan said. "This joker might be her pimp out to get even."

"It's possible." Chan rose from the sofa and stood up straight. With as much dignity as he could muster he said, "Whoever he is, I'm in your debt for what you did tonight. Thank you, Duggan."

He held out his hand stiffly. Duggan did not grasp it straight away, but simply stared at it, his facial expression a mixture of surprise and disbelief. Was his enemy really stretching out a hand of friendship? Just when Chan thought that he would ignore the peace offer, Duggan grabbed his hand.

"I'd best be leaving, Ace. I need to get back to the station. There's one last thing I have to do."

Chan opened the door. Duggan took a few steps down the corridor, then halted and swung around.

"Jeez! I almost forgot! I've still not explained why I was here at your flat to stop that joker." He reached into his pocket, removed a brown envelope. "After our meeting at the restaurant, I went back to the station and saw this on your desk — our pal Wong left the office unlocked again." He gave Chan the envelope. "I thought it might be important, so I brought it."

"Thanks."

Duggan shrugged: "Only doing my job. Like I keep saying, I'm not one hundred percent arsehole, only ninety-nine. I'm just sorry I couldn't catch this joker tonight."

"We'll get him soon."

"But this Liu Yan name means nothing, huh?"

"Nothing," Chan lied.

31

AH FAH EMERGED from the kitchen. "Okay, where did you hide the coffee jar? I've searched high and low and I still. … Hey! What's wrong, dad?"

"I'm tired."

"You're sweating! What's the matter?"

"I'm tired — tired of stupid questions!"

"No need to shout."

"But only an idiot would …" He stopped himself before he said too much to her that he would regret. He took a deep breath, calmed down. "I didn't mean to snap. I'm still shook up from what happened tonight. I thought I would rush in to find you lying here … Lying in a pool of …"

She put her arms around him: "You didn't, though, did you?" She kissed his cheek. "I'm okay." She pushed him gently onto the sofa. "Now just sit and relax, and I'll make that rocket-fuel coffee I promised. Then we can … Who are you phoning?"

"Your mother."

"Why?"

"You're going to stay with her in Taipei."

"I can't."

"You take the first flight tomorrow."

"I lost my passport — remember? That's why I couldn't go with her in the first place."

"Then I'll have to make other arrangements." Chan punched numbers on his phone: "Joe Parwani's Agency? Get me Joe please … Well ask him to call Peter Chan when he's free … Yes, he has the number."

He replaced the phone in its cradle.

"Who's Joe Parwani?"

"A friend," Chan said. "That character who tried to break in might try again. I want you safely away from here."

"I *will* be away — I go back to university tomorrow."

He shook his head: "Not safe enough. I want you where …"

The phone rang: Joe Parwani calling back.

"I need a favour, Joe," Chan said. "I need your safe-house from tomorrow — a baby-sitter too … Well if you send your people here first thing, I'll deliver the baby myself … I know our own people can do the job, but I want the best … Thanks, Joe."

Chan ended the call.

"What was that baby-sitter stuff?" Ah Fah asked.

"You're spending a few days in Silvermine Bay."

She screwed up her face: "On Lantau?"

"You leave tomorrow."

"It's a dump! Can't you get me a forged passport and fly me to Paris? Or New York, or—"

"This isn't a game, Ah Fah," Chan cut in sharply. "You take the ferry to Lantau — understood? You should only need to stay a few days; we'll have found this character by then. But until we do, I won't sleep unless I know you're safe."

"Me catching that ferry will make you feel easier, huh?"

"Yes."

"All right," she sighed. "Boring Silvermine Bay it is."

"Thank you."

"Now, *finally*, I'll make that coffee," she said. "Once you've solved the mystery of the missing coffee jar."

"The coffee's in that stone rice pot under the sink."

She slapped her head: "Silly me! I should have known. The best people always keep coffee in rice pots, don't they?"

"I broke the coffee jar last week."

She clomped off to the kitchen, still seemingly unfazed by what had happened. Duggan got it right, Chan thought. Because she never came face to face with that gunman, the danger hasn't sunk in with her yet.

The kitchen door closed. Cupboard doors banged open and shut — she never did anything quietly. He sank further into the sofa and tried to relax. Tried to block out his fears for Ah Fah by focusing on the crime he had to solve. It was hopeless, though. No way could he concentrate on victim Szeto Yip. Not when his mind was crammed with thoughts of another crime, another victim.

Liu Yan!

Would he never escape her? Never forget what had happened in China with her kidnapper? Would those events of twenty-five years ago forever haunt him? Why did that gunman yell out her name? Chan wondered. Why now, after twenty-five years? Liu Yan had a brother. Duggan said the gunman is probably in his thirties. The brother would be that age. Is it him?

"I'm making that coffee strong enough to blast you into outer space," Ah Fah shouted from the kitchen. "I hope drinking liquid nitrogen is all right with you."

Chan could smell the coffee. She was definitely making it strong. He needed something even stronger. He reached into his pocket; the key to the cabinet where he kept a bottle of rice wine would be in his wallet. He frowned. The pocket contained more than a wallet; an object was there which shouldn't be there. He pulled the object out and examined it: a photograph of a Chinese girl. He shuddered. He turned the snapshot over — he couldn't bear to gaze at her face. The back of the photograph made him shudder even more. A message was written on it.

You killed my sister!

I was right, Chan realised, swallowing dryly; the gunman is her brother. He didn't only try to break in here, either. He pushed me in front of that tram — what happened was no accident. He thrust this snapshot in my pocket before shoving me on the tramline. How did he find me? Liu Yan died twenty-five years ago in the middle of China. How did he trace me to Hong Kong? I covered my tracks. No longer use the same name. Can he access special information? Is he a policeman, or an office worker with China's Public Security Bureau? That way he would have access to confidential files and …

"Here we go!"

Ah Fah entered with two steaming cups of coffee. She put one cup down beside him. "Strong enough to put hairs on …" Her brightness vanished as she glimpsed the strain on his face. "You've gone all pale and sweaty again!" Her voice oozed concern. "Should I turn the air-con higher? You'll relax more if it's cool."

"I *can't* relax! There's too much I need to … I'm sorry, Ah Fah, I didn't mean to shout. It's just …"

"I know, dad," she said understandingly. "I'll take my coffee to the bedroom. The last thing you need is me a motor mouth like me sitting here jabbering on." She leaned over, kissed his forehead. "If you need me, just shout."

He waited until she had gone inside and closed the door. He rose from the sofa, took deep breaths. Joe Parwani's team can't protect her forever, he thought. Her long-term safety depends on me: I have to find the brother. I'll only do that if I think and act logically. I need to block him out of my mind for a while. Worrying about how he might hurt Ah Fah will make me angry and emotional. Angry and emotional men make mistakes. I need to calm down. That way I'll think more clearly.

Normally whenever he needed to calm down, he went for a walk outside and focused on events divorced from those that he wanted to forget. Impossible tonight, though. No way could he leave his daughter. He did the next best thing: he walked around the living room.

A picture rested on the bookcase: proud father Peter Chan clutching newly-born Ah Fah. Wrapped in a towel, yellow from jaundice, she stared up wide-eyed and open-mouthed at an even wider-eyed father who looked terrified he might drop her. Next to this stood a shot of Chan's estranged wife, Mei; and of his dead mother, serene-faced and beautiful; and of his dead, shaven-headed grandfather, staring out stiffly and suspiciously from the frame.

There were none of his father.

There never would be.

He had the pictures, of course — dozens. As well as sending a letter every month for thirty years, Mister Peter Collins from The Laurels, High Barnet, Hertfordshire, had sent photographs. The first few had shown a tall, thin man with hair the colour of burned gold, a mirror image of the man Chan remembered from mother's funeral, the only time he had met Mister Peter Collins. Gradually over the years the pictures had changed: to an older, sadder man with thinning hair: a man shrunk in size: a balding man wasting away: a sad, dispirited man: a man waiting for death.

And there were the letters too — he still had them. Despite various times over the years, when he had vowed to burn them, at the last minute he had always held back. Was it really my decision, though, he wondered, or did Mei decide for me?

"Burn those pictures and you burn part of yourself, Peter," his wife had told him.

He shook his head, hoping to also shake away thoughts of his father: thinking about him was as bad as worrying about Liu Yan's brother. I should focus on finding Szeto Yip's killer, he thought. Focusing on Szeto will block out thoughts of Liu Yan's brother. It will calm me down, enable me to think logically; help me to come up with a good plan to track the brother down.

He returned to the sofa and picked up one of the two manila files Duggan had given him at the restaurant. The file contained newspaper articles about deals that tycoon John Tsang had signed over the years, and pictures of Tsang at charity functions, arm invariably around the shoulders of an attractive woman.

Chan searched for links with film-maker Alan Yip, but found none. He put this file down and picked up the other file Duggan had given him. After ten minutes he found what he wanted: a newspaper profile of Tsang with pictures of him at various stages of his life. The photograph of Tsang as a young man was the one that Chan found most interesting.

So that's it, he thought, that's why Yip scrawled on his newspaper when we met at his office. It makes sense now. And this picture of

Tsang also backs up what my Filipina dancer friend Giselle told me in Wan Chai. But does a link exist between Tsang and Szeto's murder? No, there's no link there, but I still need to keep this photograph.

He folded the picture and put it in his wallet.

He opened the envelope that Duggan had brought to the flat. It contained a four-page list of locally registered owners of Colt .38s, the type of gun that had been used by Szeto's killer. Chan scanned the first page but saw nothing exceptional. Then the second page but again saw … No. Hold on. What about that name two lines from the bottom? He placed his finger against the name, read it once, twice, then a third time to make sure he wasn't mistaken.

No mistake.

One of the Colt owners was Szeto's brother, Fai.

32

ANY INTERVIEW WITH Fai would have to wait. Fai was not due to leave Taiwan until tomorrow. Even then he would not head directly to Hong Kong; his plane would land at Macau. How do I tackle him? Chan wondered. Go in hard and try to break him from the start? Or will I achieve more success by using patience and subtlety? He was debating the advantages and disadvantages of the two approaches when his phone rang.

He picked up the receiver: "Peter Chan."

"This is Miss Yeung, inspector. Alan Yip's assistant."

Chan glanced at the clock on the wall: almost ten-fifteen. Why was she ringing his home so late?

"What can I do for you, Miss Yeung?"

There was a pause which lasted for about five seconds. Then she said haltingly, "It … It's more a case of what I can do for you, Inspector Chan."

"I'm listening."

"I wanted to … Well, it's about what Mister Yip said to you when you met him today."

"What about it?"

"I thought … Well, I wanted you to know, inspector … To know the whole truth, I mean."

In Alan Yip's office she had been confident, self-assured. Now she sounded hesitant and uncertain. In fact there was a distinct edginess to her voice. Why?

"Are you still there, inspector?"

"I'm here."

"You remember Mister Yip said that his two sons had always been incredibly close?"

"What about it?"

He waited for her to answer. She remained silent. He could hear her breathing heavily, though. Her edginess was getting worse.

"Go on," he coaxed, "I'm listening."

"It's all a lie!" she blurted out. "Szeto and Fai — they both *hated* each other!"

"How do you know?"

"I know *everything* about that family," she said. "The brothers ... They were lifelong bitter enemies — and I can prove it all too. But first ... First you must promise me something, inspector."

"What?"

"Protection from Fai."

"Why do you need protection?"

"He — he scares me. If he ever learns I've been talking ... He'll be angry. And Fai ... He isn't a nice man when he's angry. He's capable of doing anything ... Promise you'll protect me, inspector, promise me."

"I'll do everything I can," Chan assured her. "You have my word on that, Miss Yeung. How can you prove the brothers hated each other?"

"I've *seen* it!"

"When?"

"Many times — I've heard Fai make threats too. I've even heard him threaten to *kill* Szeto!" She spoke more quickly and loudly. "Yes, it's true. He threatened to kill him — kill his own brother! Not just once, either … Threatened him many times … The last time just two months ago when Fai went all crazy after Szeto shot him … Face turned all purple and then he … Fai swore he would kill him … Because—"

"*Slowly*!" Chan said. "Tell me nice and slowly."

She took deep, relaxing breaths. She said more calmly, "Fai took a lot of the staff from the company's technical department on a trip to woodland near the China border — a team-building trip, he called it. They all dressed up as soldiers in those stupid camouflage uniforms and carried stupid toy guns."

"Toy guns?"

"The sort that shoot paint; Fai's keen on games, you see — a big baby who loves giving commands. He was leader of one team and Szeto was leader of the other. Then they played this stupid game. Fai had to try and make it to his camp before Szeto captured him. Szeto did capture him, of course — he was always much better at everything than Fai. Then, just because Fai had torn up the stupid magazine Szeto ordered him to read before they began playing … Szeto shot him in the face with paint and almost blinded him! Fai went crazy. He even threatened to *kill* Szeto! And Fai is a man who … He has an ungovernable temper, inspector."

"How do you know all this?"

"They needed a referee for their pathetic game. And ... Well, they couldn't waste a *man's* time on something so ridiculous, could they? It's far too precious. But I'm only a stupid woman."

"I still don't understand."

"I was *there*! I saw it!"

"That bit before they started playing soldiers," Chan said.

"I saw it all with my own eyes!"

"You say Szeto ordered Fai to read a magazine?"

"Yes."

"And then Fai tore the magazine up?"

"Yes."

"Why?"

"It was a magazine published by that cult," she said. "The cult Alan Yip told you about in his office. One of those stupid things they hand out to people in the streets free of charge — full of stuff about why people should join them."

"Yes, I know all about those Heavenly Ghost magazines," Chan said. "I've read them myself; I'm aware of the sort of stuff that's inside. What I'm not aware of, and what I would like you to make me aware of now, Miss Yeung, is just *why* Szeto ordered Fai to read the magazine."

"The brothers were never close."

"Why did Szeto almost blind Fai with paint when Fai tore up the magazine?"

"Fai hated Szeto."

"That doesn't answer my question, Miss Yeung."

"He threatened to kill Szeto."

"But why did Szeto order him to read that magazine?"

"I don't know."

"I think you *do* know. Why did you phone me, Miss Yeung?"

"I explained — to tell the truth."

Chan pressed harder: "I mean the *real* reason."

She grew defensive. "I don't know what you're talking about."

"I think you do."

"No, no, I … Look, I must go now. Someone's calling me on my mobile phone."

"Why did you call me tonight?"

"I have to answer my mobile."

"Hello … Are you still there, Miss Yeung?"

The line had gone dead.

33

ASSASSIN LIU PENG cursed as he scanned the killing ground with his field glasses. Where was General Ma? The general should have arrived fifteen minutes ago. What had gone wrong? Had Ma's security team discovered that someone lay in wait, ready to ambush him? Had they kept him away from the city?

Peng shifted the powerful Swiss-manufactured binoculars to the right, sweeping them in a smooth arc across the area situated four hundred metres away, the area where General Ma should now be standing. He glimpsed no general: only a bespectacled, elderly schoolteacher who led a group of youngsters in the direction of the Imperial Palace. The children's bright red scarves looked out of place on such a grim day; Beijing's sky had turned tombstone grey, a sulphurous tang drifted through the air of China's capital. Rain scudded across Tiananmen Square. Photographers and artists who normally touted for trade on the edges of the square had scurried for cover five minutes ago. The crowd by the Monument to the Heroes of the People wore raincoats.

Where was General Ma?

Then he saw him. At least he saw the car, a black armour-plated limousine with dark windows; the type reserved for top members of China's parliament, the National People's Congress. Peng put down the field glasses and picked up his French FR-F2 sniper's rifle. He settled the rifle's stock in the pit of his shoulder; screwed his right eye over the telescopic sights; caressed the rifle's trigger with his index finger. He started to breathe more slowly to steady himself: in-out, in-out; his tongue lolling childlike from his mouth, the way it always did whenever he concentrated hard.

The armour-plated limousine rolled to a halt. The front door on the passenger's side swung open and a stocky bodyguard emerged. The bodyguard scanned the area for signs of danger. Satisfied that it was safe, he tapped twice with his hand on the car's roof. The rear door on the driver's side swung open and the tall, silver-haired general appeared in full dress uniform, weighed down by all his medals. He snapped out a smart salute to his bodyguard and then strode off purposefully towards the Monument to the Heroes of the People.

The pathetic excuse for a security operation amazed Peng. Had the idiots in charge of protecting Ma seriously believed that no one would learn about the general's unscheduled visit? Peng eased the sniper's rifle to the left, until the general's head rested in the middle of the cross on his telescopic sights.

He prepared to squeeze the trigger.

Before he could get off a shot the attic door crashed open and a black-clad figure clutching a submachine gun burst in.

Peng screamed, more in shock than pain.

Everything went as black as the intruder's uniform.

THE SHRILL RING of his mobile phone dragged a hung-over Fai from the land of slumber. He reached out for the phone which rested on the bedside table of his hotel room.

"Yeah?" he asked sleepily.

"Where are you?" John Tsang snapped.

Fai yawned. "What time is it?"

"Why didn't you answer the phone in your flat?"

"I'm not in my flat. What's the time?"

"Where are you?"

"Macau. What time is it?"

"Time that you realized who is in charge of this operation," Tsang snapped. "I told you to go to Hong Kong and deal with that Yeung woman."

"Relax, Tsang, it's all under control."

"It's *Mister* Tsang!"

"Well relax, *Mister* Tsang, the Hong Kong problem's been taken care of … Yes, it's all done … So you can relax and go gambling … I mean you can go back to sleep … I mean—"

"You're drunk!"

"Of course I'm fucking drunk!"

"Take a cold shower. Sober up."

"Being drunk is the only way I can get through the day! In case you've forgotten, *Mister* Tsang, my brother's dead."

"I haven't forgotten."

"We were close. Yes, yes, it's true, I … We shared so much … But we'll never share anything again, will we?"

"Do you think you're the only one upset by Szeto's death?"

"What do you mean?"

"The time is now half past six," Tsang said brusquely. "I'll give you twenty-four hours. Sober up. Then go to Hong Kong and deal with that problem."

"I told you. I've already dealt with—"

"Do you think I'm a fool? I know when you're lying to me."

"And I know when you're lying to me," Fai shot back. "That stuff about buying Szeto off — it was all bullshit."

"Watch your mouth!"

"My brother would never have taken a bribe. So how did you really manage it, *Mister* Tsang? How did you really get my crazy, self-righteous brother to shut up?"

"Twenty-four hours," Tsang said. "That's what I'm giving you. If you haven't taken care of that Hong Kong problem by then, I'll take care of it myself." He paused. "Then I'll take care of you."

"Me? What the fuck do …"

But Tsang had gone

"ARE YOU AWAKE, darling?" Sergeant Wong's wife called out.

No reply.

"It's twenty-five to seven, darling."

Still no reply; she frowned. What was the matter with him? He had left a note specifically asking her to make sure and wake him at this time. Why did he not answer any of her calls? Surely he could not still be asleep. She had been shouting at him like this for the past ten minutes.

He must have woken up by now.

She walked down the corridor, pushed open the door to their bedroom: he *was* still asleep! He lay on his side, face turned towards the wall. She reached over and shook him by the shoulder.

"Get up, lazy bones."

No response.

"All right," she said playfully. "If you want to play tough, then we'll play tough — I'm going to kiss you awake."

She turned him over so that he lay on his back, then bent over to kiss him. Before her lips had travelled even half-way to his face she jerked them violently away. She threw up her hands in horror: then screamed.

34

PENG WOKE WITH a start in his hotel room. What was going on? Nine years had passed since that incident with General Ma. So why now — why dream about this one failure in his career rather than the many successes? Because of yesterday, of course: because of that catastrophe with Chan and his daughter. Those two failures had triggered this dream of that other defeat.

He rose from the bed and moved over to the hotel room's window. He opened the thick velvet curtains, peered out through the netting that lay behind them. The pale-yellow light of dawn filtered into the room. At the restaurant, on the other side of the road, one member of staff cleaned windows while another hosed down the pavement. The first customers would soon arrive at the restaurant to eat a breakfast of *dim sum.* Would film-maker Alan Yip be among them? Cream-coloured minibuses and red taxis motored by the restaurant. The buses and taxis were probably taking people to work.

Peng turned abruptly away from the window and stared into the mirror on the wall. *Amateur!* he spat at his reflection. *Amateur!*

It was the worst insult a professional, a man who prided himself on always remaining calm, could hurl against anyone. It was also the truth. Pushing someone on a tram line was what a cheap Triad thug would do. But not a professional: you always stood the chance, as had happened with Chan, of your target surviving. A professional assassin eliminated his target with a bullet in the brain. That way there was no escape. He had not meant to shove Chan on the tram line, of course. He had intended only to put his sister's photograph in Chan's pocket and then walk off. That way, Chan would realise what fate awaited him and would start to sweat and suffer. But I lost my temper, Peng thought. In fact it was more than that, I became completely irrational.

It had happened so quickly. One moment he had been dropping the picture in Chan's pocket and preparing to head away from the tram stop. Then, as the tram pulled in, he had remembered his sister and recalled her death. Liu Yan's brutal killer stood there in front of him: completely defenceless.

Rage had engulfed Peng. He had pushed Chan on the line.

It wasn't only amateurish, Peng thought, it was stupid. If that tram had crushed Chan he would have died quickly, perhaps instantly. That's not what I want. If my sister and father are ever to sleep peacefully in the after-life they must be *suitably* avenged. Chan has to suffer exactly as my sister suffered.

I didn't only act like an amateur with Chan — I messed things up with his daughter too. Not only once either, I botched it twice with her. She's still alive today; still strutting around the streets. Why? Because I went and allowed my foolish emotions to rampage out of control again.

The first time it had been the laughter. That had saved her the first time. As Peng had prepared to shoot the lock off the door at Chan's flat, she had burst out laughing in a girlish way, much like the way his sister had laughed. In that moment, someone he had been viewing as merely another target had become a living, breathing person — just like his sister had been.

To shoot the girl would make him like Chan; make him a murderer. I'm no murderer, Peng thought, I'm a professional. That's why I came here: to do a professional job and eliminate film-maker Alan Yip. As for Chan — his death is justice. The girl is different. When you consider it rationally, you realise she plays no part in …

Bullshit!

Considering everything rationally had nothing to do with me leaving her unharmed. I failed to kill her because I let my feelings take control again. I acted unprofessionally. After hearing her laugh I walked out of the apartment, went downstairs and left her unharmed. Then, after that fiasco with Chan on the tram line, Peng had realised that he must control his emotions. The girl *did* play a part in all of this — she was Chan's daughter. By killing her he would make Chan suffer. He had returned to the apartment block, determined to deal with her professionally, only to clumsily let himself be intercepted by the Westerner this time: he had botched the job with the girl again.

Am I losing my touch? he wondered. Should I scrap my original plan and just kill Chan quickly? He'll still be dead and my sister will be avenged. Then I can focus on Alan Yip. Is my obsession about taking a perfect revenge against Chan blinding me to Yip? That cult is paying me half a million dollars to kill Yip, and I promised to do the job. Father always said a man who breaks his word is a man without honour. Should I kill Chan quickly? Break into his home now — probably he's sleeping — then …

No!

Peng shook his head to clear it of such thoughts — Chan was the main target, not Alan Yip. Yes I'll deal with Yip, he told himself; I never break my word. But I only kill him *after* I have made Chan pay. There will be no quick, easy death for Chan either. No matter whether it's safer to kill him quickly or not, he dies like I always planned he would — painfully.

I make him watch as I kill his daughter. Only then do I finish Chan himself. And not until tonight, not until I … All right, maybe I am obsessed with a perfect revenge. Perhaps ensuring Chan's punishment exactly fits his crime isn't necessary to appease hungry ghosts in the after-life — my sister might sleep easy even if I kill Chan quickly. Perhaps my perfect revenge is more for me than her — the Mister Symmetry jibes about me being a crazy perfectionist could be true. But why *shouldn't* I do it for me? I suffered when Chan killed Liu Yan. Her death left me without the person who had become a second mother. Why shouldn't I do it for myself?

What about the General Ma dream, though? Father used to say dreams are sent as warnings. Is this dream a warning — a warning that I'll fail with Chan the same way that I did with the old general? No, I won't fail, because I didn't really fail with General Ma. Only treachery enabled the opposition to find my hide-out. A jealous rival on my own side gave away my location in that attic. He betrayed me. Just like the Party big-shots betrayed father after Tiananmen Square — no honour exists in this world.

The opposition team had burst into the Beijing attic as Peng had been about to pull the trigger and capture General Ma's face on the camera gun. Snapping Ma's picture would have demonstrated that he could have easily shot him. It would also have proved the truth of what Peng had said before the start of the training exercise, when he had claimed that the state's security system was hopeless.

No, Peng thought, that training exercise with General Ma nine years ago wasn't a failure. In fact it was another success. I should stop worrying about that dream. Everything is going to be all right. He checked his watch. It was twenty minutes to seven. Peter Chan had exactly fourteen hours and fifty-six minutes to live.

35

IN VICTORIA PARK the air was the colour of polished copper.

Old folk performed *tai chi*, the ancient system of physical and mental drills that make Chinese pensioners some of the world's fittest. No *tai chi* for Old Yuen, though, the caretaker at Chan's apartment block sat asleep at his desk — probably he had over-indulged in rice wine again. Whether he had or not, there was no need to wake him; Chan shut the lobby doors quietly. He walked fifty metres to the main road. For once, a taxi was cruising past when he needed it. He flagged down the cab and climbed in.

"Where to, chief?" the young driver asked.

"Mid-Levels," Chan said. "Robinson Road."

Situated between mansions on the Peak, where Hong Kong's rich and famous live because it is cooler, and the working-class tenements a hundred metres below, Mid-Levels is a large, diverse area. Parts of it contain housing built before the Second World War. Six or seven storeys high these blocks often have few high-speed elevators and air-conditioning systems, but plenty of blocked toilets and cock-roaches. They are often sited near traditional Chinese medicine stores and *mah-jong* parlours, or near corner shops selling noodles and herbal teas.

In other parts of Mid-Levels, modern apartments tower into the sky. While cheaper than luxury housing on the Peak these apartments are still beyond the reach of most Hong Kongers. Shops here sell antiques and paintings, jewellery and rare Persian carpets.

Restaurants serve minuscule portions of artistic-looking French food, or *sushi*, or Indian food costing five times what it does a few kilometres away in Wan Chai. There are trendy wine bars and trendy night-clubs, where if you pay an emperor's ransom, you can rub shoulders with trendy TV stars. And in this trendy upmarket half of Mid-Levels, Chan reflected, in one of those modern high-rise blocks, lived women who made mysterious phone calls to police officers late at night.

It was seven-fifteen. He was on his way to see Miss Yeung.

After she had hung up last night he had called back, but had got an engaged signal. His instincts had urged him to head off to see her immediately. He would have, too, if he had not been so worried about Ah Fah. No way could he leave his daughter alone. Not until half an hour ago, when Joe Parwani had turned up to escort Ah Fah to the Lantau safe house, had Chan been free to visit Miss Yeung.

It might prove better this way, he thought, as the driver moved the car past the Noon Day Gun. If I'd seen her last night she might have stonewalled me. She's a rational woman, though. A good sleep should have helped her to realise it's in her own best interests to tell me everything.

Chan had slept fitfully. He had spent the night worrying about Ah Fah, as well as struggling to puzzle out the reason for Miss Yeung's jumpiness. In Alan Yip's office she had been calm and assured. What had changed things? Why had she contacted him? To tell the truth about Yip's sons, she had insisted. Chan's instincts told him there was more to her call. If she acts sensibly this morning, he thought, I should be able to persuade her to tell me how much more — particularly what part the Heavenly Ghosts cult plays in all this. Because at the moment it makes no sense: why would Szeto order Fai to read one of the magazines that cult publishes and then blast him with paint?

Was it simply a cruel joke on a hated brother? No, there's more to it than that. Miss Yeung seized up when I pressed her about the paint-gun incident. Her behaviour suggests that it was more than just a joke. Or was it fear of what Fai might do to her if he discovered she'd spoken to me that made her clam up? Perhaps neither answer is correct. Perhaps that paint incident *was* a joke. Perhaps … He was getting nowhere. He was only giving himself a headache. Keep on beating his brain like this and he would knock himself unconscious. He needed to relax. His brain worked better when he was calm. If he walked for the last few hundred metres to the apartment it might help him to focus. Then, when he met Miss Yeung, he would ask all his questions again. And keep asking them until he got satisfactory answers.

He glanced out of the taxi's window. They were about halfway between the Peak and the harbour, the steep climb forcing his head against the seat rest and causing the cab's strained engine to splutter like an eighty-a-day smoker. A panoramic view of the waterfront unfolded below: skyscrapers swarmed and blistered in the heat, harbour waters glinted like sheet metal.

"Stop here," Chan said. "I'll walk the rest of the way."

The driver pulled up by the kerb. Chan paid and tipped him then clambered from the taxi's air-conditioned comfort. The blue-yellow sky was cloudless; another steamy day lay in prospect. But the full force of Hong Kong's strength-sapping humidity would not make its presence felt for a few hours. At the moment it was hot, but not too sticky. And the air was generally mosquito free.

He started walking.

Although early, the streets had already begun to fill with people. An aroma of garlic and freshly baked bread and ground coffee drifted through the air. Outside a row of European bars, office workers nibbled at croissants and sipped Cappuccinos and freshly squeezed orange juice. Chan swung left on to Robinson Road.

And came face to face with the assassin.

"POLICE STATION, HOW can I help?"

"I need to speak to Inspector Chan."

"We've got two Inspector Chans. Which one do you want?"

"Peter Chan."

"Your name is?"

"Mrs Wong."

"Why do you want the inspector, Mrs Wong?"

"My husband, of course."

"Husband?"

"Yes, yes … Just put—"

"Calm down, Mrs Wong! What has your husband done?"

"Nothing."

"So why do you want the inspector?"

"Just connect me quickly."

"He's not in. Can you wait until—"

"No. No … My husband … Look, I must speak to Inspector Chan now."

"Your call is urgent?"

"Yes."

36

THE ASSASSIN STOOD by Ladder Street, the stone stairway that slopes sharply away from older-style houses and shops in Mid-Levels and leads down to the gleaming modern office towers of Central's business district. In fact there was not only one assassin standing there, but two.

Chan smiled as he saw them. They were the strangest pair of assassins you might meet anywhere: the oldest hired killers in town, perhaps in the world. These eighty-year-olds disposed of more people in a year than he had arrested in his career. Yet they had never fired a shot, never stabbed anyone. As far as he knew, they'd never even struck anyone in anger.

They were the *man mai por*, friends of the dead.

He was surprised to see them. Not because of the early hour; there was always some business to be had in Hong Kong no matter what time of day. But Mid-Levels was not their normal pitch. They usually hunkered down outside Wong Tai Sin Temple, on the other side of the harbour in Kowloon. Dressed from head to toe in black, they would wait silently for temple visitors to approach them about enemies they wanted to dispose of.

Some people wished to get rid of a rival at work, some of them a rival in love; others had lifelong enemies in the neighbourhood. The women's assassination technique was brief and simple. Clients handed over a photograph of their enemy. The *man mai por* would then mutter something, perhaps accompanying their words with a whiff of joss smoke, before grabbing a *kung fu* shoe and then beating the photograph. The enemy was then pronounced 'dead'. He or she would spend the rest of their life in abject misery, clients were cheerfully assured. When not killing people here on the street, the two old women cleaned the police station, which was how Chan had got to know them.

They grinned. "It's lover boy!"

"Want anyone killed?" One of the old crones brandished her shoe. "Give me the police commissioner's picture — I'll kill him for you now."

"I always thought you were such a wise woman," Chan teased. "Surely you know by now, grandmother, that the commissioner's my oldest and dearest friend."

He left them to their business. The traffic din grew louder. Taxi drivers jabbed their horns, purple-grey exhaust fumes choked the air, a 747 jet roared overhead: just another ordinary day in another sweaty Mid-Levels street.

He swung left.

The apartment block stood about fifty metres away. He walked over, pushed open the double swing doors, and then stood for a moment in the lobby, letting the breeze from the air-conditioning system cool him. Sufficiently refreshed, he took the lift to the tenth floor — the second door to the right was the one he wanted. He rang the bell. No reply. He tried the iron security grille — it slid back with a grunt. The wooden door that lay behind the grille was also unlocked. He nudged it open, moved inside the flat.

"Hello? Miss Yeung? This is Inspector Chan. We need to talk about last night."

No reply.

He glanced around the living room. Drawers had been ransacked, the display cabinet's glass doors yanked open. Clothes, books and magazines littered the floor. An armchair had been overturned, an umbrella stand knocked over.

Where was Miss Yeung?

Three doors led from the living room. Chan opened one of them: it led to a small kitchen. He closed this door and opened another:

Miss Yeung's bedroom. He entered the bedroom and discovered why she had failed to respond when he had called her name a moment ago. She lay on her back on the double bed. Her mouth gaped open. Her eyes had the faint stale glitter of death.

PENG PATTED HIS left shoulder.

Satisfied the snub-nosed 9mm Makarov rested there snugly, he nodded contentedly to himself. He reached to his jacket pocket and traced the outline of the powerful Leica binoculars. Then his hand moved to the polished briefcase at his side: he caressed the case's metal locks, gave another contended nod. Both locks were secure. No way would they suddenly burst open and disclose the contents of the case: the French FR-F2 sniper's rifle, the telescopic sights and six snub-nosed 7.5mm bullets.

He offered up a silent prayer to his dead father. He had asked father to help him today, to help him make certain that Liu Yan's killer did not escape justice. Father had faithfully answered the call. An hour ago, while heading for Chan's home, Peng's taxi had been blocked by heavy traffic on Hennessy Road. On the spur of the moment, he had decided to get out of the car and walk the rest of the way.

The decision had been crucial.

Had I stayed in that taxi, Peng thought, my plan to avenge Liu Yan would lie in ruins. But I walked and everything still remains perfect. It wasn't me who made the decision to walk, though, it was father. From his place in the after-life, he saw that if I stayed in the car I would fail in my mission. He realised that when I got to Chan's home, Chan and his daughter would be gone.

So he sent me a message from the after-life, ordering me to get out of the taxi. I didn't know at the time that it was father who was telling me to walk; I thought I had made the decision myself. Now, though, I know that it was him. Thanks to father, I arrived in time to see Chan put his daughter in that car with the two Indian bodyguards.

Peng had hailed another taxi, tailed the car to the harbour and then followed the daughter and her guards on board this ferry. In a few minutes the ferry would sail for Lantau. His plan was still working perfectly. Once the ferry sailed Peter Chan's daughter was doomed.

37

THE BODY WAS cool to the touch: she had been dead for some time. To determine exactly how long a time, Chan would need his friend Eddie Gallacher's assistance.

He phoned the police surgeon. He would be grateful for Eddie's help in establishing when Miss Yeung had died. He did not need Eddie to say *how* she had died: those leech-like bruises on her neck showed she had been strangled. Her yellow silk blouse had been torn, exposing both breasts, while scratch marks scarred her right breast and shoulder. White lace underwear hung around her knees.

Using a handkerchief as a makeshift glove, to avoid leaving any fingerprints, Chan examined the items on her bedside table. The ashtray brimmed with stubbed-out cigarettes. He picked up one stub and sniffed it: marijuana. Strange, he mused, although on second thoughts, perhaps not strange; he knew many people who smoked the stuff to escape Hong Kong's stresses.

A glass held golden-brown dregs: whisky or brandy? He swirled the glass, and then raised it to his nostrils. Brandy. He checked the wastepaper basket. A red carrier bag, stamped with the words 'Mid-Levels Wine and Tobacco Stores', lay inside — probably the bag that she had taken her brandy home in.

He opened the wardrobe. Inside were business suits, an evening gown, a pair of leather … He stiffened at the sound of footsteps. Then relaxed when he realised they came from the adjoining flat; the walls must be paper-thin. He closed the wardrobe, returned to the bed and checked underneath: nothing. He went back to the living room. His gaze was drawn by a set of glass tumblers in the display cabinet. There were seven tumblers, all stood neatly in a row, all similar to the tumbler he had examined in the bedroom: made of expensive Italian crystal. Probably she had bought them from a luxury goods shops in Tsim Sha Tsui's Ocean Terminal; or perhaps she had purchased them on holiday, then brought them home and stacked them neatly in her cabinet. And here they all were, still neatly stacked.

His gaze moved to a spot near the door. He walked over, reached down to the floor and picked up the object which had drawn him there: a wad of hundred-dollar bills, fastened with brown elastic bands; two thousand dollars in all. The money must have been positioned behind the door. He had knocked the thick wad to one side when he opened the door, which had prevented him from noticing the cash immediately. Had a burglar killed Miss Yeung after she confronted him? They had struggled — which would explain all the mess — then he had killed her and fled, dropping this wad of money on the way out?

Did a neighbour or the security guard see him? Judging from the struggle Miss Yeung had put up neighbours must at least have heard something. Chan tried the flat opposite. A sleepy-eyed man in his early thirties answered the door. No. He had heard nothing unusual.

"Are you a heavy sleeper?"

"Not particularly."

"But you heard nothing unusual?

"No."

"No furniture being knocked around?"

"No."

He tried two other neighbours and got the same reply. He went downstairs and spoke to the aged security guard.

"Think hard, grandfather. Did you see anyone who doesn't live in this block come in late last night then go to the tenth floor?"

"No, chief."

"You're sure?"

"On my mother's life!"

So the killer had climbed Spiderman-style twenty metres up the apartment block's smooth concrete face then got in through a locked window. Or the old boy had been asleep at his desk. You didn't need to be Einstein to work out which was more likely.

Chan went upstairs and surveyed the living room again, taking his time, making sure not to overlook anything. His gaze settled on the overturned chair and umbrella stand, books and magazines scattered on the floor. Then on the display cabinet, its doors yanked open, and on the Italian glasses in …

"*You fool!*" he cried out loud. "*You fool!*"

It's true, he thought, I'm a fool. Use your brains! No struggle took place here — it's a set-up! Look at those glasses, still in a neat row — if someone had banged against that cabinet during a struggle the glasses would have crashed to the floor and shattered. They didn't, *because there was no struggle.* The killer overturned the chair and made that other mess *after Miss Yeung was dead,* to give the impression of a fight. He could easily knock a chair over and scatter books without making much noise. He couldn't include those glasses in his act. If they'd been dragged from the cabinet they would have smashed and alerted neighbours. I noticed how thin these apartment walls are when I heard that character walking around next door. Yet no neighbour heard a struggle last night: because there never was one.

So if the killer wasn't a burglar who dropped those two thousand dollars, then what and who was he? Did Miss Yeung herself reveal his name to me? Chan wondered. Did she tell me when she phoned last night? She was terrified of what Fai might do. Did he kill her? Chan played out a scenario in his head. Miss Yeung is in her bed, struggling to sleep, smoking marijuana and drinking brandy to make herself feel more drowsy. The doorbell rings and she gets up and … No. She hated and feared Fai — no way would she open the door. He must have broken in here. Or perhaps the booze and marijuana made her so muddled that she forgot to lock up.

Anyway, somehow Fai gets inside. He strangles her then tries to cover his tracks by dropping that cash to ... Hold on! Fai couldn't have done it. He's in Taiwan. He doesn't return until today. No way could he have been here last night.

Unless he left Taiwan early!

Chan pulled the mobile phone from his pocket. He called the Mandarin Hotel in Macau.

"Has Mister Yip Kwok Fai checked in yet? … He arrived this morning … What room is … Not in his room at the moment … No, there's no message."

Fai *had* left Taiwan early. He could have caught a jet cat from Macau — journey time to Hong Kong was one hour — strangled her and then returned to Macau. Providing that all the drink and drugs had left Miss Yeung so muddled that she had left her door unlocked last night; or if the lock on her door was easy enough for an amateur like Fai to pick.

Chan walked over to the entrance door, bent down and examined the lock. He pulled a pen and notebook from his pocket and jotted down the lock manufacturer's name. He tried to pick the lock with a credit card and penknife. He couldn't do it, but that was no guarantee that no one could — he had never been any good at such delicate jobs.

Fortunately, he knew someone who was good at them: Snakefingers Sung would know if any amateur could pick that lock. A retired housebreaker, Snakefingers had often proved a life-saver. Ever since the January day eight years ago when Chan had been a character witness for Snakefingers' drug-taking daughter and saved her from prison. Snakefingers had proved eternally grateful, willing to help whenever he was asked.

Chan called him and explained the situation. Then he listened carefully while the former housebreaker gave him his expert opinion.

"But if you want a second opinion, Inspector," the housebreaker said, "then you should get in touch with—"

"No, it's all right," Chan said. "I don't need to double check with anyone else. If you say that's the way it is with those locks then that's good enough for me, Snakefingers."

He ended the call. He checked his watch: ten past eight. If the ferry was on time Ah Fah might have reached Lantau by now. He phoned her. Mechanical problems had delayed their departure, she explained. They were just leaving. Apart from that, everything was fine. Yes, she would call the moment they reached the safe house. Satisfied by this assurance, he said goodbye. He settled down to await police surgeon Eddie Gallacher's arrival.

PENG GLANCED AT the girl as the ferry pulled away.

She sat about ten metres away. Smoking a cigarette and talking loudly and laughing, doing all these three things at the same time it seemed, waving her arms animatedly as she made a point.

She won't laugh for much longer, though, he thought, a lump forming in his throat as he recalled how his sister had died screaming in pain when she had been the same age as Chan's daughter. Once this boat has docked and I decide the time is right I make my move. Her bodyguards can't protect her. Judging from the jackets they're wearing despite the sticky heat, both of them are armed. That won't save either of them, though — or her.

Then I turn to that final confrontation with Chan.

He checked his watch. The final confrontation with his sister's killer was now less than thirteen hours away, a confrontation with only one possible outcome. At thirty-six minutes past nine tonight, Peter Chan would die.

38

A QUEUE HAD formed outside the restaurant. But because the owner wanted to stay friends with the police, Chan managed to bypass the crowd. A booking captain wearing a pristine white jacket and black bow tie escorted him to a table by the window.

The restaurant was big, at almost a hundred tables, and decorated in glitzy Cantonese style: chandeliers, red carpets, red wallpaper — a fish tank in the corner to bring good *feng shui.*

Dozens of waitresses wheeled trolleys crammed with bamboo baskets containing *dim sum.* The waitresses chanted the names of items available to eat and drink; s*iu mai, har gau,* came a cry from one part of the room; *chow fan, po lei,* another waitress sang out from another part. When someone at a table thrust up a hand, or called out to a waitress, she would wheel her trolley over to them.

The restaurant was one of the most popular in Hong Kong, which explained the queue. Chan had only suggested coming here because he knew Wong loved dumplings; Chan was no fan of *dim sum.* He disliked most Cantonese food. Despite twenty years of living in Hong Kong he'd never got used to the stuff, it was too bland. He preferred peppery Sichuan dishes, or the thick buckwheat noodles and wholesome cooking of Beijing.

He had no time for the atmosphere of the *dim sum* restaurants, either; too steamy and loud. It was so noisy in here — the trundling of food trolleys up and down the floor, the non-stop jabbering of customers, the shouts of waitresses as they moved between tables, the banging open and shut of doors — it was all giving him a splitting headache.

And where was Wong?

Last night Chan had left a message on his sergeant's phone to say he was rearranging the meeting for eight-thirty. It was almost nine, so where was he? It was crazy sitting here wasting time. There was work to do. As well as question Fai they needed to tackle Alan Yip. Yip's police station spies would soon tell him about Miss Yeung — perhaps they already had — but the news must still be delivered officially. How would Yip react? The answer would have to wait. Yip was in China on business, not due back until tonight.

Chan dragged his mobile phone from his pocket and punched Wong's number. To his surprise, Wong's wife answered.

"Ah Lau? It's Peter."

"Hello, Peter."

"I must have rung your home number by mistake. I was trying to reach Ah Wong on his mobile."

"Didn't you get my message?"

"What message?"

"When I couldn't reach you at your flat, I thought you must be at work. I rang there and spoke to Sergeant Duggan. He said he would explain. About Ah Wong, I mean."

"Is something wrong?" Chan asked anxiously.

"He's caught the chickenpox bug. He's covered in spots. Didn't Sergeant Duggan explain?"

"I think he may be about to," Chan said. "He's just walked into the restaurant. Make sure that husband of yours takes care, Ah Lau. Tell him I'll call round to see how he's doing."

Chan put the phone in his pocket.

Duggan sauntered up to the table. "Morning, Ace," he announced breezily. "Mind if I grab a pew?" He pulled up a chair and sat down. "Got things to tell you: three things, actually."

Chan stared at him levelly. "Why didn't you call to tell me about Ah Wong?"

"You already know about that stuff, huh?"

"I just spoke to his wife."

"Thought I'd better come in person," Duggan said, continuing in his breezy manner, "seeing as we've got important stuff to discuss."

Chan frowned: "Important stuff?"

"The fat man catching chickenpox is the first of three things I have to tell you," Duggan said; "seeing as you know that already, I'll move to the second. Wong can't work this case, but the chief super reckons it's too big for you *not* to have a partner. So he's giving you me."

"You?"

"No need to sound so surprised. I'm a good cop."

"That's a matter of opinion."

"And the chief super's opinion is what counts. He knows I'm all clued up about the case. That's why he decided I was the ideal replacement. Especially when I said we're friends now. I mean it's true, isn't it? Last night—"

"I said I was in your debt. I said nothing about us being friends."

Duggan looked anxiously at him. "Working on a big case like this one could help to get me promoted, Ace. And you owe me too, remember?" Duggan paused. "Surely you haven't forgotten about last night."

Chan had not forgotten. It's true, he thought, I owe him. If not for Duggan, Ah Fah might have died. No way can I object to him replacing Ah Wong. Besides, he probably isn't so bad. He has faults — but who hasn't? A certain Inspector Chan has more than most.

"Relax, Duggan, I won't mess things up for you."

Duggan breathed a sigh of relief: "You won't regret it."

"But we play by my rules," Chan told him firmly. "You do what I say when I say. And you ditch the rough stuff too."

"There are times when you need to get tough with people," Duggan protested. "Sometimes you—"

"You do *exactly* as I say."

Duggan held up his hands in surrender. "You're the boss."

"You had three things to tell me," Chan said. "What's the third?"

"I circulated details of the guy who slugged me," Duggan said. "I even sent them to our Security Bureau friends over the border."

Chan nodded. "Good work."

"I'm a good cop." Duggan leaned forward. "Now it's your turn to show how good you are. I need you to fill me in on the Yeung woman. How about we eat while you do it? I've had no breakfast and my old mum warned me not to work on an empty stomach. I could murder some *cha siu bau* — I'm crazy about those barbecued pork buns."

"I didn't know you liked Chinese food so much."

"I told you last time. I like everything Chinese."

"Including Chinese women."

The words came instinctively. Chan regretted the childish insult as soon as he had made it, but by then it was too late.

Duggan groaned. "Let's not start that again."

"Sorry," Chan said. "Like you say, let's not start again. We've got more important … Where are you going?"

"I need to take a leak."

Duggan headed for the washroom. Chan signalled to a waitress, who was busy serving a group of Europeans four tables away. The clientele here was mainly Chinese, though, mainly families; noisy families. At one table, a baby began screaming. At another table children demanded Coca-Cola. There were a lot more children here than you usually saw in restaurants, even in the child-friendly Cantonese places. More old people, too, because it was traditional to take your parents or grandparents for *dim sum.*

That was why some extended families here were fourteen strong and stretched back for four generations. Po-faced old men and women in such family groups sat so stiffly upright that they looked glued to the backs of their chairs, only occasionally lowering their heads to sip tea, or to gnaw at a chicken's foot. Younger men read the newspapers, smoked cigarettes, or gabbled on mobile phones; sometimes doing all three together. Children, when they weren't screaming their heads off for large glasses of iced Coke, scurried between trolleys full of hot tea and steaming food, narrowly avoiding being scalded to death.

The waitress arrived at the table. Chan ordered Duggan's food and also asked for a pot of tea. "*Po lei*, not jasmine," he told her. She reached over to her trolley and removed three bamboo baskets

— four dumplings in each — and then placed the baskets on the table. Then she left, saying she would get someone to bring the tea.

Duggan returned. He sat down and hungrily chewed a pork bun. He said, "Tell me about the Yeung woman."

Chan told him.

"So Eddie Gallacher says the killer topped her between eleven-fifteen and a quarter after midnight, huh?" Duggan said.

"Yes."

"And you reckon Fai killed her?"

"I only said that he *could* have," Chan replied. "Fai's plane landed in Macau at six-thirty last night."

"I thought he wasn't due until this morning."

"He left Taiwan early. He booked himself into the Mandarin at Macau's airport and sent his bags on. The bags reached the hotel at eight-fifteen last night. Fai didn't arrive at the hotel himself until two this morning."

"Meaning he could have got a cab from the airport to the ferry terminal, and then caught a jet cat to Hong Kong?"

"Those jet cats run all night," Chan pointed out.

"Then he tops her and high-tails it back to Macau, huh?"

"The journey from Macau takes less than an hour," Chan said. "He could have got there and back in time."

"I thought your safebreaker pal said an amateur couldn't have broken that lock on the Yeung woman's door."

"Maybe Miss Yeung forgot to lock up."

"And maybe pigs will fly."

The tea arrived. Chan poured for both of them.

"I don't buy Fai taking a jet cat," Duggan said. "I reckon he headed straight from the airport to a casino or brothel. Gambling and whoring is why most people visit Macau."

"Aren't you forgetting that Colt Fai owns?"

"The Yeung woman was strangled," Duggan pointed out. "It's Fai's brother who was plugged with the Colt."

"Supposing the same person killed both?"

"That person's Fai, huh?"

"I don't know," Chan replied. "But I know that when Miss Yeung called me she sounded scared. She claimed Fai threatened to kill Szeto. Supposing Fai did?"

Duggan chewed another pork bun. He dabbed his greasy lips with a napkin. "So we're suddenly just scrapping all this cult stuff, huh?" He sounded surprised. "I mean … I thought it was cut and dried — death threats against Alan Yip, and then those cult papers found under his kid's body. I thought we were just waiting for the clinching piece of evidence before arresting those temple weirdoes."

Chan drank some *po lei* tea. He preferred this strong, dark brew to the more fragrant jasmine tea his wife had always ordered.

"We're not dismissing the stuff about the cult," he said. "We're simply making sure we don't let those cult death threats blind us to other possibilities."

"Possibilities that include Fai topping her?"

"We have to check out every possible angle," Chan said. "That means we need to quiz Fai about that Colt, and also about Miss Yeung's claims."

"When do we do that?"

"Now."

WITH A LOUD convulsive shudder the ferry docked at the pier.

Passengers sprang up from their seats and bolted for the exit. Peng remained sitting. There was no point in behaving like these losers. The crew would not lower the gangway for two minutes. He would only have to wait standing up instead of sitting down.

Besides, if he jostled for space there was a risk of him being shoved up against another passenger; that passenger might feel the outline of the Makarov and summon the police. Only an amateur would take that sort of needless risk. Peng prided himself on his professionalism. On a meticulous attention to detail that had kept him alive for so long in such a deadly business: a business where the smallest mistake meant the difference between life and death.

He stayed in his seat.

The girl's bodyguards had also decided to remain seated. Peng silently praised their professionalism. The girl dug them both in the ribs and gestured impatiently for them to move to the exit.

The older man calmly shook his head.

I got it wrong about those two bodyguards, Peng thought, as he disdainfully flicked a mosquito from one ear. I thought they were amateurs, but they're not. They both know their business. They still can't save her, though. I've met tougher opposition and succeeded. I'll succeed this time, too. Especially as father is watching me and guiding me from the after-life, helping to ensure that Chan's crime doesn't go unpunished — helping make certain Chan suffers like Liu Yan suffered.

The crew had lowered the gangway.

The crowd at the exit began to thin out. The older of the two guards signalled to the girl that it was also time for them to move. Peng allowed them a gap of ten seconds. Then he rose calmly from his seat and followed them off the boat. Once clear of the pier, the older man turned right, gesturing for his fellow bodyguard and the girl to follow him. Were they heading for the taxi rank? No, they planned to walk. That meant they must not be going far. No one would walk far in this sweltering heat.

Peng allowed them a gap of about forty metres. They walked three abreast, the girl in the middle. The two men were both slim and short, the girl tall and muscular. She towered above them. She shot out a foot to kick an empty beer can which littered the pavement, missed the can and stumbled, and then burst out laughing at her clumsiness. The older bodyguard pointed to a spot in the distance. Was that their destination — a bungalow by the beach? Perhaps they …

Peng broke from his thoughts as someone seized him by the shoulder. He swung round — what fool would dare grab him so roughly? He glimpsed a peaked cap, smartly pressed green jacket and green trousers, shiny black leather holster containing a Colt service revolver. The man who gripped his shoulder was a police inspector. He was trapped.

39

PORTUGESE SAILORS FIRST weighed anchor off the coast of Macau in the sixteenth century: so as a European trading colony it predates Hong Kong by three hundred years. Yet Hong Kong has never afforded Macau the respect for age that is such a traditional and important part of Chinese culture. In fact it has constantly overshadowed its neighbour.

Hong Kong is Southeast Asia's finance centre and is where multinational companies have established Asian headquarters. It is far bigger than Macau: some six million people live there while Macau is home to only around half a million. Hong Kong has more luxury hotels, more restaurants, more office towers, more apartment blocks, more cars, more buses, more noise; more pollution — more of everything.

Apart from casinos.

Because it is believed to feed organised crime, gambling other than on the government-run Mark Six lottery, or on government-regulated horse racing, is banned in Hong Kong. You will not find any glitzy casinos there. Recognising that there was a pent-up demand for casinos, Macau businessmen built lots of them. In recent years American tycoons have got in on the act, financing glitzy new 'super' casino-and-hotel complexes like those found in Las Vegas.

That is why casinos and gambling dens can be found on almost every Macau street, and why Macau has taken over from Las Vegas as the world's gambling capital. In the glitzy Macau casinos you won't find gamblers wearing dinner jackets and elegantly sipping their James Bond-style vodka martinis as they pause between games of *baccarat.*

What you will see, if your eyes ever become accustomed to the fog of cigarette smoke, are red-eyed, down-at-heel gamblers who have not slept in twenty-four hours, and who are down to their last dollar and sweating with tension; gamblers chewing at cigarettes; gamblers spitting on the greasy floor; gamblers begging other gamblers to lend them the measly few dollars that will offer one last chance to get rich; gamblers spilling beer, smashing glasses — arguing with and fighting each other. And what you will hear above the noise of shattering glass are gamblers screaming with delight on the few times they win, or cursing with despair on the many times they lose.

Chan and Duggan were bound for Macau's most famous casino — the roulette-shaped Lisboa. But not to gamble; they wanted to interview Alan Yip's son, Fai. He had been missing from his suite at the Mandarin when they had called there ten minutes ago. He had gone gambling in the Lisboa, the pretty young girl on the Mandarin's reception desk had informed Chan.

"Reckon he'll still be in there?" Duggan asked, as they tramped along the waterfront.

"We'll soon find out."

They crossed the road, avoiding an old man whose bony legs looked ready to snap with the strain as he pedalled a rickshaw taxi towards the jet cat terminal. Chan wiped sweat from his face. *Aheya,* it was hot today! The sun burned from a cloudless turquoise sky and sent fireballs blazing across the waters of the estuary; waters that were coloured grey-brown not blue, because of the tonnes of mud deposited in the estuary by the Pearl River.

On Chan and Duggan's left, a few hundred metres away, the humpbacked steel bridge which links Macau to the islands of Taipa and Coloane, glinted like a huge silver bracelet in the fierce sunlight. The humpbacked bridge was an attractive, even a graceful design, Chan thought. But there was nothing even remotely attractive or graceful about all the cranes and scaffolding which scarred the skyline. Hundreds of workers clambered up and down scaffolding, looking like human ants as they erected yet more and bigger and bigger new hotels and 'super' casinos. Would the crazy pace of construction work never slow here?

The aim of all this frenzied building activity was to turn Macau into a more upmarket and beautiful place. As far as Chan was concerned, it had made Macau look uglier.

He brushed more sweat from his brow. He was pleased when, after another five minutes, they finally reached the Lisboa's air-conditioned comfort. They moved through the lobby and into the hotel's huge and cavernous casino.

"Busy, huh?" Duggan said. "Spotted him yet?"

"We'll be better off splitting up," Chan said. "You check the right side, I'll take the left."

Chan wiped more perspiration from his face; the lobby might be air-conditioned, but not this place. Or perhaps there were simply so many people crammed inside here that the air-conditioning system had been neutralised by their body heat, and those foul cigarettes they all seemed to puff.

He waved a hand to clear the cigarette smoke away from his eyes. As the thick tobacco fog lifted, pasty-faced men and women with smudged make-up hovered like a bunch of phantoms in front of him. Judging from their haunted appearances, most had already lost next month's wages. It was always the same story. When they had set off from Hong Kong they would have been confident of getting rich. Yet most of them would leave Macau tomorrow broken and dispirited.

He pushed his way past a blackjack table. Two women stood hunched over the table. They were probably in their mid-twenties but looked nearer forty. Loser was written on their sad, frightened faces. Tomorrow they would be at the money lenders in Mongkok, or Yau Ma Tei, begging for a few thousand dollars to get them through the month. The money lenders would charge huge interest. If the women failed to repay on time the money lenders would get Triad red-pole heavies to rough them up.

Beyond the blackjack table, red and yellow lights flashed on a regiment of buzzing and beeping arcade slot machines. An army of old crones in flowered pyjama suits patrolled the machines, pumping a steady stream of coins into them. Occasionally one of the machines coughed back a measly few dollars, which the old women immediately pumped back in.

Chan was more interested in what was happening at the roulette tables. A crowd had gathered at one roulette table. He pushed his way over and peered between the shoulders of two middle-aged women. A roulette player in an electric-blue shirt seemed to be the centre of attention — a high-roller judging from the pile of twenty thousand dollar chips stacked in front of him. The high-roller grabbed the chips and handed them to the Filipino croupier. The nonchalant way he did this suggested that there were plenty more chips where these came from.

The young croupier's dark brown eyes widened in disbelief: "Are you sure about it, sir — *really* sure?"

The man in the electric-blue shirt shifted in his seat. Chan could see his face now: Fai. With a loud slap, Alan Yip's son put more chips on the table. He turned to the girl beside him.

"Sure we're sure — aren't we, darling?"

The girl laughed brightly. "Sure we're sure."

"But ... I mean ... It's half a *million!*" the croupier said.

Fai nodded. "And I want it stacked on number four."

The croupier shrugged, as if to say: I've warned you, but if you insist on being a fool, then be my guest.

"Okay, sir, I'll take your bet."

The croupier cracked his knuckles and prepared to spin the wheel. An air of hushed anticipation descended. Fresh cigarettes were lit, full glasses of whisky and beer downed. Chan noticed the bald-headed Malaysian gambler who stood opposite him touch a jade pendant for good luck. A few feet away, a leathery-faced old Chinese woman mumbled what sounded like a prayer. Probably she had only bet a few dollars, but her gamble would be more a matter of life and death than Fai's half million — these few dollars might be all she had. If the wheel proved unkind she could finish up destitute. Fai would always have Alan Yip to bail him out.

"No more bets!" the croupier announced in a loud voice. "No more … Stand back! Stand ..."

He spun the wheel.

The crowd held its breath. Unshaven men who looked as if they had not slept for several days gazed intently at the spinning wheel, as if by doing so they might somehow will the white ball into the correct slot. The wheel stopped spinning.

"Stand back!" the croupier ordered. "Stand back!"

The white ball rolled four times around the rim of the wheel, making a low whirring sound, before gradually slowing down and trickling into slot twenty-seven, then bouncing out and landing in another slot three places away.

"Stand back! Number ..."

The table erupted into confusion. Yells of delight from the few people who had won became fused with groans of despair from the many more people who had lost. There was an explosion of breaking glass, as some of those who had lost hurled their whisky tumblers to the floor; a babble of men and women cursing loudly in both Cantonese and Mandarin. The young croupier cried out for order. Chan pushed past the two middle-aged women. He walked over to where Fai was sitting, leaned over and tapped Fai on the shoulder. Fai swung around. Chan showed his police ID card.

"We need to talk, Mister Yip. Let's go somewhere quiet."

Duggan nodded at Chan from across the room.

40

PENG STARED INTO the inspector's face.

What he saw there told him that he must kill the man. The inspector's square-jawed face was set hard as flint. His keen brown eyes brimmed with suspicion. He knows, Peng thought; knows who I am and why I'm here — he has to die. It's because of that fiasco with Chan's daughter yesterday. That European who intercepted me on the stairs got a better look at me than I thought he did.

He's given police a detailed description of me. That's why this officer grabbed me. Why I have to kill him. Unless I act now it'll be too late. In a moment he'll seize his radio and summon help from other officers — I can glimpse the danger in his eyes. I can't allow him the moment. One quick, hard blow to snap his neck; that's all it will take. Then I head quickly down the road. No one will stop me. They'll be too scared to intervene.

Now! Do it now!

He focused on the part of the inspector's neck that he would break. Flexed muscles in his right hand. Felt the edge of his palm stiffen and grow harder. Felt his heart beat quicken.

Then the inspector released his grip on Peng's shoulder.

The inspector smiled: a bashful, apologetic smile.

Peng hesitated — supposing the inspector was *not* a threat. Have I misjudged the situation? Peng wondered. Did I get it wrong about the European at Chan's flat? Maybe he never got a good look at me. Supposing no description of me has been circulated. Supposing

... But if that's true, then why did this officer grab me?

"Terribly sorry, sir." The inspector spoke as bashfully as he had smiled. "I thought you were someone else."

Peng relaxed. So that was it. That was why the police inspector had grabbed his shoulder: a simple case of mistaken identity.

"My boss sent me here to meet a passenger off the ferry," the inspector explained. "The chief superintendent said the passenger would be carrying a case like yours — but my man's a foreigner." The inspector raised a hand to his peaked cap in an apology. "Sorry to have bothered you."

Peng nodded understandingly: "That's all right, officer, there's no harm done."

The inspector moved off.

Peng shot a glance down the road. The girl and her guards were a good hundred metres away from him now, approaching a sharp bend. He quickened his pace — if they swung out of sight around that bend he might lose them for good. Fortunately, they did not go as far as the bend. They turned into the entrance to a bungalow. Peng slowed to a halt. Now that he knew their destination he did not need to rush.

He turned around and walked back casually in the direction of the ferry pier, until he reached a wooden bench by the side of the road. He sat on the bench, pretended to gaze out to sea. He was really watching the groups of visitors from Hong Kong as they filed past on their way to the beach, or the hills. It took five minutes before the special group that he was waiting for passed by: a mother and three young children, but no husband or father.

Peng rose from the bench and attached himself to the family group. Together in their company, he strolled past the bungalow where the girl and her two bodyguards had holed up. If anyone inside the bungalow was on the lookout for threatening characters, they would disregard him; they would assume that he was the children's father.

As he ambled past the bungalow, he checked for guards — were there more than two of them looking after the girl? He also searched for alarm systems and security cameras. No guard stood on duty outside, but a security camera was fixed to the whitewashed wall. The wall stood roughly two metres high and ran all the way around the bungalow. Peng walked for about another fifty metres with his adopted family until they came to a fork in the road. Here they split up and went their different ways: the family headed for the beach while he strode off purposefully towards the hills.

He made for a place that he had noticed immediately after walking past the bungalow. A place that all his years of experience told him would prove ideal for the job he must do. The best place from where he could take a long-range shot at that bungalow with his French FR-F2 sniper's rifle: a perfect killing ground.

"SO I THREATENED to kill him — it was only words! Szeto knew I never meant it. But he'd fired paint in my face for fuck's sake! What was I supposed to do — run up and kiss him?"

Fai swallowed more vodka. He drank the stuff as though it was as harmless as water; no wonder his face had become so flushed. They were in his hotel suite. Twenty minutes had passed since Chan had approached him at the roulette table in the casino. Chan surveyed Fai's flushed, square-jawed face for signs that he was lying. He found none. Did this mean Fai had spoken the truth? No. He might simply be a skilful liar.

"But if you think it went further than me running off at the mouth, you're crazy. Get it through your thick head, Chan — I *loved* him! Yes, we were different. Szeto took after his mother: a crazy idealist. Me, I take after my father — we're both of us bastards and cynics. Yet there were times when I would look at my crazy idealist brother and … Yes, I envied him. Because I saw the man I wanted to be. I won't envy him again, though, will I? He's gone and …"

His voice trailed off.

Is that genuine pain? Chan wondered. Are those real tears? Or is it all an act? Fai is a good actor. That's why he looks impressive when he appears on TV as a spokesman for his father's company. How do we discover if he's acting now? By making him angry? It might work. Angry men can often make mistakes. If his grief is a mask, anger might cause the mask to slip.

Chan said, "Szeto was your father's favourite, wasn't he?"

Fai stiffened. "Who said that?

"Answer the question," Duggan said roughly.

"Who told you Szeto was—"

"Yes or no?" Chan said sharply.

"It was that bitch Yeung, wasn't it?"

"Answer the inspector's question," Duggan snapped.

Fai swallowed more vodka then wiped his wet lips with the back of one hand.

"I never had anything to do with that bitch's death," he said heatedly. "I couldn't have. I've never left Macau since I checked into my hotel."

"I didn't ask about Miss Yeung," Chan said. "I asked you if Szeto was your father's favourite. Was he?"

"The Yeung bitch — she was pure poison!" Fai almost spat out the last word. "As poisonous as a snake; and she planted all her venom in Szeto."

Chan frowned. "What do you mean?"

"I mean she's your killer. That bitch murdered my brother."

41

AFTER TREKKING UPHILL for ten minutes, Peng halted to survey the scene. To his left, about half a mile away and roughly six hundred feet below, lay the ferry pier; the boat he had arrived on had just begun its journey back to Hong Kong. To his right was the beach, its golden sands dotted black with sunbathers and swimmers.

Peng was more interested in what lay in front of him.

He took the Leica binoculars from his pocket, raised them to his eyes and focused on the whitewashed bungalow where the girl and her guards had holed up. From his vantage point it was about four hundred metres to the bungalow. The girl splashed about in the bungalow's swimming pool. The younger bodyguard sat at a table overlooking the pool. Peng could not see the other man. He must be inside the bungalow because …

Voices from behind him: Peng removed the binoculars from his eyes and turned around. The voices belonged to a group of ramblers. He smiled as they passed by but none of the ramblers smiled back. I got it wrong, he realised, as he watched the group of about a dozen men and women move out of sight around a bend in the hillside. This spot isn't going to be the perfect killing ground I thought it would be. A long-range hit from here will be difficult. In fact it will be almost impossible. Not because of the distance: I could take someone out from this range, I've done it before. The problem is this spot is on a popular nature trail. Those ramblers gave me some strange looks when they saw me in action with the binoculars. Other hikers would do a lot more if they stumbled on me when I was using the sniper's rifle. It's too risky to take a shot from here. I'm going to have to work from close range: I need to get inside the bungalow. That camera on the wall makes it difficult, but I *will* get inside — I must. Liu Yan and father depend on me. Failure means they'll never rest easy in the after-life.

I won't fail them, though. The passengers who arrived on the same boat as me will be sunning themselves on the beach now, or hiking up here in the hills. No one will be walking past the girl's bungalow — I won't be disturbed. First, I deal with the security camera: one well-placed shot will do the job there. Next, I take out the two guards. Then, finally, I get the girl. I won't fail. I'll succeed like I always do. Chan's daughter is as good as dead.

"THAT YEUNG BITCH hated Szeto," Fai said.

"How do you know she killed him?"

"She hated him as much as she hated me, inspector."

Chan eyed him keenly. "How do you know she killed him?"

"She was always trying to put us at each other's throats. Always painting us both black in the eyes of my father. Me and Szeto … We were a threat to her, you see."

"How?"

"We had influence with my father. She wanted rid of us. So first she killed Szeto. Then, when Szeto died …"

His voice quivered then trailed off. He gulped vodka.

"What happened?" Chan pressed. "What happened when Szeto died?"

Fai shook his head. "No, I can't ... Questions about Szeto … Hurts too much." He looked at the vodka as if it might help him forget. "It won't work, it won't—"

"How can you prove she killed him?" Terry Duggan cut in.

"I can't, sergeant, but I know she did."

"How?" Duggan asked roughly.

"I just know."

"Bullshit!"

"No, I can feel it. I feel it in my bones. I—"

"We're wasting time," Duggan said. "He's pissing us about." Duggan punched a fist into the palm of his hand. "Give me five minutes alone with him and—"

"Shut up," Chan said.

"Anything happens, we say he fell — it's our word against—"

"Shut up!"

Duggan held up his hands in a gesture of surrender. "Okay, okay, whatever you say."

"Let's go outside," Chan said. "The fresh air might help us all to think a bit more clearly."

Duggan opened the double glass doors. They stepped onto the balcony. The sky had changed in the half hour since they had entered the suite: from vivid turquoise to hazy blue-white. A jet trailing plumes of vapour had begun its descent into Macau's airport. Chan and Fai sat opposite each other at a white marble table. Duggan stood with his back against the balcony's wall.

"So, Mister Yip." Chan made his voice friendlier in the hope that it would encourage Fai to co-operate more. "Tell me about …"

Fai held up a hand to halt him: he had forgotten the vodka. And he needed it, he said. It might not have wiped out the pain of his brother's death, but it had helped numb that pain.

Duggan went inside with him.

"Remember, Duggan," Chan said. "We do it my way."

"Relax, Ace, I'm only grabbing a beer."

While he waited for them to return, Chan glanced from the balcony. Macau looked as tawdry as one of the fake Rolexes which Tsim Sha Tsui's hustlers pressed on tourists. Many tourists bought them, pleasantly surprised by how much the fakes resembled the real thing and by a price tag fifteen times cheaper than for the genuine article; only to be equally surprised six months later, though less pleasantly, when plastic parts in the watches snapped.

It was amazing how Macau had changed so dramatically in such a short a space of time. Ten years ago, it had not been tawdry. It had possessed a tranquility and elegance that had made a refreshing change from Hong Kong's hassles. But a construction boom had spiralled out of control, ripping both the heart and soul from

Macau. The waterfront, which not long ago had oozed old-world charm, had turned new-world ugly. Where once had stood the low-lying whitewashed buildings which had given Macau a relaxed and Mediterranean-style feel, garish hotels and casino complexes now jutted up from the shore.

In the past few years American tycoons had been opening casinos and hotels here at the rate of one a month. And these were no ordinary casinos or hotels: one 'super' casino was made of burnished gold; another layered in gold, silver and bronze, while the latest hotel to be built was the largest in Asia and boasted three thousand luxury suites.

The sunlight gave up on the impossible task of making the casinos and hotels look any more beautiful. Instead it danced across the estuary waters and over the silver humpbacked bridge that links Macau to the islands of Taipa and Coloane. A cargo ship ghosted underneath the bridge. A ferry chugged back to China, overtaken by a jet cat which knifed through the sea bound for Hong Kong.

"I grabbed you a beer too!"

Duggan and Fai had returned.

Duggan tossed him a Carlsberg. "Catch! It'll cool you down."

He returned to his place by the wall. Fai sat opposite Chan. Fai refilled his glass with vodka. Did he really need so much to help him over his brother's death? Yes, Chan thought: assuming he told us the truth about his love for Szeto. For a man who loved his brother and had who nothing to do with his death, Fai's behaviour is understandable. Alcohol helps you escape reality, and the pain of losing a loved one which reality brings. But supposing Fai lied about his relationship with Szeto? Is the vodka to help him escape the guilt he feels about Szeto's murder? It was time to try and find out. And the friendly approach was not going to work. Duggan had been right. They must get tougher.

"Where were you last night?" Chan asked sharply.

"I've already told you where I was," Fai said. "I had nothing to do with that bitch Yeung's death."

"You own a Colt .38." Chan said

"No I don't."

"We checked the records," Duggan said. "Your name's there."

"Your records are wrong, sergeant. I admit I *used* to own a gun — I bought that Colt when I joined a shooting club last year. But I sold it three months ago."

"Why?" Duggan asked aggressively.

"Blasting toy soldiers was as exciting as watching paint dry."

"Are the Mandarin's records also wrong?" Chan said.

Fai gave him a puzzled look. "What are you talking about?"

"Reception says you checked in at two this morning."

"Is that a crime?"

"Your plane landed at six-thirty last night."

"So?"

"Why the eight-hour gap?"

"I needed time to myself."

"Eight hours?"

"It's not as unbelievable as you make it all sound, inspector. I wanted to remember the good times with Szeto. I went to Taipa. We used to drink at a bar there — a place called Ah Yat's."

"So someone at the bar can vouch for you?"

Fai shook his head. "It was shut. I walked along the waterfront."

"For *eight* hours?"

"I thought solitude might help me cope with Szeto's death. As well as help me puzzle out that other stuff."

"What other stuff?"

"Whether he was shot by mistake."

Chan's eyes narrowed: "Mistake?"

Fai nodded: "Perhaps I was the real intended victim."

"What the fuck are you talking about, pal?" Duggan said from his place by the wall.

"Szeto was wearing a general's uniform," Fai explained. "That uniform was mine. I collect military artefacts. It was the best piece in my collection: worn by the general who led the Yalu River attack during the Korean War."

"You gave it to Szeto?" Chan said.

"He won it, inspector. We had a paint-balling contest. We agreed the winner could demand anything from the loser — Szeto won."

"And demanded the uniform?"

Fai nodded. "He did it to spite me."

Duggan gave a loud snort. "Spiting you hardly fits, does it, pal? Not with all the lovey-dovey stuff you spouted two minutes ago."

"He's right," Chan said. "You told us you and Szeto were close."

Fai poured more vodka. But he didn't take a drink he merely twisted the glass in his hand, staring blankly at the colourless liquid as it swirled around. He said haltingly, "We *were* close. Until a few months ago when … Well, Szeto had been having some emotional problems and been acting irrationally ... Drugs doctors gave him made him worse … Made him act childishly. He knew how fond I was of that uniform. So …"

"What?" Duggan demanded.

"He took it the way one child takes a favourite toy from another." Fai gulped vodka. He added heatedly, "But it never stopped me loving him." He shook his head. "I could never have done anything to hurt Szeto."

"This stuff about you being intended victim," Chan said. "Did your *eight* hours of walking help you puzzle it out?"

"No. It never helped me cope with Szeto's death either. So I took a cab to the hotel. Then I decided to try something else that helps when I'm low — I thought gambling might help me forget."

"Did it?" Chan said. "Did you manage to forget?"

Fai shook his head in disbelief: "Half a million! I went and lost five hundred *thousand* dollars! Any other time and I'd shoot myself for being so stupid — I've never bet anywhere near as big before. But I never had a dead brother before, did I? I was so upset about … Well, I wasn't thinking straight and—"

"Answer the inspector," Duggan snapped. "Did gambling help you forget your brother's death?"

"No."

"You've forgotten that paint-gun incident," Chan said.

Fai looked puzzled. "I told you about it."

"Not everything."

Fai stiffened. "What do you mean?"

"Miss Yeung said that before Szeto blasted you with paint, he ordered you to read a magazine."

"So?"

"Produced by that cult on Lantau — the Heavenly Ghosts. Why would he do that?"

"Surely it's obvious, inspector."

"Not to me," Chan said. "Enlighten me."

"He was one of them. Szeto was a member of the cult."

42

JOE PARWANI TENSED.

What was that?

He grabbed the remote control from the sofa and pressed the button for security camera number two: a close-up of the hallway appeared on his TV screen.

Everything looked normal.

He jabbed another button on the remote. It brought up the street outside the main entrance. Nothing wrong here either. Two more buttons brought up areas at the back of the bungalow: again, everything perfectly in order. Did I imagine the noise? he wondered. No, I heard something. So why don't I see anything? Have those cameras gone on the blink? It's happened before; twice this year. I was crazy to opt for that cheap Shanghai system. I should have bought the expensive Japanese one.

He rose from the leather sofa. I need to check out the hallway, he thought. Need to make absolutely sure about it. He pulled the snub-nosed Smith and Wesson 9mm automatic from his shoulder holster, slipped off the safety catch. Clutching the gun in his right hand, he moved over to the living room door and peered cautiously around it. He glanced down the hallway, to where he was certain he had heard the noise come from.

Nothing.

He moved to the entrance door. Bent down and gazed through

the glass spy-hole that allowed him to view the area outside. No one was there. He blew air from his cheeks. You *are* hearing things, you daft bastard, he thought, replacing the gun in its worn leather holster. You're getting past it, Joe, too old to handle the pressure.

He tramped into the kitchen, cursing as he brushed beads of sweat from his forehead. Screw this bungalow! The air-con was even worse than that lousy security system! No wonder Pete's kid had headed straight for the pool — it was like a sauna in here.

He grabbed a Carlsberg from the fridge and took a hefty gulp; he needed a beer badly. Not just to cool down, but also to relax; his heart was racing as fast as one of the runners at Happy Valley's race track. No two ways about it, he thought, I'm getting past it. Pete should have hired a much younger man for this job. The days when Joe Parwani was the best in the business seem another lifetime away.

He returned to the living room, sat on the leather sofa and resumed the monotonous task of monitoring the TV set. None of the images he summoned up from the bungalow's four security cameras showed anything out of place anywhere.

A shout from the swimming pool made him turn away from the screen and gaze through the living room's open double doors. The girl squealed with delight as she splashed about in the turquoise water. She seemed untroubled by any danger. Is that because no danger exists? Parwani wondered. Has Pete Chan overreacted? He's always been protective of her, maybe a bit *too* protective. Has he imagined all of these threats? He's almost as old as me. Maybe he's become as senile as me too.

Parwani turned back to the TV set. He picked up the remote, pressed the ... Jesus Christ! No sodding picture at all now. Only grey blankness. He angrily jabbed one button, then another: still no picture; just the same dull grey blankness. He cursed silently: the son of a bitch has gone and loused up for a *third* time! Well, enough is enough. First thing tomorrow, I phone up the manufacturer and demand a full refund. Something that keeps breaking down is no good. A man in my business needs something precise and reliable. My own stupid fault, though. If I hadn't been tight-fisted, I'd have bought the Japanese system: I would have an alarm network that guarded me against major criminals. Instead I save a measly few dollars, but get a lousy security system that wouldn't even deter a teenage vandal. A system that ...

Vandal!

Is that it? he wondered. Is that what has happened here — vandalism? Maybe I didn't get it wrong about that noise. Supposing someone outside has vandalized the security system. Someone who wants badly to get in here, someone …

He grabbed his Smith and Wesson.

"Sanjay!" he shouted. "We've got trouble!"

DUGGAN WIPED BEER foam from his mouth: "What do the guys at the station say?" he asked Chan, who was replacing his mobile phone in his pocket. "Are the Colt records wrong?"

"They're double-checking."

"You reckon Fai lied, huh?"

Chan blew air from his cheeks. "Why don't you tell me the answer? My brain has stopped working."

"Drink up, it'll help you think."

Chan swallowed some of his *San Miguel* beer; he needed it. Not only to improve his focus but also to help him stay cool. They sat outside *Henri's Galley,* a popular waterfront restaurant which serves Portuguese food.

"Fai *could* have killed his brother," Chan said. "He was in Hong Kong when Szeto was shot. He also had time to go to Hong Kong and strangle Miss Yeung last night."

"Do you reckon he *did* strangle her?"

"Snakefingers is sure only a professional could have picked that lock on her front door."

"Might be like you told me last time," Duggan said. "She might have got so drunk that she forgot to lock up."

"And it might be like you told me last time — pigs might fly."

"And Szeto?" Duggan queried.

"What about Szeto?"

"Do you think Fai killed him?"

"What I think isn't important," Chan said. "What's important is being able to *prove* Fai did it. And at the moment we can't, can we? Especially if no link to the murder weapon exists; if he told the truth about selling his Colt he's virtually untouchable."

Duggan flicked a mosquito from his ear "What do you make of that stuff Fai told us about Szeto joining the cult?"

"It would explain certain things," Chan said.

Duggan leaned forward in his chair. "Like what?"

"Like why all that cult stuff we found under his body only had Szeto's prints — he put those cult pamphlets in the car himself."

The waiter, a fat young man in a grey tee-shirt and blue shorts, both of which fit so tightly that they made him look even fatter than he actually was, arrived at their table. He told them the food would be soon on the way and asked them if they wanted anything more to drink. Duggan said their glasses would soon be empty so the waiter should bring two more beers. He told him to make certain the beer was ice cold.

"What I don't really get," Duggan said thoughtfully, after the waiter had left them, "is if it was so easy for Fai to know all about Szeto joining the cult, how come dad didn't?"

"Dad?"

"Alan Yip."

"He wasn't Szeto's father."

Duggan had been in the process of lifting the almost empty beer glass to his lips when Chan began his reply. As the inspector's words sank in, Duggan froze, leaving his arm stranded in mid-air, glass half-way between his chest and gaping mouth. Then, like a man in a trance, he slowly lowered the glass to the table.

"Come again, Ace."

"Alan Yip wasn't Szeto's father."

Duggan frowned. "Care to expand on that, inspector?"

"John Tsang was Szeto's father."

43

PARWANI FLICKED OFF the safety on his automatic.

"Get her out of the pool, Sanjay," he shouted. "And watch the wall in case anyone comes over."

Parwani moved down the hallway, his right hand gripping the gun: he halted about six feet from the main entrance door.

"Who's there?"

No reply.

"Who's there?"

Still no answer.

He moved cautiously to the door. Bent down and gazed though the glass spy-hole: someone *was* outside, a man in his late twenties or early thirties. The man held a black briefcase in his left hand while his right hand clutched an object which he pointed at the door. Parwani's brain barely had time to register that the object was a gun, before the door exploded in his face.

DUGGAN SHOOK HIS head: "I wanted it made clearer not more confusing."

"John Tsang and Alan Yip's second wife had a love affair," Chan said. "Szeto was the outcome of that affair."

"Is this fact? Or inspired guesswork?"

"It's professional judgement," Chan replied. "A judgement I've made for two reasons. Reason number one: when I talked with Szeto's girlfriend in Wan Chai, she said he liked Shanghai food and had got the taste from his father — Szeto told her that his father came from Shanghai."

"So?"

"Alan Yip is from Chengdu. It's John Tsang who comes from Shanghai. He …"

The tinkling of a bell made Chan swing round in the direction of the waterfront; an old man pedalling a trishaw taxi, his puny leg muscles straining despite the trishaw's empty passenger seats, touted for business. Chan waved him on. Out at sea, a jet cat carved a trail of foam as it headed for Hong Kong. A plane full of tourists landed at the airport on the other side of the estuary.

"That's one reason," Duggan said. "You mentioned two."

Chan took his wallet from his pocket. He opened the wallet and removed a piece of paper.

"Take a look." He handed Duggan the paper. "It's from the file that I had Ah Wong put together for me: it shows John Tsang as a young man before he became fat. A young man who bears a very striking resemblance to … Where are you going?"

"For another beer; I need it to calm down after what you said."

Duggan entered the restaurant. Chan sat back and struggled again to make sense of it all. After Fai's claims that his brother had been a paid-up member of the Heavenly Ghosts, Chan's impulse had been to drag cult guru Brother Li to the police station and sweat the truth from him.

Then he had recalled grandfather's advice about how wise men waited patiently for lead to turn to gold. Only hotheaded fools would charge into the cult's temple wearing size-fourteen boots. Supposing Fai had lied? Perhaps the cult had no links to any murders — Fai might have just been trying to divert suspicion from himself.

Blundering about in the cult's temple was not the thing to do, Chan had decided. Besides, he had no need to rush there. Li was not about to suddenly go into hiding. And a cold beer might refresh the brain cells. So Chan and Duggan had come here and …

"Here you go!"

Duggan had returned, two *San Miguels* clinking in his hands.

Chan grabbed one of the stubby brown bottles. The coating of frost on the bottles meant that they had come straight from the fridge. Chan refilled his glass, took a long, thirst-quenching drink. Ah, that was good! The beer was so cold that it stung his throat.

The waiter brought the food: garlic bread, huge grilled sardines, crab cooked in coconut, stewed codfish; spicy African chicken. The sardines were fat, smoky and succulent; the chicken beautifully moist and tender. The crunchy bread oozed garlic butter.

"I should have asked earlier," Duggan said when the waiter had left. "How's your kid?"

"Fine."

"No delayed shock?"

"She's fine."

"Really care about her, huh?"

"Doesn't every father care for his children?"

Duggan gave a snort of laughter.

"Not if he's Paddy Duggan! My dear old dad loved us eight kids like a dose of the clap." Duggan swallowed some beer then wiped his lips. "I can't remember a day he didn't kick shit out of one of us — particularly me. I'm oldest, see, so I tried to protect the smaller kids. Not that it did any good. He just beat crap out of two of us instead of one."

Is that it? Chan wondered. Is that why Duggan likes rough stuff — because it's second nature? Because he grew so used to it that he thinks it's normal? We're all conditioned by childhood experiences. Mine left me with a hang-up about westerners. Despite trying to convince myself that I'm not prejudiced against *gweilos*, deep down I know I am. At least I'm prejudiced against *certain types* of westerner. Tall Englishmen with swimming pool-blue eyes and blonde hair like the hair my father had. Englishmen like Terry Duggan.

"Finally got even, though," Duggan said proudly. "At seventeen, I was as big as Paddy. I caught him lurching from the Red Lion one night even more pissed than usual. I came up behind the bastard and smashed him with a brick. Then I kicked him and kicked him — I kicked him till I hadn't the energy to kick him any more. He spent two weeks in hospital. He never spoke about it after, but he knew who'd done it. Knew I'd do it again too, unless he left the other kids alone — he never touched them after that."

Duggan stared dreamily at his beer glass, as though he was seeing everything happen all over again with his father. Then he shuddered and shook his head.

"Screw it!" He gulped his beer. "Paddy's dead and rotting in his grave. Forget him. Let's eat."

He loaded his plate with stewed codfish, salt-dried and flown all the way from Portugal. Chan dabbed garlic bread in the extra-virgin olive oil, put a chunk of smoky sardine on the crunchy bread and took a bite. He grabbed another crust of bread, another sardine chunk. They ate and drank in companionable silence for a few moments. Then Duggan paused to wipe greasy lips.

He said, "Do you reckon the Yeung woman was lying?"

"About what?"

"Being scared of Fai?"

"She sounded genuinely frightened," Chan said.

Duggan scooped the last pieces of the African chicken onto his plate: "Supposing she was lying? Supposing Fai didn't kill her or his brother? Let's assume those cult jokers did it. I mean … Well, it seems you're dismissing them all of a sudden."

"I'm not dismissing the cult."

"Seems that way to me," Duggan said. "Is it because you reckon Alan Yip lied about the death threats he says the cult made?"

Chan shook his head. "I'm *not* dismissing the cult. I don't think Yip lied about the threats either. Records show he shopped three cult members in China. All three were shot — it rings true the cult would want revenge. But we can't ignore the fact that things have changed since Yip spoke to me, can we?"

Duggan frowned. "Have they changed?"

"If Fai told the truth, Szeto was a cult member. Why kill one of their own?"

Duggan stared at him as though the answer was obvious. "They're a bunch of loonies."

Chan shook his head. "It's not so simple. We need to visit that temple in Lantau."

"Why?"

"To discover if ..."

The ring of his phone interrupted him. The caller was his police surgeon friend, Eddie Gallacher.

"You asked me to ring you when I'd finished the tests on your Mid-Levels victim," Gallacher said.

"Have you finished?"

"No, I'm calling to see if you want a game of tiddlywinks. Do you want her details now, or will you wait for my written report?"

"Now, Eddie."

Gallacher explained what he had discovered.

"That list of things you found in her stomach," Chan said after his friend had finished.

"What of it?"

"You never mentioned brandy."

"Correct."

"Why?"

"For the amazingly simple reason I found none."

"None?"

"Not a single, solitary drop."

"Brandy would have showed in your test?"

"If it had been in her stomach," Gallacher said. "But it wasn't. What the hell are you twittering on about brandy for?"

"No particular reason ... Look, I have to go, Eddie. I'll call in at your office when we get back."

He switched off the phone.

"What was all that brandy stuff about?" Duggan asked curiously.

"Nothing important," Chan said.

They ate in silence for the next few minutes until they had finished their meal. Then Chan said, "I want you to go and talk to the restaurant manager."

Duggan looked puzzled. "Why?"

"Ask if he knows where we can hire a boat to take us to Lantau."

"You're the boss," Duggan said.

He got up and headed towards the restaurant. Chan waited until Duggan had gone inside the restaurant and had closed the door.

Then Chan phoned directory enquiries and asked for the number of the Mid-Levels Wine and Tobacco Stores in Hong Kong.

He rang the store.

"This is Inspector Peter Chan, are you the store manager? … No, nothing serious, sir … I just want to ask some questions about your customers, that's all."

He questioned the manager for several minutes. When he had got what he wanted from the man, Chan ended the call without bothering to say goodbye.

He phoned the Mandarin Hotel's reception desk.

"I want Mister Yip Kwok Fai in … Checked out? … When? … I see … Yes, thank you."

His heart started to beat faster as he switched off the phone. He silently cursed his stupidity. He had tackled this case completely the wrong way. Got everything screwed up right from the start. No longer, though. Because now he …

"We're in luck!" Duggan had returned. "The head waiter knows a guy with a boat. This guy will take us to Lantau for—"

"We're not going to Lantau."

Duggan frowned: "I don't understand."

"We're going home."

"You said we had to check out that temple."

"Things have changed," Chan said. "Our killer is in Hong Kong."

AH FAH GLARED at her bodyguard.

The bastard still sat there pretending to read his newspaper. Only he wasn't — he was mentally undressing her with sewer-rat eyes. The older guy was a real sweetie, but this one a sleaze-ball. Enough is enough, she thought. If he doesn't stop leering, I'll drown him. I'll give him one last chance. I'll swim underwater for a while. If he's still leering at me when I come up for air, I'll soak him good. She gulped air then dived to the bottom of the pool. When she resurfaced, he no longer sat by the table. He was walking to the bungalow. In fact he was *running*.

A gun in his hand.

Then he was spinning around, clutching his stomach.

He said something she couldn't hear too clearly, dropped the gun and staggered towards the pool. For a moment he teetered on the edge, arms flailing like windmills as he fought for balance. He lost the battle and splashed heavily into the pool.

The turquoise water around him turned a dull pink.

Panic gripped her. "Joe, Joe!"

A man emerged from the bungalow; but not Joe Parwani.

"Dad, dad!" she screamed.

44

"I DON'T GET it," Duggan said. "Why are we scrapping that trip to Lantau?"

"I told you. Our killer is closer to home."

They were on the jet cat bound for Hong Kong.

"What makes you sure?" Duggan's deep blue eyes narrowed. "It's that call you made when I was in the restaurant, isn't it? You still haven't told me about that call, Ace. Who did you call? What—"

"Relax. I'm going to tell you."

"When?" Duggan asked testily; "this week? Next year?"

"In Miss Yeung's flat I found several items on her bedside table," Chan said. "The items included a glass with dregs of brandy."

"What about it?"

"Eddie found no alcohol in her stomach."

"So?"

"There was brandy in the glass; so who drank it?"

"That's what I want *you* to tell me." Duggan stared levelly at Chan. "So how about you tell me now, huh? Who drank the brandy?"

Chan did not give him an answer. Instead, he turned away from Duggan and stared through the cabin window and out to sea. They were passing the coast of Lantau. The Hong Kong jet cat terminal was ten minutes away.

"Is this a dumb-arse party game you're playing with me here? Duggan's impatience was turning to anger. "Do I get thirty guesses at the truth?"

Chan turned away from the window. "The killer made a mistake. He tried to make it look like it was a break-in in that had got out of control."

"What killer? What's his name?"

"He wanted to give the impression that a thief had broken in — that Miss Yeung had woken up and confronted him and the thief had panicked. But the killer tried too hard."

"Give me a *name!*"

"He got so focused on throwing things around the living room, trying to make the break-in look realistic there, that he forgot the most important item — the one that actually linked him to her murder — was in the bedroom," Chan said. "Or maybe he didn't forget. Maybe he thought wiping the brandy glass to clear his prints would be enough. Or maybe he knew it wouldn't be enough; maybe he meant to do the job properly. Only he heard someone moving around in the next apartment and got scared he might be discovered. So maybe he ran, leaving the job half done."

"And *maybe* if I give you three fucking weeks *maybe* you'll finally answer a few questions," Duggan said. "Only I don't want to give you three weeks. Not even three minutes. In case I forgot to mention when I signed up, I'm not the world's most patient person. So how about you tell me now, huh? How about ..."

Chan's phone rang.

"Inspector … Oh it's you, Ah Fah." His voice softened when he realised it was his daughter. "What did you … Hello … Are you still there, Ah Fah?"

"There's a man, dad ... Wants to talk."

Chan stiffened. "You're frightened."

"Do everything he says."

"Everything *who* says? Who's there? Who—"

"Listen, dad, just listen."

"Why are you crying? Has he hurt—"

"*Everything*, dad, or he'll kill me."

FAI SAT AT home full of guilt, remorse — and fear.

The vodka bottle he had opened twenty minutes ago stood at his side, half-empty. But fear, remorse and guilt continued to fester. He was surprised. Normally vodka eased his conscience, killed the fear — made him a new man. This time it had failed to perform its magic. He had hoped that getting drunk would enable him to drift into self-pity and that the self-pity would be so strong it would drive out guilt and remorse.

It hadn't happened.

Should he really be surprised? Should he be the slightest bit shocked that his guilt remained? He should have known it would be impossible to escape it. And what chance was there of self-pity, with him alive and Szeto dead? Because I'm to blame, Fai thought, I'm to blame for everything that happened to Szeto. I told those policemen Miss Yeung killed Szeto. But I lied.

I murdered my brother.

"YOU LOOK LIKE you saw a ghost."

"I'm fine."

"Don't look it," Duggan said. "Is your kid in big trouble? Is that what's shook you? Is—"

"I'm fine," Chan snapped. "Everything's okay — understood?"

Duggan raised his hands in surrender. "Hey, hey, relax. If you say you're okay, that's okay with me."

But Chan guessed from the way in which Duggan looked at him that the tall, blonde-haired sergeant was unconvinced. To avoid Duggan's unnerving gaze, Chan stared through the cabin window. He could see the Hong Kong shoreline. Five minutes more and they would be at the terminal.

"So what's next, Ace?"

Chan turned from the window.

"We arrest our killer, huh?" Duggan said. "A*fter* you've told me his name, of course — because I'm getting more than a bit pissed off with all this secrecy. I mean, I thought you were a professional. But a professional wouldn't hide things from his partner."

"First you go back to the station," Chan said flatly.

Duggan frowned. "What?"

"You go back to the station."

"What the fuck are you talking about?"

"You wait for my call and—"

"You bastard!" Duggan's face turned red with fury. "You're *double-crossing* me! You plan on arresting him solo, don't you? Want to keep all the praise for yourself."

"You wait for my call."

"I never figured you for a lousy—"

"You wait there," Chan snapped. "I told you at the start that we do things my way. You go to the station and wait for that call — understood?"

Duggan opened his mouth to protest again then thought better of it. He held up his hands in surrender. "Whatever you say; you're the boss."

AH FAH'S LUNGS felt ready to explode.

At the start of her ordeal, half an hour ago, she had ordered herself to breath slowly and calmly. But she had known it would be tough. Since childhood she had suffered from a nasal allergy, which always got worse during periods of stress. For the past five minutes her nasal passages had been blocked, which meant that she'd had to suck air through her mouth. That saliva-coated gag meant this had become harder and harder to do. Soon it would be impossible.

Dad, dad! Help!

She wanted to reach up and wrench the gag from her mouth. Impossible: her hands were bound so tightly to the chair that the rope cut her skin. Her captor could do it, though, his hands were free — he could undo the gag. She stared at him, her liquid brown eyes imploring him to free her. He continued to stand in silence by the car he had used to drive her to the garage, watching her strain hopelessly at her bonds. He's enjoying it, she thought, he's enjoying watching me die!

Dad, dad! Help me!

No good. He would not come. Only unconsciousness and death would come, a hard and a painful death. I don't want to die, she thought. I can't die, I'm only eighteen. Please, Lord Buddha, please don't let me die.

She could no longer hold back the nausea.

Vomit gushed into her throat.

She began to choke.

A picture of her mother, tall and elegant flashed through her brain. Then one of her father, arm protectively around her. Then another of her mother, more beautiful than before.

I'm sorry, mum! Sorry I loved dad more!

No more pictures, only blackness.

FAI PUT DOWN the phone.

I can't, he thought — I can't confess. If I do I'll be punished. But I *should* be punished — I'm guilty! If I hadn't told Szeto about Tsang he would never have rushed off to confront Tsang. He would be alive today and ... Of course he wouldn't be alive. Szeto would be dead. His fate became sealed when he joined that crazy cult. It changed him forever, turned him into someone with crazy ideas of right and wrong. That's why he could never understand that last time, could never understand about the deal I cut with Tsang — it was never fraud like Szeto claimed. It was a business deal, just me getting back some of the millions my father owed me.

Why could Szeto not understand? Why did he never realise it was only me getting my reward — payment for all the slave-labour I've done for the company? That lousy cult screwed up his mind, that's why. But I knew they'd done that before I spoke to him. So why tell him all about Tsang? I was scared, of course, I *needed* to tell someone. And ever since we were kids, whenever I was in trouble and had to talk things over, it was Szeto I went to.

Chan and his English police sergeant thought I never cared for Szeto, but they were both wrong: I loved my brother. I loved his gentleness, sense of fun; his ability to forgive and forget, his loyalty and affection. At least I did before those cult screwballs drove him insane; after they poisoned his mind our relationship changed. I still loved him — but now I hated him too.

I hated all his self-righteousness and his certainty, his unwillingness to compromise, his stubborn refusal to understand that everything is not always as black and white as this new Szeto said it was — I hated him so much I wanted to kill him. I *did* kill him too because I … That's what's so insane. Can you both love *and* hate someone — and feel both emotions at the same time?

Yes, it's possible. That's why I did it — betrayed Szeto. And in sending him to his death I also betrayed myself, or at least that better part of myself if such a thing still exists, which now will always be dominated by feelings of guilt and remorse; feelings that I'll only overcome through longer sessions with the vodka bottle.

Suddenly Fai wanted to weep, both for himself and the brother he had loved and hated. But tears refused to flow.

AH FAH'S CHEEKS stung from where he had struck her.

"You're lucky," Peng said. "No one slapped my sister back to consciousness. She never was *unconscious*, see. She was awake when she burned to death." His voice shook with emotion. "And your father — he killed her!"

"It's not true!"

"All of it's true," Peng shouted. "That other man — he started the fire. But your father was his accomplice. He's equally guilty."

"No!"

"*Yes!* Your father killed my sister. And now he's going to suffer like Liu Yan did."

"Please," Ah Fah begged. "Don't hurt him."

Peng checked his watch: ten past seven.

Almost time.

Five more minutes, he thought, and then the final confrontation begins. I make my last call to Chan, then order him here and force him to watch — make him suffer as I slowly kill the girl. That's why I couldn't let her choke, why I removed the gag. She has to be alive when he arrives. Chan has to see her die, has to endure what father and I endured twenty-five years ago.

He moved to the other end of the garage, to where three large petrol cans stood on the floor. He bent down, grabbed one of the cans, then returned to the car and sloshed petrol over the boot. He put the empty can on the floor.

"My sister burned to death in a car just like this," he said. Bound hand and foot like you." He pointed at the boot of the car: "In a cramped space like this."

He put a key in the lock of the boot then turned the key. There was a click as the lock sprang open. He raised the lid of the boot.

"No!" Ah Fah screamed. "No!"

45

HEADLIGHTS BLINKED IN the blackness.

The lights were switched off. Everything went dark again. It was the signal Chan had been waiting for. He started walking down the narrow road. His throat felt as dry as parchment, his heart beat at twice its normal rate. He breathed slowly to try and relax: in out, in out — that's it, Peter, try to shove the fear to the back of your mind. Try to think logically and unemotionally: angry and emotional men make mistakes. Any mistake tonight might cost Ah Fah her life.

He reached the garage door: knocked twice. The door swung open and he moved inside, straining his eyes to see: it was pitch-black. He couldn't glimpse anything. Not Ah Fah. Not her captor.

Nothing.

Then the garage exploded into dazzling white light. He thrust up his hands to shield his eyes from the glare. He heard the garage door slam shut, then a man's voice: harsh and commanding.

"Move to the wall and shove your face against it."

Chan did as ordered.

"Where's my daughter?"

No answer. Feet crunched across gravel on the garage floor. Hot breath scorched the back of Chan's neck. Strong young hands moved over his body. They searched for a gun.

"I came unarmed," Chan said, "just like you said."

"Turn around; slowly."

Chan turned. His eyes had begun to adjust to the light. He could see a car now: a red Ford Escort about eight feet away. Next to it stood three large fuel cans. At least one of the three cans must have sprung a leak because there was a strong smell of petrol. Ah Fah's captor stood by the car. He cradled a semi-automatic pistol in his right hand.

"Where's my daughter?"

"She'll stay safe, providing you do as I say."

"I want to see her."

"After we talk."

"No. I see her now."

Peng pointed the gun at Chan's head. "You see her when I say. And you do *what* I say *when* I say — or you'll never see her again."

Keeping Chan covered with the Makarov in his right hand, Peng reached to his jacket pocket with his left hand and pulled out what looked like an envelope. He tossed the envelope on the floor.

"Pick it up and take a look, Chan. Take a *good* look."

Chan reached down and picked it up: it wasn't an envelope, it was a black-and-white photograph. The half-smiling face of a Chinese teenager: thick-rimmed spectacles, hair tied in pigtails, braces on her teeth. More a profile than full-face shot, because she had tilted her head to the right, tilted it so far that Chan got the impression she had tried to escape the camera; perhaps the unfashionable thick-rimmed glasses and wire braces had made her self-conscious.

There had been no need for such bashfulness. She had not been beautiful, but she had not been ugly either: just another gawky teenager experiencing the bitter-sweet pains of growing up. Neither outstandingly pretty nor exceptionally plain, her face was another of those ordinary, everyday faces that you encountered without taking too much notice on the streets of Shanghai, or Beijing: or even here in Hong Kong. At least it would have been an ordinary, everyday face for most people — but not for Chan. This face had haunted his dreams for twenty-five years.

"Her name was Liu Yan. She was my sister and ..."

Chan couldn't hear him — Chan was no longer in the room. No

longer even in Hong Kong. It was twenty-five years ago and he was a naive Security Bureau officer in China, trying to rescue the Party official's daughter from her kidnapper.

He felt icy wind lash his cheeks; felt the wind whip snow in his eyes, one moment freezing them the next burning them; heard the kidnapper assuring him the girl would stay safe if he did as ordered; watched the kidnapper disappear into the icy-grey distance; glimpsed the parked car containing the girl and began running towards it, eager to free her quickly. The car exploded, the kidnapped girl still inside; flames shot into an oil-black sky; screams ripped the night; burning rubber …

A bullet thudded into the floor by his foot.

He jerked back to the present.

"Answer me, you son of bitch! I asked why you killed my sister. And you'd better tell me, Chan — quick! Or you'll never see your daughter."

"I didn't kill her."

"I found my father's diary. It's in there."

Chan shook his head. "I was too young and ambitious. I thought I could free her myself. I thought I would be a hero."

"Bullshit! You worked with that kidnapper. How much did he pay you?"

"You've got it all wrong!"

"My father had proof, Chan! Proof *you* killed her. You worked with that kidnapper — that's why you let him escape."

"The Security Bureau chiefs lied to your father — they blamed me to hide all their own mistakes."

"If you were so innocent you would have stayed. You wouldn't have run to Hong Kong."

"I *had* to run. I faced prison — maybe a bullet. The operation had been a disaster. Your father wanted some heads to roll. My bosses invented that story — the one of me and the kidnapper. It meant they could pretend their plan would have worked. That Liu Yan would have been free, if it hadn't been for a crooked young cop."

"You're lying. You …" Peng stiffened. "What was that?" He glanced at the garage door. "You brought someone."

"No."

"You said you would come alone. You broke your word. That means your daughter dies."

"I came alone."

"You're lying, just like you lied about Liu Yan."

"I swear I—"

"You killed her. So now you're going to suffer like me and father suffered. Your daughter's going to die like my sister."

Keeping the Makarov trained on Chan with his right hand, he grabbed a petrol can with his left hand. He sloshed petrol over the car. Images speared Chan's brain: a freezing January morning in China twenty-five years ago: a girl burned alive trapped in the boot of a car: a car like this one.

"Ah Fah!"

"Too late," Peng shouted. "You can't save her."

"Ah Fah!"

Chan charged blindly forward.

Bang!

Hot air burned his cheek as a bullet from the Makarov zipped past. He dived for cover, hit the gravel of the garage floor hard; made an instinctive grab for the Walther in his shoulder holster. But he was wearing no shoulder holster tonight. He had come here to the garage unarmed. He glanced up from the floor. Peng grinned triumphantly at him, Makarov in one hand, cigarette lighter in the other.

"She's going to burn!"

The garage door exploded.

Chan saw an object fall through the air. A small, round object: it hit the ground with a dull thud about ten feet away from him.

There was a blinding white flash.

A stun grenade! he thought. *Someone has thrown a stun grenade!*

Everything began to happen in slow motion. Like the events of an action scene in one of Alan Yip's *kung fu* movies. A black-clad figure burst into the garage, gun in his hand; then another black-clad figure, and another.

Peng got off a single shot with his Makarov.

One black-clad figure fell.

"Stay down, boss!"

Duggan's voice — he was one of the black-clad figures.

Peng turned his Makarov towards Duggan. In this new, slow-motion world it seemed to take him forever to turn. Duggan was about two metres away from Peng; crouching. Right hand outstretched like Peng's; a gun in it.

"Stay down, Pete!"

Bang!

Chan saw Peng's right hand fall to his side, saw the snub-nosed Makarov fall from it.

Bang! Bang!

Peng opened his mouth to say something, but no sound came. His mouth closed again. He took two steps backwards.

Bang! Bang!

Duggan's fourth and fifth shots not only drove Peng backwards, they lifted him off his feet and hurled him against the wall. He slid down the wall like a drunk and rested on his back on the floor. He made no sound. With five bullets in his chest, he was probably dead.

Then Duggan was standing over Chan. Shouting.

"You okay, Pete? Speak to me — you okay?"

"Ah Fah," Chan croaked, "in the car."

"They're pulling her out."

"How is she? Is—"

"Alive."

46

"HER ORDEAL HASN'T caused lasting physical damage," said the doctor. "But she's still in a state of shock, of course."

"But she'll be all right?" Chan asked anxiously. "She won't suffer long-term effects?"

The silver-haired doctor judiciously weighed his words. "Each and every patient is different, inspector. Some patients suffer from these long-term effects and others don't."

"But my daughter … Will she …"

"She seems a strong character," the doctor said. "As long as you and your wife both show patience, and both give her the support that she needs while she's recuperating ... Well, then I don't foresee lasting damage."

"Can I talk to her?"

The doctor shook his head. "Not tonight. She needs peace and quiet. I've given her a sedative."

"She'll be all right to talk tomorrow?"

"Yes," said the doctor. "You can talk to her tomorrow."

"Then I'll say goodnight," Chan said. "And thank you again for everything you've done."

"And your wife?" queried the doctor. "Will she ..."

"I'm sorry," Chan said. "I should have explained the situation more clearly. My wife's in Taiwan visiting relatives. I spoke to her there half an hour ago. She plans to catch the first available plane to Hong Kong."

"She'll also be here tomorrow?"

"Yes."

"Until tomorrow then," said the doctor."

"And thank you again," Chan said.

They shook hands. Then Chan turned and headed for the hospital's main exit. As he walked down the whitewashed corridor he experienced a mixture of emotions: guilt that he had allowed his daughter to suffer the way that she had suffered: hatred of her kidnapper: relief that it was all finally over and that everything had now been ... Hold on! It wasn't all over. Not yet.

A killer still had to be brought to justice.

While Ah Fah's life had been at risk in that garage, nothing else had mattered to Chan. Murder victims Szeto Yip and Miss Yeung had been irrelevant — their killer too. Nothing had mattered to Chan apart from ensuring his only daughter's safety. He had done that now, though. Ah Fah was safe. No one would hurt her again. Now he was no longer only a father with a teenage daughter to protect. He was also a police officer. He had a job to do: a killer to arrest.

THE PHONE LINE was poor. John Tsang could not hear clearly. He asked Fai to repeat what he had said.

"I'm going to confess."

Tsang could not believe his ears: "Are you crazy?"

"I can't live with it, Tsang! All the guilt — it's killing me! I can't sleep. Sometimes I can't even breathe. It's no—"

"Have you been drinking?" Tsang asked sharply.

"It's no good," Fai said. "I can't handle it … Not any longer … I have to tell someone what—"

"You're drunk!" Tsang's voice was a mix of anger and contempt. "You've been drowning yourself in vodka again. How many times must I order you to stay off it? Getting drunk won't help with anything, you fool."

"It's no good," Fai insisted. "I *have* to tell someone! I have to say what happened. I can't cope with it. The guilt — it's all too much!"

"Shut up!"

"My brother's dead!"

"Do you *want* to go to prison?"

"I'm to blame!"

"That's what will happen if you go squawking to the police — you have to keep quiet. The police would never understand why you did it."

"I'm to blame!"

"Don't be a fool."

"Yes, yes, it's my fault — your fault too. We're both to blame — both of us guilty for what happened to Szeto."

"Listen," Tsang said angrily. "You're going to say nothing to the police — understood. Or I'll—"

Fai no longer listened. He had put down the phone. He did not need to hear Tsang say any more; his mind was already made up. He reached down and picked up the phone again. He punched the number for the police station. A woman answered.

"I want Inspector Peter Chan," Fai said.

"May I tell him what your call is about?"

"I want to confess."

DUGGAN PARKED THE car and they got out and walked across the empty parking lot into the building. They gave their names to the night-duty receptionist and then showed her their official police identification cards.

"He's expecting you, inspector," the receptionist said. "It's on the third floor. Room number—"

"It's all right," Chan said. "I know where it is."

Duggan pressed a button to summon the lift. It arrived and they shuffled inside. They got out at the third floor, turned right and moved purposefully down the long, narrow corridor, the red thick-pile carpet muffling the sounds of their footsteps. The door at the end of the corridor was their destination.

Duggan rapped at the door.

"Come in," said a voice from inside.

Duggan pushed open the door. Alan Yip sat at a desk at the far end of the room. In front of him was a large window which overlooked the film set. The film set stood empty, illuminated by two pairs of giant security floodlights; the misty orange-white glow which these lights produced floated in the air like dry ice and gave the set a ghostly feel. Yip turned slowly away from the window and stared at the detectives.

His face looked haggard and drawn.

"A complete tragedy," he croaked in a tired, old man's voice. "What happened to my personal assistant Miss Yeung, I mean. That's what you're here to see me about, I suppose — to question me about Miss Yeung."

"No," Chan said. "We're arresting you for murder."

47

"SZETO WAS VERY highly strung," Chan said, "maybe even a bit crazy."

He was at the police station with Duggan. It was ten minutes after midnight. They were in Chan's office. Duggan had just brewed two large cups of coffee. He placed one of the steaming blue cups on the desk in front of Chan.

"Being crazy is partly why Szeto did what he did," Chan said. "Why he agreed to go on that revenge mission to kill Yip."

He picked up his cup, took a sip and then winced. Duggan's coffee was as lousy as the rocket fuel which his daughter Ah Fah brewed.

"Szeto hated Alan Yip," Chan continued. "He blamed him for his mother's suicide. He told his girlfriend Giselle that if he got a chance he would kill the man who'd bullied his mother to her death — the cult gave him that chance. They trained him and armed him, and then sent him on a revenge mission."

Duggan said, "Killing Yip would avenge the cult members Yip betrayed, huh? Those three men executed in China?"

"It would avenge Szeto's mother too," Chan said. "But Yip found out about Szeto's plans — he killed him."

"And John Tsang is the joker who went and told Szeto the truth? About his mother, I mean?"

Chan nodded. "Fai had swindled millions from his father's company. Tsang helped him do it. Tsang saw it as the perfect way to bankrupt Alan Yip and destroy him slowly. But Fai grew frightened that Yip would discover what he had done. He needed to unburden his fears to someone. He got drunk and told Szeto everything. Then Szeto went and confronted Tsang and said it all had to stop. Tsang tried to buy Szeto off. Not with money but with the truth — that he was his real father and that Yip had driven his mother to her death."

"So Szeto tries to kill Alan Yip? But he screws up and Yip ends up killing him?"

"Yes."

"Yip killed the Yeung woman too, huh?"

"She was against his idea of pinning Szeto's death on the cult," Chan said. "She wanted to implicate Fai. That way, not only would she save Alan Yip's skin, she would also dispose of a rival for his affections. Yip thought she was getting too much out of control. He was scared she might do something that would put his freedom at risk."

Chan paused for another sip of coffee. It tasted no better than first time around.

Duggan grinned at his discomfort: "Nice, huh?"

"Beautiful," Chan said dryly. "You've definitely got the coffee-maker's gift."

"I'm a man of hidden talents."

"I don't doubt it. But next time just one spoonful for each cup, not half a dozen."

Duggan took a bottle of milk from the fridge. "A squirt of this might make it taste less like diesel oil." He handed Chan the milk and then took a swig of his own coffee; unlike Chan he liked it. He smacked his lips. He said,

"So Alan Yip tops the Yeung woman? He tears her clothes, scratches her, messes up the flat and tries to make it look like a burglar or maybe even a rapist has topped her after a struggle?"

"But he tries *too* hard," Chan said. "Perhaps it was the film-maker in him — the perfectionist wanting every shot to be the best. He got so focused on scattering things around the living room, making the break-in look realistic there, that he forgot the most important item — the one that actually linked him to her murder — was in the bedroom. Or maybe he didn't forget; he might have thought that wiping his prints would be good enough. Or maybe he knew it wouldn't be good enough and meant to do the job properly, only he heard someone moving around in the next apartment — the walls in that block are paper-thin — and ran because he thought he might be about to be discovered. He should have washed that glass out as well as clearing his fingerprints from it. Eddie Gallacher found no alcohol in her stomach, but I found brandy in the glass."

"Meaning someone else drank the brandy?"

Chan nodded. He followed Duggan's advice and splashed milk into his coffee: it still tasted like diesel oil. He shoved the cup to one side.

"Before arriving at Miss Yeung's place, Yip bought brandy from Mid-Levels Wine and Tobacco store in Robinson Road," Chan said. "He carried the bottle off in one of their bright red plastic bags. When I first saw the bag at Miss Yeung's flat, I thought nothing of it — I thought that she had bought and drank the brandy herself, you see. After Eddie called me in Macau about his tests on Miss Yeung, I realised the bag *was* important."

Duggan drained his coffee. He lit a cigarette. He said, "I got it wrong about the Yeung woman — I thought Fai topped her."

Chan declined Duggan's offer of a Marlboro. "No way would she have opened the door to Fai. And that lock on her apartment is a top-of-the-range German design. My housebreaker friend Snake-fingers says only a professional could pick it."

Duggan took a pull from his cigarette. He blew out blue-grey smoke. "So *no one* broke in, huh?"

"That's right," Chan said. "She opened the door willingly to her killer because she wasn't afraid of him. Alan Yip poured a drink, took it through to the bedroom, got her to lie on the bed, whispered sweet words in her ear, stroked her neck and …"

"Then topped her?"

"Yes."

Duggan took another slow, thoughtful pull from his cigarette. He said, "Reckon we'll ever prove it, though — in court, I mean? Alan

Yip is one extremely powerful guy in this town."

"Proving it in court is someone else's job. Ours is done."

Duggan said enthusiastically, "We celebrate? Wash away the taste of my lousy coffee with a beer or six?"

Chan shook his head. "I need to visit the hospital."

Duggan frowned. "I thought the doctor said your kid's going to be okay."

"I still want to pay a last visit before going home," Chan said. "Just to double-check there are no problems."

"We'll sink those beers tomorrow, huh?"

Chan did not directly answer Duggan's question. Instead he said softly, almost dreamily, "It could have been much worse — Ah Fah, I mean. If you hadn't burst into that garage when you did, then Ah Fah might … By the way, how did you know I was there?"

Duggan grinned broadly. "Followed you to your apartment and stuck a transmitter to your car," he said, as though the answer was obvious. "You don't seriously think I swallowed all the bullshit you gave me on our way back from Macau, do you?" He shook his head. "Seeing you turn as white as a sheet on the boat … I knew something was wrong."

"In other words," Chan said slowly, "you *deliberately* disobeyed orders." He fixed Duggan with a level stare. "I ordered you to go directly to the office and wait there for—"

Duggan threw up his hands in disbelief. "Jesus Christ! What's wrong — *your kid's safe!*"

"Relax," Chan said. "I'm not angry. You saved her life. You were right to do what you did. I was wrong not to trust you."

Duggan grinned again. "Some things never change, do they? Me always being right and you wrong, I mean."

Chan shook his head. "Things change. This afternoon you asked if we were friends. I only said I was in your debt, I said nothing about being friends. I hope that's changed."

Duggan nodded.

IT HAD JUST gone two in the morning when he arrived home.

The phone's flashing red light meant someone had left a message:

it was Wong, apologising for falling ill and asking Chan to call back. Chan had already phoned him from the police station two hours ago — Wong had left a message there too — and told his friend all about Alan Yip. Chan had assured Wong that he had nothing to apologise for; it wasn't his fault that he had caught chickenpox.

No there's nothing for him to apologise for, Chan thought. In fact I should thank Ah Wong for falling ill when he did. Him catching chickenpox helped me. It gave me a chance to get to know Terry Duggan better and to make amends with him. Duggan isn't the only person who I need to make amends with, though. It's time for me to do what I should have done twenty-five years ago.

He moved over to the chest of drawers beside the living room's door, pulled open the top drawer and took out a box of thumb tacks. Then he walked over to the wall, to the place where the portrait of his serene-faced mother stared down at him. He reached into his pocket, took out the picture of Liu Yan that he had retrieved from the garage where her brother had died. He placed this picture on the wall, next to the one of his mother. He bowed three times and asked Buddha to allow Liu Yan to enjoy wealth and prosperity in the after-life.

Later today he would travel to the Buddhist temple at Tsuen Wan. He would walk to the temple's furnace and hurl in silver and gold ghost money to keep Liu Yan wealthy in the after-life. He would bow his head and beg forgiveness for the tragic mistakes he had made in China twenty-five years ago. And Liu Yan's spirit *would* forgive him — Chan was sure of it.

Her angry ghost isn't the only one I need to stop from haunting me, he thought. It's time to do what, for years, Mei told me to do. Before journeying to the temple, I'll write to my father. It won't be easy, but I'll force myself to do it — and this time I'll make sure to post the letter. I could be too late — Mister Peter Collins might be dead. But if he's alive … I'll send the letter and try to make my peace with him.

Yes, he would do all that later. Now, though, he would sleep. He felt tired; exhausted. Yes, he would sleep. And he was sure that because he had made that pledge to write to his father, and had promised Liu Yan's spirit he would keep her happy in the after-life, sleep would come easily this time. There would be no nightmares.

Printed in the United States
148704LV00001B/151/P

9 781849 237949